The Six
and
Anwyn of Ialana

Katlynn Brooke

Copyright 2014

Book Three of the Ialana Series

Thanks and appreciation to my husband who has unfailingly supported my writing career without complaint, and also for all my friends and family who have helped me hang in there with advice and encouragement. You know who you are.

Contents

FORWARD I

1. Rhagat Rise 1
2. Anwyn, Three Rivers 8
3. Three Rivers 16
4. Rhagbeneth 26
5. Yor Swamps 33
6. Three Rivers 36
7. Making Plans 43
8. The Arrival 48
9. Anwyn 52
10. Secrets 57
11. Departure 65
12. Anwyn 70
13. Anwyn 76
14. The Farm 79
15. Ambros 85
16. Fire 90
17. Pursuit 94
18. The Elemental Kingdom 97
19. The Six 106
20. Goodbye 111
21. Flaming Fury 120
22. The Cave of The Sentinel 126
23. Glahivar 130
24. The Mines of Amrafalus 135
25. Ambros, Yor Swamps 142
26. Anwyn 150

27. Zephan   156
28. Glahivar   161
29. Yor Swamps   165
30. Cold Bone Clan, Rhagbeneth   170
31. Yor Swamps   174
32. Shegami   181
33. Ardvale   184
34. The Battle of Yor Swamps   187
35. Blaidd   190
36. The Weapon   195
37. Glahivar and Shegami   198
38. Beginning of the End   202
39. The Sentinel   205
40. Mu'A   209
41. Aftermath   214
42. Anwyn, the Six   220
43. Anwyn   227
44. Zephan   233

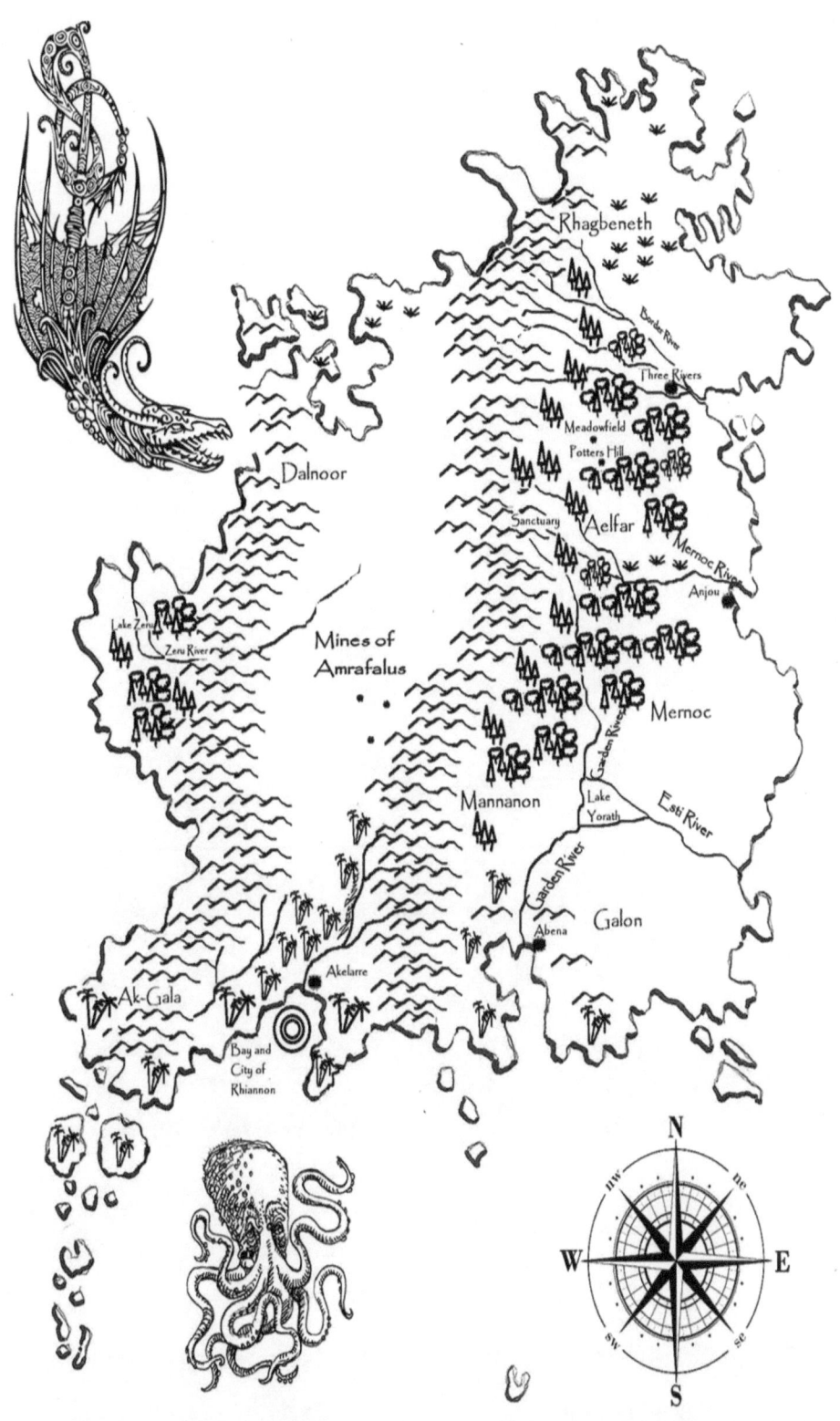

Rhagbeneth

Dalnoor

Three Rivers

Border River

Meadowfield

Potters Hill

Sanctuary

Aelfar

Memoc River

Anjou

Lake Zeru

Zeru River

Mines of
Amrafalus

Memoc

Garden River

Mannanon

Lake
Yorath

Esti River

Garden River

Galon

Abena

Ak-Gala

Akelarre

Bay and
City of
Rhiannon

N

nw   ne

W   E

sw   se

S

FORWARD

In the third of the Ialana Series, Astrobal, the demon-lord of Iocho-dran, has set his sights on Anwyn, the thirteen year old daughter of Jar-ah and Tegan. Not only has he dispatched an old enemy of the Six from the past to kill her, but he now has his eyes on a larger prize: a deadly weapon that only a few genetically coded humans are able to control.

As the healers, who are now also adept in healing and merkaba use, set off on their journey back to Galon from their six year sojourn in Three Rivers, they must not only discover why Anwyn is a target for the forces of evil, they must also protect her, and themselves, from the malevolent assassin sent from Iochodran. A powerful assassin who can disable their merkabas at the worst possible time.

Ambros, the Queen's Consort and their temporary escort, has plans of his own, plans that Queen Catrin is not meant to know about, but nei-ther he nor the Six have any idea of the trouble they will run into. Will Ambros find his match in Moran Blacktooth, the Yor Swamp warlord? And how will Anwyn and the Six stop Astrobal from using a weapon that can destroy a planet with merely a touch?

1.

Rhagat Rise

If I am dead, I don't want to know it.

Glahivar opened her eyes and looked around. She was aware of movement and light, but her vision was not the way it was supposed to be. Perhaps her eyes did not actually open, at least, not with a pair of eyelids. She felt a stab of alarm as she moved her hand to her face. What, by the gods, was this? Black pincer claws, like a crab, invaded her vision. A thick miasma that reminded her of mountain fog swirled around her body, a body that felt strange and alien to her.

The last thing she remembered was running into the . . . *where*? She couldn't remember. She felt as if her head was stuffed with wool.

It had been a building. There was a city . . . a city called Rhiannon. She . . . there was something urgent she needed to do. The battle was lost, and her shape-shifting raven body was not working the way it was supposed to. She couldn't shape-shift back into . . . Oh yes, it was coming back to her now. She could not get her female human form back. Something terrible had gone wrong, and it was all the fault of . . . Udfa. The last thing she had seen was a sword descending towards her neck. And then she'd woken up. Here.

Pain and horror mounted like a flood as each scrap of memory unfolded. Each disappointment and unexpected event cut into her brain like a fiery sword.

She screamed. It felt as if the doors into hell had opened. Her eyes had no tears to shed, but she sank down, panting, into the grey dirt beneath her body.

She remembered. Everything.

There had been pleasant times, times before the betrayals that had brought her here, when she had called herself the Raven. She'd once been a beautiful woman, one whose beauty could have been legendary. Her body, in that life form, reminded her of the carved marble statues depicting the goddesses in the temples of Rhiannon. She had been able to shape-shift into any form, but now, she remembered, she'd always preferred her raven form. She'd sometimes use her merkaba, the spirit body vehicle or capsule, to transport herself quickly to places when time was of the essence, but winging over the mountains and soaring in the air currents with raven wings gave her more pleasure than an enclosed and speedy merkaba vehicle ever could.

But, all that aside, nothing gave her more joy than to plot and plan. Manipulation was her game, and she'd been skilled at it. With her body and face, there were few who could resist. These were pleasant thoughts, yes, but she must not dwell on them. Her end, those were the thoughts she now tried to forget, but they crowded back into her mind like insistent beggars.

All her plans had gone awry. How could she not have seen even loyal Blaidd turning on her with his mutants? They'd destroyed the army of King Brenin, her willing, but stupid pawn. Udfa, the admiral of her fleet, he had betrayed her trust as well. All her and Brenin's plans to conquer Galon in the east, and then Aelfar and Mernoc in the north, had come to naught, thanks to Udfa's betrayal.

He was to have supported Brenin's less-powerful navy by attacking Ortzi's fleet in Galon with Rhiannon's navy while Brenin and his army attacked from the north. Instead, Udfa had allowed Brenin's navy to be decimated, and he'd not shown up at all. She would never forgive him for that.

He had plotted her destruction, and her end had been undignified and hideous, but how he'd accomplished that, she had no idea. Only the use of crystals could have destroyed her so utterly. Udfa would have had access to Amrafalus' death-dealing crystals. She'd been unable to shape-shift back into her glamorous queen form, and instead was slain by a soldier—a common soldier—who had looked on her failing half-human, half-bird form with horror.

She knew her name now. It was Glahivar. It had always been Glahivar, but in her previous form she'd also taken the name "Branwyn". She looked down and noticed that her human form was no longer. She shuddered. This form was not recognizable to her. The stench from it—from her—rose into the mist around her, and she gagged.

"Get used to it, dear."

The thin voice sent shivers through her, and a dark form rose above her from the mist. Reddish-orange eyes glittered in a swirling darkness.

"This is your eternal body now. Your spirit body. It's what fits your template best, and you should consider yourself lucky to have it. A formidable body. It will be useful to us."

"Who are you?" Glahivar's voice shook.

"Shegami the Putrid. You will come to know me as your closest friend, sweetheart." A snarling hiccup that could have been a chuckle emanated from the form. "The next question is, obviously, *where* are you? That's what they always ask." The hiccupping snarls sounded again. "You are in Iochodran. And where is that, you ask? You were in the Severed Universal Fields for some time, building your present form, and then were released here to do the Master's bidding. You won't remember much of it, but some of it may come back to you, eventually."

"Iochodran . . . yes, I remember. The counterpart to Ardvale, is it not?"

"Go to the top of your class my dear! Few remember that. Ardvale, the accursed place, it undoes much of our work on the material plane. Well, we've come up with a solution to that, and you are part of it."

The darkness shimmered, and Glahivar jumped as it changed into a reflective surface. "Look into the mirror," the voice commanded.

Glahivar cried out as an enormous creature reared in front of her.

"It's you, you idiot!" The chuckles came again, gleeful. "*Look! Look and see what you've become!*"

An image appeared of the body she now wore. Eight eyes stared back at her. Eight eyes in a spiny face, a mouth with two dripping fangs and saw-toothed mandibles behind them. The body was segmented into two parts; a large abdomen with a stinger on its end, and a thoracic segment with six arms and two legs. The arms all ended in claw-like pincers. She was a spider, but nothing like a spider that she had ever seen.

She trembled again. How she missed her beautiful raven form! She would never have that again, but now she understood Shegami's reasoning.

The Raven had little offensive power, and it had been impossible for her to choose aggressive forms due to her previous template coding. Coding she had rejected. Now she must make the best of what she had, to use it to the best of her ability.

She sank back onto the blistered ground and genuflected before the darkness known as Shegami.

"Mistress! I am proud of who I am. Glahivar, your humble servant and devoted slave. Show me what I must do."

"*Humph!* You're laying it on a little too thick, my dear." A cackle emerged from the gaping black hole that was the mouth of Shegami. "No one in Iochodran is ever sincere, and don't think it will work with me. I know *exactly* what you are up to. You covet my position here, and maybe one day, if you do as you're told and pay me all due respect, you may be successful in your ambitions. But it won't be until you've carried out your mission. If you fail, you'll get a transfer to the household of Gobenach of the Shadowlands. If you think *I* am tough, just wait . . . You are a newcomer here. Never forget that." She cackled and gestured with a tentacle. "Follow me."

Glahivar trailed the darkness over a landscape that never seemed to emerge from shadows and mists. Towering cliffs rose around them as they sped over the cratered earth. There was nothing green here. Nothing that lived. Only dark shapes that skittered and scurried from them as they approached.

She could not see a light source, but there was a dim light coming from somewhere. Either that, or her eyes could see without light. As if reading her mind—which there was no doubt in Glahivar's mind that she was—Shegami spoke.

"You are able to see in all energy ranges, my child, including the ultra-violet and infra-red. We don't need light here as you were used to in the material spectrum. You will find it an asset in your mission."

Glahivar could now see strange waves and shimmers that emanated from every object when she moved her eyes a certain way. She could refocus them to observe other flickers and lights that showed her the temperature of all around her, including her own body. She practiced this focusing and re-focusing as they sped across the blight, and by the time they arrived at their destination, an enormous mountain, she was quite proficient in her observations of the visible and invisible spectrum.

Maybe, she thought, *I could even enjoy my new form.*

"Raghat Rise," was all Shegami said, as the mountain rose in front of them.

Austere, needle-like spires reached towards a lavender sky. She could see the red and orange heat impressions that came from within, but also the deep indigo-black of bone-chilling cold.

She did not feel the heat, or the cold, as they flew into the castle-mountain. Guardians stood at the doorway. A portal to the gates of hell, she thought. These guardians, frightening to even her, would discourage all intruders.

Who would want to die of fear, assuming one *could* die here? Wasn't she already dead? But her consciousness still lived. She wished she had gone into oblivion instead.

They entered into an immense hall. It reminded her of the Hall of Amrafalus in the fallen Citadel of Rhiannon, only much larger and darker. An invisible force pulled and tugged at her as they moved down the hall. She could not stop her scurrying legs from moving, as if they'd taken on a life of their own.

At the end of the hall was a coldness that she felt first before seeing it. An unpleasant odor grew into a choking stench as she flew down the hall towards the seated figure. She gagged. She had never smelled anything like this before, not even from her current body. Nostalgia enveloped her as she remembered the rose perfume that Branwyn had used in her old life, but it would have not helped her here.

At last, the force released her, and she sank to the floor in terror. She didn't want to look up.

"Speak!"

The hideous voice pierced her hearing organs. She placed her claws over them, but the voice would not allow her to block it out.

"Look at me when I speak to you, *worm*!"

She looked up, and cringed. This was worse than even she could imagine. She had heard of demons from the Shadowlands, but had never felt the icy grip of one before. If something could be the embodiment of fear, it was the monster that crouched, yet still towered above her, its body a crawling mass of maggots and worms. But the slimy things that crawled around the body of this creature did nothing to hide the gleaming fangs and claws, or the red holes that were the eyes.

"State your name," it continued.

"Glahivar, my Liege!"

"I bring her to your Lordship as your new servant," said Shegami. "She is our latest addition to the Army of Astrabal."

Astrabal—now that Glahivar knew his name thanks to Shegami's help—pinned her with a stare that would have turned a lesser mortal to stone. Fortunately, she was no mere mortal.

I can handle this, she thought. *I am not the idiot they think I am. I will show them!*

"You may not be an idiot," Astrabal sneered, his words thick and wet through the rotting flesh surrounding the vent-hole that was his mouth. "But you aren't far from one if you think your thoughts are private. Nothing is private here. I will know at all times what you are doing, and Shegami will be responsible for you."

Shegami whimpered. "Yes, my Lord. I will ensure this one does what is required of her. She will feel my punishment if she disobeys!"

"You will both feel my punishment. Now, tell me. What exactly, is her mission?"

Glahivar was curious about this too. She had apparently forgotten that part.

"It involves Anwyn, the Child of Ardvale, my Lordship. She is the daughter of two of the six healers that so recently plagued us."

The demon let loose a roar that shook the rafters of the hall, but Shegami continued, undeterred.

"She has been released from the elemental kingdom of our opposite polarity, and is back in Three Rivers with her parents. An ideal time for us to strike and render her useless."

"You will render her *dead*!"

"Oh yes, my Lordship. Dead, of course, yes! She will not stand a chance against Glahivar."

"But, but . . ." Glahivar couldn't help speaking. "How will I get near the child in this," she looked down, "this body? I use deception as one of my skills, and—"

"Silence!" Astrabal thundered. "You will not address me directly unless I tell you to. Shegami, you will take her to our Chambers of Disruption." His gaze shifted back to Glahivar. "We have the skills to give you a new shape-shifting ability, to enable you to choose a more pleasing form to the human eye, but one that will be as deadly as the one you wear now. The form you wear now will only be your form when you need it, but you will have all the tools to do your job. I assume you're not too stupid to handle that?"

"No, my lordship. I can definitely handle that. It is my skill, as I said—"

Dismissively, Astrabal's immense form rose, and he turned to leave. Some of his maggots fell off his body and plopped onto Glahivar as he moved.

Shegami tugged at Glahivar. "Come on, quickly, before he tires of us and feeds us to his beasts!"

They too left, heading to the Chambers of Deception, in the bowels of Raghat Rise, as Glahivar, disgusted, used her claws to swipe at the crawling insects on her body.

2.

Anwyn, Three Rivers

nwyn opened her eyes. She'd had such a terrible dream. She could hear her brother, El-Azar, breathing softly in the next bed. All was quiet. She rose from her bed and walked to the window, her bare feet silent on the cold, stone floor. She opened the shutters, and they creaked a bit, but no one stirred. In the courtyard below the brazier fires of the queen's palace guards sputtered as they cooked their night-watch meals. She could hear a soft murmur of voices and the occasional burst of laughter.

All was well, but the dream disturbed her. What should she do? Was it a premonition? Or maybe she had just eaten too many sweets before dinner. Mother had told her to be careful, but she was a thirteen-year-old, and she had wanted to eat them. Now it had given her a bad dream, not to mention a stomach ache. She would expect that of El-Azar, but not herself.

She returned to her bed and tried to go back to sleep, but the images of her dream were still imprinted upon her mind. They had not gone away, and closing her eyes only made them more prominent.

THE SIX AND ANWYN OF IALANA

She could still see a dark landscape with looming shapes that flew under a lavender sky. She jumped. This too had appeared in her dream.

One of the shapes in particular frightened her; a spidery shape with waving legs and glowing eyes. *Oh*, where was Finn when she needed him? She could call her mother, but she did not want her mother to know she was having bad dreams. Mother would worry and, she had to admit, she would feel silly for calling her. She was almost grown up now! She could go to Finn, it would only take minutes, but he too would just laugh and tell her she had eaten too much pudding.

Alright, she thought, Mother would do the same. But it was not the same. Finn would find the right words to say.

She lay awake for hours, wondering what the dream meant. She closed her eyes again until she could not see the ugly place or the spider thing anymore.

She fell asleep.

The Mines of Amrafalus

Abban panted. His parched tongue lolled in his wooly, sheep-like face. His half-human, half animal body could not sweat, so the moisture ran off his tongue instead. The air was stale, and it felt as if he baked in an oven. All he could think of was how thirsty he was, of dipping his head into a cool bucket of water and taking a long, long drink, but water was only passed around twice a day. They got food once a day.

He didn't know how he'd made it this long, but, then again, he had no idea how long he had been here. All the days and nights in the mines ran together, and the passage of time no longer mattered to anyone.

The only thing he wished for, besides water, was death. It would be soon. Slaves dropped around him all the time, and they were removed like so much trash. The only thing that mattered to the overseers was production. Dirt was valued more than the life of a man, whether human or Trueni. There were plenty of humans here too, but they never lasted long. Trueni, the mutant slave force of Rhiannon, were bred for this type of work, and it took more to kill a Trueni than a human. He wished it wasn't so.

Abban was sorry now he had not taken the opportunity to remain in Galon all those years back, after helping Blaidd escape the vindictive Branwyn by taking him in his fishing boat to Ibai. Horrified, he'd witnessed the mutation of Blaidd as Amrafalus' crystals changed him into a beast, the likes of which had not yet been seen in Ialana. But instead of remaining where it was safe and opting for healing, he'd returned to Akelarre, his Trueni fishing village and, home, outside Rhiannon.

He had been satisfied with his lot as a Trueni fisherman, and had not felt the need for healing. He'd been a mutant all his life, as were his parents, and their parents before them, back into a past that had no beginning.

For a while, everything had continued as normal. His life returned to the way it had always been, and he was happy. He understood why many Trueni had left for Galon. They seemed freer there than the Rhiannon Trueni were, but he'd thought those in Akelarre who were free could not complain. They sold their fish at the markets and were able to survive.

It was only once or twice a year when the soldiers came and rounded up slaves for the convenience of the non-mutant citizens of Rhiannon, and for the mines. They were a pool of free labor, and they could lose their freedom at any time. He'd been willing to take the risk that he would be overlooked in these round-ups. Now, he wished he hadn't.

Not too long ago, he wasn't sure how long it had been, he'd been one of those who'd lost their tenuous and illusory grip on freedom. The soldiers had come in the early morning darkness while he still slept and broken down his door. This had been no general round-up. They had come especially for him.

The soldiers had taken him to the seat of government on Rhiannon, to the buildings still left standing from the destruction of the Citadel. He had been interviewed personally by Udfa and the Council. They had wanted to know where he'd taken Blaidd, the human boy, friend of both the Raven and Amrafalus. The boy who had turned into a monster.

At first, he'd not wanted to talk. But Udfa had his methods, and after three days of enduring excruciating pain and fear, he couldn't stop talking. He'd not only told them where he'd taken Blaidd, but also what he'd learned in Ibai from other Trueni regarding the six healers.

He thought that once he talked, he would be killed, but instead he'd been thrown into a wooden cage on the back of an ox cart and taken to the mines in central Dalnoor. He wondered if his revelations had caused problems for anyone. He hoped the six healers and Blaidd were able to escape. As frightened as he'd been of Blaidd, he had recognized that deep down, in spite of his alarming appearance, Blaidd was not a true monster. He'd been weak, and had made bad choices. He'd been a victim of the *real* monsters—the rulers of Rhiannon.

Abban felt as if his arms were dropping off. He could barely lift them anymore. Since approaching this new tunnel area this morning, he'd felt a weakness in his limbs that was not normal.

They'd just had their scheduled sleep, and he shouldn't be this tired. He lifted his pickax and brought it down on the rock face in front of him. The lamp next to him guttered as if in a breeze. There should be no breeze here. They were too far underground. He slowly lifted his arms again before the overseer could slash him with his whip, and the pickax struck the rock.

Crack!

He jumped. The noise was different. Louder now. It sounded hollow, and he heard the distant rumble of falling rocks just behind the rock wall. Now the overseer had heard it too, and he moved closer to Abban. He did not enjoy the extra attention of an overseer, and it sounded like they were going to have a cave-in. There were spots in front of his eyes and a roaring in his ears as he lifted his pickax again. With a final effort, he swung it down onto the same spot. As it connected with the rock he lurched forward, the rock face disintegrating in front of him.

Astonished, he stood there, his mouth agape. A black cavity, about the size of a man's head, had opened up in front of him. He could not see how big it was inside, as it was too dark, but he saw sparkles. Something that glittered. It was so beautiful! *He must touch it.* He dropped the pickax and stretched a heavy arm towards the glittering object. It felt cool to the touch, but it also burned.

A hot pain shot up his arm, and then there was nothing but blessed blackness.

It was another beautiful day in Rhiannon, and Udfa drew the fresh sea breezes into his lungs as he surveyed the work on the site of the Citadel. Here would rise a new Citadel, and it would be named after him: The Citadel of Emperor Udfa.

The slaves had cleared nearly all the rubble away of the old Citadel that had once risen with pride in the central ring above the City of Rhiannon. Now, it was only a gaping hole filled with sea water.

Six years ago, the Citadel had collapsed, thanks to the deliberate sabotage of the generator crystals by those infernal healers. How they had escaped was a mystery to all. The only one who knew, the Raven, had taken the secret with her to her grave. He wondered if they would recover the remains of Amrafalus, the erst-while reptilian ruler of Dalnoor and Ak-Gala, in the cavern. Probably, by now, there would be nothing left of him, but maybe they'd find a skeleton down there somewhere. It would make him feel better to know for sure that he was dead.

Amrafalus had been trapped in the cavern during the collapse. Udfa remembered that day clearly. How, after the discovery that the Six had escaped, he'd only just escaped himself as he'd followed the traitorous Blaidd out. Fortunately, he'd realized a split second before it would be too late, that something unexpected had happened, and that his desire to murder Blaidd had saved his life.

But the news he'd received today from the mines had ruined his day. The Mines of Amrafalus were at least ten days' travel from Rhiannon. The news was so bad they had used a series of relays using messengers and horses to do it in half the usual time. The exhausted messenger had handed the scroll to Udfa.

It was from Petosiris, his mine overseer.

"Your devoted servant, Petosiris, sends greetings and wishes for good health to venerable Emperor Udfa from the mines in central Dalnoor.

THE SIX AND ANWYN OF IALANA

An unexplained event has halted the workings of one of our mines, the gold mine. I am at a loss to know what to do, and wish your sage advice, my Emperor. We have experienced sudden death and loss of life at this mine, and a blue light penetrates to the sky from the ground. Anyone who approaches this light, this mine, or area, is killed instantly. We have roped off the danger area and set guards.

Please advise as quickly as possible.

Your devoted overseer."

He had read it again and again, but could make no sense of it. He called his assistant, Zephan, and showed him the message. Zephan looked nonplussed. His mouth opened and closed, fish-like. *Of course he would have no idea*, thought Udfa. The man was an idiot. But he did know who might know.

This situation required the best wizards he could find, and there was only one option open to him. He had no faith in local wizards. They were charlatans, all.

He looked at Zephan. "We need to find them," he said.

Zephan looked distracted. "Find who?" He found the news confusing, but he couldn't let on that he had no idea what to do. He was Udfa's most trusted lieutenant and advisor, and appearing perplexed would not help his ambitions.

"The Six healers, you fool. The kids who brought the Citadel down."

"Oh. Why?"

Udfa sighed. He would give anything for an assistant with some intelligence, but if anyone close to him had even half a brain, they'd be too threatening to his reign, and would need to be eliminated. Zephan was both slow and ambitious, and as a result, was unaware that Udfa thought this of him. But Udfa could handle ambition as long as he himself was smarter than the potential usurper of his throne. It's what kept Zephan alive.

"This—this death ray thing," he said. "We have to find out what it is and how to control it. How did it arrive at the mine? It is evidently the work of wizards, and we need the best wizards in Ialana to tell us what it is, and how we can use it. I want you to find them."

"But—but, my emperor, we *have* been trying. I traced them to Galon, and found the man who'd taken Blaidd there, too."

"Yes, I remember. We questioned him."

"He's in the Mines now. Our spies in Galon have told us that the warlord, Ortzi, left them in the crystal caves, thinking to use them, and they were buried alive during an earthquake. It is possible they escaped that too, but just in case, we could use the parents of one of them to track them. The Trueni, Abban, told us that the parents still lived in Ibai, the fishing village near Abena. I put a watch on them in case their daughter might be alive and attempt to contact them."

"Yes, I know. And she hasn't been back in six years. They are either dead, or someone is falling asleep on the job, Zephan. I want you to go there, personally, and bring the parents here."

The look Udfa directed at Zephan made Zephan's spine tingle with fear. He knew Udfa would not tolerate failure.

"We also need to know what Ortzi is up to, but your first task now is to find the healers."

Ortzi, the leader and warlord of Galon, had been an enemy of Rhiannon for years. Udfa had tried, unsuccessfully, to discover his secret of the exploding metal fireballs he had used to defeat King Brenin's navy in a battle six years ago. Fortunately for Udfa though, he had been too wily to allow the Rhiannon fleet to go up against Ortzi.

Brenin, without the expected backup promised by Udfa and The Raven, had lost the battle both at sea and on land. He'd heard sorcery was involved in the land battle, and this was where Brenin had lost his life, and most of his army to dark and dangerous creatures of the underworld. Creatures that still roamed Mannanon.

The stories that came out of this battle had frightened even his most hardened troops, and he knew it would be impossible to get them over the mountains to do battle with Ortzi or Catrin, the Queen of Aelfar and Mernoc.

But Udfa wanted more land, and he wanted it badly. He wanted to rule all of Ialana, but he'd need better weapons than those he currently possessed. For that, he needed the help of sorcerers who knew what they were doing, especially with crystals, and now this mysterious death ray.

He needed the Six. They'd proved their abilities beyond doubt. He'd find them.

And this time, he would not lose them.

3.

Three Rivers

"Yes, I am happy here, Jarah, but how much longer do we need to stay?" They sat side by side on the banks of the River Mair. It was late spring, and Tegan's hazel eyes narrowed as she looked out over the bright, sun-dappled water that flowed past the palace.

Jarah sighed as he sat up. He'd almost been asleep.

"We can go back to the palace if you're tired of being out here," he replied.

"You know what I mean." Tegan playfully threw a clump of grass at him. "We've been back in Aelfar years, now. Six years of distraction. Our work here is done. We have had time to rest and practice our skills. We can use our merkabas more easily now, and—"

"*Um* . . . yes. I've been thinking about it too. Catrin has been kind and generous to us, and given us the shelter we've needed, but I think we're all ready to pick up our mission once again."

"Don't let her hear you call her *Catrin*. She's still the Queen, and prefers to be addressed as such."

"None of us are into this royalty business, but I understand what you're saying. She's our benefactor, and we have to show her respect for that. You and I may both know all life is equal, and that no one should be able to place themselves above another, but most people here *don't* know that."

"They've forgotten who they really are," said Tegan. "If they only knew—"

She stopped speaking as a young girl ran up to them, her reddish-blonde hair gleaming in the sunlight. She led a small boy by the hand from the bank where they'd been skipping stones across the water.

Tegan frowned.

"Anwyn, take El-Azar back to the palace and get him into clean clothes. He's covered in mud!"

"Mother, he's making his acquaintance with the earth elements. They've promised not to linger."

Jarah grinned and winked. He and Tegan always joked with Anwyn about how the earth elementals were overworked and needed some time off. "Go make your acquaintance with the water elementals, then. They've seen little of you both lately."

Anwyn laughed. She enjoyed this banter with her parents, and even though the joke was stale by now, she never tired of it.

Jarah and Tegan watched the children as they ran towards the palace walls, to the door within that was still almost hidden by growth and discoloration from the elements. The Queen had shown them the secret passage she'd discovered so many years ago, and the children insisted on using it rather than the conventional palace entrances. To them, it was exciting and different. It was now no longer a secret passage, but a rather well-known one. Catrin had forbidden its usage by palace staff, and only the healers and their children were allowed to use it.

"I've been thinking about us returning to Ibai, or even Akelarre," said Jarah. "Our original mission after finding the healing crystal was to heal Trueni back into their human form. We've been doing none of that for the past six years."

"Being afraid of Ortzi was always the reason, especially since Djana's parents still live there. Putting them in danger was never an option."

"But now we are knowledgeable enough to avoid Ortzi, and any other potential traps, and protect her parents."

KATLYNN BROOKE

"We were so naïve six years ago, Jarah. Irusan had to bail us out at every opportunity. I too think we're ready to take care of ourselves, but I'm still a mother. I worry about Anwyn and El-Azar. Are we going to take them with us, or leave them here? I couldn't bear to be parted from them, but I don't want to put them in danger."

"Danger? *Anwyn?*" Jarah laughed. "Anwyn is more skilled than all of us. She knows almost as much as Irusan, and I feel sorry for anyone who gets in her way."

Tegan smiled, but her eyes betrayed her concern. "I know. I still can't help but worry though. El-Azar shows no signs of other skills, but he's young yet. I worry for him too."

"He'll be fine. With the friends and family he has, he won't lack for protection. Djana and Tristan will be back from Ibai soon. They promised not to stay long, and they will let us know if it looks safe enough to return."

"Well then. Let's fire up our merkabas and go!"

"Where?" Jarah asked. "Back to the palace, or to Ibai?"

Tegan shook her head in mock frustration. "To Ibai, of course."

They gathered up the remains of their picnic and walked to the door of the secret passage. They decided they'd have to tell Catrin, but not everything. It was too dangerous, and she wouldn't understand.

Ibai, Galon

The children were asleep. Djana and Tristan sat quietly at the table with Djana's parents, Holgar and Adne, as they ate the familiar Ibai supper of rice and fish. The bustle of the fishing village had settled down as darkness fell, with only an occasional footstep or call of a passerby on the street to disrupt the quiet.

They knew it was better to keep their visit under wraps for now. If Ortzi discovered them in Ibai, he would not go easy on them. There were spies everywhere, especially amongst the as-yet unhealed Trueni. Ortzi and Udfa paid well for information.

"We've all read the papyrus notes Blaidd gave you," said Djana.

Her mother nodded. "It's what he wanted. For you and the others to learn from his mistakes."

"His knowledge of crystal programming is impressive," Tristan added. "He knew far more than we gave him credit for."

"Well, he was our teacher in Mu'A at one time!"

"Yes, I am aware of that, Djana. But we had no idea of that, and when we did find out, we didn't think he'd regain his memory of what he knew," said Tristan.

Djana smiled. "A rather strange thanks to Amrafalus' memory crystals, but he did. I'm grateful to him for these notes. We spent a lot of time in Mu'A, but not enough to learn absolutely everything there is to know about crystal programming."

"I am sure he doesn't remember anything now as that frightful beast he turned into, but at least he wrote down what he knew before he changed" Tristan remarked. He didn't know whether they could ever completely trust Blaidd again, or the beast, Yagmak, he had turned into. He had betrayed them so many times, but he'd also saved their lives in Mannanon. His thoughts about Blaidd were interrupted by Adne.

"I am a little confused about what you call 'past lives,'" she said. "I don't understand it. It all sounds like fairy tales or sorcery to me. Like the dreams you always told me about, Djana. But I believe that you believe what you're saying. That's all that really matters."

"Mother, we've told you that Blaidd and the six of us—Jarah, Tegan, Kex, Adain, Tristan, and myself—all lived on an island named Mu'A, in other bodies. Five hundred years ago, we lost our lives when we arrived in Ialana with a healing crystal that we lost in the Osgoi tunnels. Our mission had been to heal mutants. We reincarnated here so that we could find the lost crystal again, and continue our mission to heal. We accomplished that, and if it wasn't true, how did we find the lost crystal?"

Adne nodded. "It makes sense, but I still find it difficult to wrap my mind around it. I have no such memories of past lives."

"Maybe you have no actual desire to remember your past. A past that could be quite painful, and to what end?"

"Tell us again about that . . . flying chariot, or conveyance, that you used to get here so quickly," Holgar requested. "I am trying my best to understand exactly what it is. I don't want to feel you are using sorcery, but I agree with your mother. It's difficult not to."

"I know, Father. It's called the *merkaba*. For the average person out there, it's a difficult thing to comprehend without the basic knowledge that has been lost to the masses for so many eons. You already know that while in Ardvale and Mu'A we spent a lot of time learning how to use our merkabas. We did not become skilled in their use until a year ago, when first we visited with you."

"I remember how shocked we were when you suddenly appeared in the house," said Adne, her voice stern. "I thought you were ghosts! I still haven't quite gotten over that."

"Sorry about that," said Djana, smiling. "But we've had a lot of time to practice and refine our abilities. Even then, it took some time to get here. We'd need to make many stops on the way, and sometimes we just got lost. Now, we have programmed the route into our vehicle and can get here and back almost instantaneously—"

"They know that already, Djana. They're asking us *how* it works," said Tristan. "I'll tell you."

Djana wrinkled her nose at him, but she smiled.

"Everyone possesses one of these merkabas, whether they're aware of it or not," said Tristan. "Usually, it's dormant in our subtle energy bodies, and can only be used by spiritual adepts."

"But we've learned how to activate them," Djana interrupted. "*Mer* means light, *Ka* means spirit, and *Ba* means body, or 'moving light body'. So, it is a vehicle for your spirit body, but can be used by those who know how as a physical conveyance as well."

Tristan continued.

"We have five capsules that surround our dimensional bodies. When we activate one of them, it allows our physical body to de-manifest and enter the dimension of the capsule that corresponds to that dimension. We are then located in that dimension, but can also see and interact with the dimension below us: this one. It allows for thought projection to get us to any destination we desire, at any speed. We are no longer controlled by the physicality of this world. At the moment, we are only able to use one of them to move around in the physical world. The others are for higher dimensions, but our physical bodies are not yet ready for those."

"If you knew what to look for, you'd see us out of the corner of your eye as little specks or flashes of light," said Djana.

"But to most, we'd be invisible." Tristan reached out for Djana's hand. They enjoyed their verbal duets.

Holgar and Adne sat silent for a while, not appearing to notice the one-upmanship that was going on in their midst.

"Whether or not what you're saying is the truth, that it is not sorcery, I'm only happy that you are able to visit us," Adne said after a while.

"Your mother and I really did think you were dead after all these years," added Holgar as Adne wiped a tear from her cheek. "I've seen the power of your healing crystal, and understand that there are things in the world that are difficult for us to comprehend. And it's undeniably true that you're able to reach us quickly now."

Holgar appeared to be digesting what they'd just told him. No one said anything for a while, but then, as they got up from the table, he spoke again.

"I'm concerned the wrong people will discover your abilities. It will be dangerous for you if anyone knows you have strange powers." He remembered his betrayal in Akelarre by his trusted business partner to the soldiers of Amrafalus.

"Not only for us, but for you too," said Tristan. "Trust us. We'll not allow anyone to see us disappear or appear magically!"

"I would never expose our children to any danger, either," said Djana. She looked over at the sleeping children nearby. Kara was the baby, and her brother, Imhotep, age two, lay next to her on a blanket. They were the most precious things in her life. She hated taking them away from the safety of Three Rivers, but as long as they remained out of sight, they were safe. If someone unknown came to the house, she and Tristan would pick up the children, pull up their merkabas, and remain invisible until the visitors left.

Adne had already told an inquisitive passerby that the crying child he heard in their house belonged to a neighbor, and that she was taking care of it for a while. She knew that Ortzi thought the six healers were dead, killed in the earthquake at the crystal caverns, but it would only take one sighting by the wrong person, such as Mikel, who hated them, and Ortzi would hunt them down again. Worse, he could use her parents as hostages, just as Amrafalus had done.

Before falling asleep that night, Djana's thoughts went over the past six years since the fall of the Citadel in Rhiannon, and their escape from the reptilian ruler, Amrafalus, by fishing boat to Ibai.

They had spent many months in Ibai healing the mutant Trueni before coming to the attention of Warlord Ortzi in Abena. Ortzi had found his own uses for them and their skills after their capture, and taken them to an enormous crystal cavern in the hills north of Abena where he'd stranded them so they could tell him how to harness the power of the crystals.

She smiled as she thought how they'd escaped with the help of Irusan, their shape-shifting cat-man friend, and the crystals themselves. The crystals created an earthquake that sealed the cave, and Ortzi thought they had all been killed. Irusan arranged for their healed Trueni fisherman friend, Askia, to transport them up the Garden River by raft, where they'd been left to find their way home to Aelfar.

This is where they'd encountered the wolf-men, and almost lost their lives to the monstrous creatures. If they had not been rescued by Finn, the elemental from Ardvale, they would not have survived the attack. Their stay in Ardvale, a place with no time, was where Jarah and Tegan's child Anwyn had been born. But once they'd left Ardvale after what felt like years of training in elemental command, only a few months in the real world had passed.

She remembered how astonished they'd been, and how they had still felt fear as they journeyed across Mannanon towards Aelfar. This is where they'd found Catrin, who had been searching for them so they could heal her son. They had saved her from the vengeance of the wolf-men by healing the wolf-man Catrin had nearly killed.

THE SIX AND ANWYN OF IALANA

Unfortunately, they'd been captured again, this time by King Brenin and his army. Brenin and Branwyn had their own plans for the six healers, but Catrin was to be killed the next day. Thanks to the assistance of Blaidd, now a fearful mutant known as Yagmak, the leader of the wolfmen, they'd escaped their capture by King Brenin. The King had lost his life in the battle with the mutants.

Their journey back to Aelfar had been long and arduous, but with the help of Catrin, who no longer wore her boyish disguise, and her bandit friend Ambros, they had made it safely to Three Rivers in northern Aelfar.

Sheltered and protected by the Queen and her son Deryn, the heir to the kingdom of Aelfar and Mernoc, they'd spent their time practicing with the merkaba and honing their healing skills. Although there were no Trueni in Aelfar or Three Rivers, the Six had worked, studied, and practiced hard, and now, at last, they felt ready to set out on another journey to Ibai. She and Tristan had volunteered to be the first to travel that far in their merkabas, taking their children with them, to scout out things in Ibai and test their abilities.

Besides herself and Tristan, all three couples, Jarah and Tegan, and Adain and Kex, now had very young children to care for. Jarah and Tegan were lucky to have an older daughter, Djana thought, who was able to help in caring for the younger children. Anwyn had become their teacher and mentor, teaching not only the children about the ancient knowledge she had been taught in the elemental world where she had spent most of her life, but the adults too.

She far surpassed any of them in skill, was proficient in elemental command, and had been able to use her merkaba vehicle from a young age. Djana thought if their secrets reached the wrong ears, Anwyn was the one that most likely would become a target. However, she did not feel that Anwyn would be an *easy* target. With her skills, she had abilities that matched those of Irusan, their mentor and teacher, the shape-shifter who had so often helped them in the past.

They'd seen Irusan occasionally for brief periods since he'd helped them six years ago. The energies of the outer worlds affected his body pattern, and to heal, he needed to remain as much as possible in his other-dimensional home.

Anwyn had also spent a brief time on the island of Mu'A, taken there by Irusan. It was imperative to all that she not suffer the fate of the Raven, who had remained in the outer world far too long for her template to heal.

According to Irusan, the Raven had suffered the effects of Udfa's crystals, the crystals he'd had a tailor sew into the hem of her garment. They had altered her template, or energetic fabric, in a way where she could no longer operate her merkaba or change back into her human form. As a result, the Raven, also known as Branwyn, became unrecognizable as the Queen of Rhiannon upon her return, and had shape-shifted back into a monster. Her own soldiers had put her to the sword, burned her body, and scattered her ashes to the four winds.

Holgar and Adne knew everything about their daughter now, and her husband and friends. There were no secrets between them, and there was no need to hide their abilities from them. But Djana's parents, although hesitant to accept the ancient knowledge from their daughter and her friends, were the exception to the rule.

The remainder of the Six had not informed their parents of their new skills. Adain, Jarah, and Tegan had reunited with their parents in Meadowfield and Potters Hill, but they explained their visits in ways that would not cause their parents alarm. Their families would react badly to the perceived witchcraft had they known the truth about them. Their understanding of healing was vague, and they had made it quite clear they did not want to know more.

All they knew was that it had something to do with Tegan's herbal skills, and they and their friends seemed no different to many of the other fake healers who pushed their dubious wares from village to village. Fake healers were more acceptable to them than the real thing, and they were more willing to accept strange powers from the gods and goddesses that they worshiped with offerings and prayers.

Their fears that the gods would be angry and punish the families of anyone who claimed a god-like ability was not underestimated by the Six. It was not their intention to cause their parents debilitating fear. Djana knew that Adain, Jarah, and Tegan's parents would understand nothing of their newfound abilities or experiences with the mystical elements of their world. They felt it safer and kinder to explain many things away in terms they could understand.

Anwyn was a puzzle to them. They had learned of her existence shortly after her release from Ardvale, as a child of nine years. Although her parents had left the land of Ardvale six years ago, Anwyn was already, in both development and in appearance, a child well advanced for her years.

Ardvale existed on another plane, and was not affected by earthly time. They had explained Anwyn away to their parents as an orphan whom Jarah and Tegan had adopted as their own. Their parents, except for Holgar and Adne, who knew the truth, accepted that explanation and asked no further questions about Anwyn.

Kex's parents, still in Rhagbeneth, did not know that Kex was alive. Having run away from them at age fifteen because of a forced marriage arrangement, she had not returned, although Djana and Tristan knew she often grieved over the loss of her family.

Djana breathed deeply and her eyes closed. She needed to get some sleep. Tomorrow was their day of departure for Three Rivers, and she did not want to fire up her merkaba while tired. Not with her children's lives at stake.

4.

Rhagbeneth

Kex allowed her tears to flow freely. She had not cried since she had left her clan and her home as a young girl. Below her, she felt sure, was the village of her clan, the Stone Wolf tribe. It had to be. She'd searched for months for her family, and this settlement felt right in the way the hide tents were arranged and decorated with large mammoth tusks and bones.

Each clan had their own signature style when it came to constructing their temporary abodes. In a few months, they would be deconstructed again as the tribe moved southwards. They would rebuild their village in the comparatively warmer areas of the South Rhagbeneth plains. In front of her stretched the Okeks Ice Plains, towards the northern reaches of the Osgoi Range. If she looked up, towards the far horizon, she could see a white band to the north, the hulking mass of the great ice wall. Her tribe seldom ventured that far, preferring instead to stay in the warmer, grassy plains where food was plentiful. Kex had spent months searching for her clan, but today she had located them in their summer lands.

THE SIX AND ANWYN OF IALANA

To say it was summer in Rhagbeneth was a bit of a stretch, since there was still snow and ice on the ground, but it was habitable, and hunting would be good. She thought the village looked prosperous this year. There were more tents, their conical, hide-covered shapes stretching below her across the plain, and smoke arose from cooking fires below. She felt underdressed in her Aelfar clothing of linens and silks, but she was warm in her insulated and invisible merkaba vehicle.

She used her linen shawl to wipe the tears away. She missed her mother and father, her brother and sisters, and her clan. She could not recognize anyone on the ground. From this height, they were merely tiny shapes that moved around the camp.

She had forbidden Adain to come with her. She did not want him to witness her sorrow if and when she located her clan. Before she left, he begged her not to contact them.

"I know you're really skilled in merkaba control, Kex, probably better than any of us, but what if you were captured and could not bring it up again? That happens to us, sometimes, when we're afraid. We're not yet completely skilled at merkaba travel."

"Yes, I know that, Adain. Don't fret. I don't plan to reveal myself. I only want to see how my family is doing. I know if I suddenly appeared I would be considered a witch. The clan does not treat witches or their families well, and there is still the matter of my refusal to marry a man from the Cold Bone Clan. I hope he did not make things difficult for my family. In our society, a promise is a promise."

With the conversation still fresh in her mind, Kex slowly lowered her merkaba to the ground. She could now smell the cooking fires and hear the chatter of children as they played in the snow. It didn't feel like that long ago she had been one of them.

A large stag lay on the ground as men gathered around it. They were busy skinning it and cutting it up. Not a part of the deer would be wasted, she thought. Everything, from the horns, bones, sinew, guts, hoofs, and skin would be used, and the meat would be cut in strips and dried on wooden racks in the cold, dry air.

Was her father, Keckryn one of these men, she wondered? She drew closer. Their thick hide coverings and furs made it hard to tell them apart. She could hear their chatter now.

"How do you know that, Olar?"

"They always attack when the weather's good, that's how. If you used your senses, Arik, you'd know that too."

"You're crazy, Olar. I only believe what my eyes and ears tell me. If I didn't, I'd never be the great hunter I am."

The group guffawed and one of them slapped Arik on the back.

"Did *you* bring this Elk down? He talks as if he did it all by himself. I think he'd wet his skins if we sent him out there alone!"

The group laughed again, and Arik turned red.

"It was my spear that brought this stag down, not yours. And you're only changing the subject because you know I'm right. The Cold Bone Clan will attack tomorrow, I tell you!"

Another voice spoke, one that Kex immediately recognized. She almost forgot to keep her shield of invisibility up she was so excited, and remembered just in time.

"We'll ask the medicine man. Yes, Gugun will know. Not you, Arik. You tell us every day the Cold Bone Clan will attack tomorrow. We're tired of hearing it. One day you'll be right, but Gugun is the only one in this Clan that truly knows what the eyes and ears cannot."

"Like your daughter?" snickered another man, and the group fell silent. Keckryn slowly rose, his bloodied, bone knife in his hand.

"You keep my daughter out of this," he said.

His voice was quiet, but it sent chills up Kex's spine. She knew when her father meant business. She had been at the receiving end of his wrath many times before. The man fell silent, and so did the other men. Keckryn sat down again, and they silently went about their task of deer-skinning.

Kex wondered what daughter Keckryn was referring to. Was it her? But she had never professed to have special powers. It was only her dreams . . .

She moved away from the group and began to search the tents. Finally, she found it; a tent on the outskirts of the camp. *Not good*, she thought. Only tribal outcasts lived on the outer edges where they were vulnerable to attack from man and beast. One could tell a lot about someone's status in the clan by their tent location. She knew it was her family tent because she saw her youngest sister, Saran, playing outside by herself. *Saran must be about eleven years old now*, she thought. She did not want to go inside the tent, so instead, she waited outside. It was too risky. She could not guarantee she could keep her merkaba invisible if her emotions ran away with her concentration.

She hid behind a rack of drying meat just in case she lost her focus and suddenly appeared. At least this way, she may not be noticed, and she could quickly regain her invisibility again. She didn't have long to wait. A woman came out of the tent and Kex gasped. It was Jax, her mother!

Losing her focus, her merkaba flashed off in the visible spectrum of light, and Jax's head jerked towards her hiding place. Kex drew in a deep breath, closed her eyes, and refocused. Jax walked, as if mesmerized, towards the drying rack and looked straight into Kex's eyes. Kex held her breath, not daring to breath or move. Was she still visible? Jax had a puzzled look on her face, but she shook her head and walked back to the tent.

"Saran, come inside and help me with the dinner. Your sister is working on the hides to make clothes for you to wear, and you're wasting time with your toys!" Kex knew her mother referred to the bone doll Saran was playing with. It had once been hers. Kex felt the tears welling up again, but angrily told herself to get a grip on her emotions.

It had been years since she'd seen her family. She was surprised she even recognized them, but she felt a sense of recognition that went beyond the way they now looked. There was a strong emotional connection with family, and a part of herself that did not rely on her eyes and ears told her she had found them.

Arik must be correct. She did have this ability. Did someone else in her family have it too? She had two sisters, Saran and Alaqa. Alaqa was obviously still at home. She was glad to know that, since Alaqa would be long past her marriageable age by now. Was Alaqa as resistant to marriage as Kex had been? Kex had been the oldest girl. She had a brother,

Khulan, but he had married a girl from another tribe before she had left. His tent must be around here too, somewhere, but she was more interested in her sister's and mother's fate to look. She decided to stay.

Saran put the bone doll down, but she didn't get up. She looked around her, as if she was searching for something. Then, she looked up. Kex almost lost her concentration again, but she focused. Saran looked straight at her, gasped, and ran inside the tent. *Had she been seen?* She drew closer to the tent.

"Mother, I saw a strange lady watching me! She was standing in the air!"

"Your imagination will get you into trouble, young lady. You must stop that. People will think you're a witch. It was bad enough with your sister and her dreams . . . Here, take this bird and get the feathers off. Put it on the fire when you're done, and don't burn it like last time!"

She must possess inner vision abilities to see me, Kex thought. *It's not possible for an ordinary person to see me if my merkaba surrounds me!*

She wondered if Saran was one of them, another birth-in from a place far, far away. If so, she needed to keep an eye out for her. It would be dangerous for her here in Rhagbeneth.

Darkness fell, but still Kex watched as her mother, father, and sisters went about their duties both inside and outside the tent. She could not hear any more conversation, and it was not until the moon rose before she decided to return to Three Rivers. Her husband would be worried about her, and she wanted to be with her children. They were her family now, not this one, but she had not forgotten them, and she never would.

City of Rhiannon

The Council sat slackjawed, too stunned to speak. The news was astounding.

Udfa had just told them about the discovery in the mines. Udfa could tell none of them knew what to make of it. He didn't know what to make of it either, but he felt that the find would mark a turning point for him.

The fortunes of Rhiannon were not gaining momentum, and citizens were restless with his leadership. He understood better than anyone just what that meant for his future. He needed some good news and what had seemed like bad news at first might be exactly what he needed.

"I told you, we need to *find* them," he said for the tenth time. "I will not accept '*they are dead*' from you, Zephan. Ortzi thinks they are dead, but how does he really know? Did he find the bodies?"

"Our spies tell me he did not see the bodies," admitted Zephan, "But no one could have escaped the earthquake in those caves!"

"No one human," said Udfa. "I tell you, *again*, that these six are not human. They are sorcerers. Remember, it was they who brought the Citadel down that killed Amrafalus. They probably caused the earthquake to cover up their escape, and you fools bought it! Get back to Galon today. Get as much information as you can, or better still, bring the parents back here. I'll get it out of them. Go on! You know what to do!"

He frowned as Zephan leapt out of his chair and ran to the door. Zephan knew Udfa would not tolerate any failures from him. He wasn't that stupid.

Udfa turned back to his Council. "Anyone here disagree?" The Council was silent. "Good. Then we also agree that the situation in the mines is still a problem. The problem is, no one can get near whatever it is. It has already killed the slaves and overseers who got too close. Whatever it may be, it's powerful indeed. That is why we need those six healers. They're the only ones who know how to control things like this. They must go in there using their magic so that it won't kill people, but ensure that we can control it. Only us. Ialana can still be ours for the taking."

"From what we've been told, getting too close is fatal for all," said one of the braver council members. "How are these wizards and witches going to get near them without . . ." His voice trailed off as he noticed the black look on Udfa's face.

"Did you not hear me? They are *sorcerers*! We take them there and make sure they do not escape. If they want to live, they'll find a way to control it. Of course they can do it. They made the crystals under the Citadel do their bidding, they can put their spells on this . . . this . . . *whatever-it-is*. If they live, and I'm sure they are alive in Ialana somewhere, they will have only become more powerful."

He rubbed his chin and smiled. He couldn't wait to counter Ortzi's flaming balls with a powerful weapon. He wouldn't stand a chance. He'd put the sorcerers, and it, on a ship with a minimal crew and send them into the harbor. They'd kill everyone in Abena if they had to.

He'd find a way.

5.

Yor Swamps

The whip cracked again over the bare back of the slave. From his ringside, arena seat, Moran Blacktooth watched. His mouth was a slash of broken and blackened teeth. His pink tongue flicked over his thin lips with anticipation as the slave screamed again. Moran enjoyed the whippings before his morning meal. If his soldiers did not find enough slaves to whip, he'd have them whipped instead. One way or another, he'd have his desires met.

Dawla sat next to him on the dais that overlooked the arena. Her face was expressionless. She did not get as much pleasure out of the whippings as he did, but she did not object to them either. Her cold eyes were unreadable, but they lingered on the bloodied back of the slave. This slave had displeased her. He had not lowered his gaze when she'd entered the room. He was new, recently captured from a raid into Mernoc, and did not yet understand the protocol of the court of the Yor warlord.

He would soon understand. Perfectly. For the rest of his short life, he'd bear the scars that would remind him of his disrespect.

Moran pondered the news he'd recently received from Three Rivers. King Brenin was dead six years, but his widow and son now ruled the kingdom. Moran had respected the King, but not so the Queen or the Prince. He had heard the Queen had remarried, but no one seemed to know much about her new husband except that he and the Queen did not approve of slave trading.

It's a shame, he thought. He and Brenin had had a profitable arrangement: that the Yor hordes would not raid north into Aelfar and Mernoc for slaves and plunder if Brenin sent him slaves, and shared the looted treasure taken during his own raids in his own kingdom.

They had always made forays into Mernoc, though. Brenin had done nothing to stop him. The treaty had always been meaningless, and he and his raiders still boldly ventured into southern Mernoc to take slaves and plunder, and then cross south over the Esti River and raid northern Galon. It was his right. He would show the new queen, her husband, and her sniveling son who was the real ruler of Ialana, but he first had to be rid of them both. He gave little thought to her new husband. According to his spies, he was rarely seen in public. He was only known as the Queen's Consort, and to Moran it indicated that he was ineffectual and of no consequence: that he allowed himself to be subordinate to a mere wife.

After taking Aelfar, he would be free take Mernoc, and after that Galon, and possibly even Rhiannon. He'd heard Emperor Udfa was no push-over, but by that time he'd be strong with the territories and armies needed to expand his territory.

The disease-ridden swamps were becoming even more unsustainable for his people, and he was sick of swatting mosquitos. People were dying of swamp miasmas, and their best healers could do nothing. He had to keep replenishing his subjects with new ones by raiding for slaves, but now the raids were producing less and less in plunder. He could no longer afford a treaty made years ago with a long-dead king. He needed the fertile lands of Aelfar and Mernoc to support him and his people. He had already made his plans.

Moran rose, and Dawla dutifully followed. The whipping no longer interested him. He needed to consult his generals and plan the raid into the heartland of Aelfar. There was much in the way of untapped resources he could benefit from. It would make a change from the ignorant peasants and their meagre possessions in north Galon. He knew he could not yet venture further south to Abena. Ortzi was a strong leader, and his navy had recently defeated Brenin, although he'd heard there was sorcery involved.

It was time for breakfast. He licked his lips again.

6.

Three Rivers

The Queen had returned home, the sunset in the western sky in front of her a pink and orange glow. Catrin looked forward to the end of her trip to the Mernoc region. She was seldom in the Palace now, and spent more time on the road than she did at home. Deryn, her son and heir, rode next to her. Not so many years ago, she never would have thought that her son would heal and turn into this strong young man, the future King.

She wished Ambros had traveled with her, but he did not venture out in public often, and when he did, he avoided getting close to people. *No doubt a by-product of his days as a bandit*, she thought. He was a powerful man too, both in spirit and body, and one whom she respected. Not just for his physical strength, but for his heart and soul. He was also the gentlest man she had ever known.

She remembered the day she'd met Ambros, the day six years ago when he'd seen right through her boyish appearance to the feminine spirit beneath the disguise. It was the day he had protected her from the cut-throats and bandits into whose village she'd strayed.

THE SIX AND ANWYN OF IALANA

The scar-faced man had become her best friend, mentor, and now her husband. She'd discovered much about Ambros since that day, and what she had discovered was shocking. But there was no time to dwell on that now. She had a kingdom to run. Her son's coronation would take place soon and she wanted to hand over a kingdom to him that was free of poverty, war, and discontent.

Her trips to the far reaches of her domain told her more than any second-hand reports could. She met personally with the farmers, peasants, and populace in all walks of life and listened to their concerns. She encouraged Deryn to do the same, and Ambros became her adviser and protector. She surrounded herself with trustworthy people.

Her Witan, or Counsel, consisted of people who had earned her trust. Ambros was her adviser and liaison to the Witan, and Callum, the husband of her Lady in Waiting, Corrick, was now the head of the Witan. Deryn was in charge of the military, but she still had the last word in any military decisions made.

Of course, Brenin's previous head, Thane Awstin the Forkbeard, had been none too happy about losing both his King and his position. Once Catrin returned from the war with the Beasts of Mannanon, and Awstin had learned of Brenin's death, he had gone to her to jockey for a position in the new government, but Catrin had seen right through his maneuvering. She knew he had been Brenin's puppet, and she did not trust him. She allowed him to retire with a generous salary if he promised to stay out of her business.

Thane Awstin knew when he was beaten, and he agreed, taking most of his Witan with him. He was no longer a threat to her. Life was, at last, the way she had always dreamed it would be.

She looked forward to seeing her friends at the palace. She always missed them during her trips, but did not feel it safe to take them with her, and felt they were well-guarded in her palace, surrounded by trusted servants and staff. She did not know which, if any, of their enemies were still alive, and perhaps still looking for the healers.

The Six had restored her son to health. She had put her own life on the line and sacrificed all she had to find the healers. It had all been worth it, and she wanted them to stay with her forever. Her kingdom was prospering, and she had accomplished her goals: to leave a wealthy and peaceful land to Deryn.

His father notwithstanding, Deryn had much of her in him. He, like Ambros, was an honorable man, and under Ambros's tutelage, she had high hopes for their future.

The Six

Tristan and Djana met with their friends as soon as they returned from Ibai.

"What do you think about us returning there permanently?" Jarah asked. "Will we, and our children, be safe?"

"No, we'll never be safe there," said Tristan. "But how much longer are we going to put off our mission—to heal—because we're afraid?"

"I'm not afraid for myself," said Kex. "I am afraid for our children."

"Me too," said Tegan. "How are we going to do healing work and not be discovered?"

Anwyn, who had been sitting listening to the meeting, spoke up.

"When I was in Mu'A," she said quietly, "we learned a little about shielding technology. I'm not skilled in it yet, but with Finn and the elemental's help, we can be taught to use it. We'd be able to live closer to Ibai, but we'd need to use shielding to live, and we'd use our merkabas to travel back and forth."

"We can use our merkaba's right now, to go back and forth from here," said Tristan. "We can get there in an instant and be home again in time for dinner!"

"True," said Jarah, "but if something goes wrong, we're a long way from home. That's months of dangerous travel over mountains and through deadly forest. We're skilled, but we're still living in a world where things malfunction, and let's face it, none of us are perfect in merkaba travel yet. At least in Ibai, if we're forced to move on the ground, we won't have far to go."

"And I like your shielding idea, Anwyn!" said Adain.

"Well, it's agreed then," said Jarah. "We'll go, and when we get there, we'll ask Finn to teach us how not to be found."

THE SIX AND ANWYN OF IALANA

The day after Catrin's return, the Six had asked for a meeting with her, Deryn, and Ambros.

"You all look so serious! I hope nothing untoward has happened in my absence?"

"No," said Jarah. "All is well. I suppose that's the problem though, if you could call it one. We have all talked and come to a decision, and we'd like your opinion. You have treated us all so well since we got here, and without you it would have been so much more difficult—"

Catrin laughed. "But my friends, I am the one beholden to you. You healed my son and he is now as healthy as I am." She looked at Deryn who sat next to her. "For that, I am eternally grateful. If I provided you with a safe haven through eternity, I would still not have repaid you. You'll always be in my debt. Oh, and don't forget how you saved my hide in Mannanon! I certainly did not forget that!"

"We don't see it as a debt," Jarah replied. "We would have done it no matter what. I am glad we helped you, Deryn."

Deryn silently nodded. Jarah thought him a man of few words, but he showed wisdom in his dealings with others, and he had been a friend to them too.

"But that is not why we're here. We have had time to develop our skills in healing, and feel strong enough now to return to where we are really needed—in Ibai and Akelarre."

"You mean you want to go back to those dreadful places?" Catrin asked. "Where you'll still be hunted by Ortzi, and the rulers of Rhiannon?"

"Mother, I agree with Jarah. Our friends need to move on. Someone else besides me, perhaps, could use their healing skills." Deryn looked at them and smiled. "If there is anything I can do to help you as king of this land, just say the word. I can provide you with a military escort to wherever you need to go."

Jarah hesitated. He looked at the other five. They each knew that they could leave in their merkabas along with their children, but no one else knew about their abilities. They had deemed it important that as few people knew about it as possible. It was safer for all that way.

Even though they trusted Catrin, Deryn, and Ambros, they did not know who they might talk to about it, and then it would become a rumor, a rumor that would reach the ears of those who still wished them ill, and people would be looking, again, for them. Right now, they were only known at the palace as herbalists, six of at least two dozen more in this city alone, they just happened to be the Queen's favorites. But they'd carefully concealed their skills—except for the professed healing of their future king. Many said that Deryn would have grown out of his childhood affliction anyway, and it was only a matter of luck on their part that he did heal. They did their best to encourage this rumor.

Jarah hesitated. "Thank you, Deryn. We appreciate your offer. We'll discuss it, and let you know."

"I will also help with an escort if you require one," said Ambros. "I know how dangerous the roads still are in Aelfar, and if you need to return to the southlands, it will be my pleasure to provide an armed guard along with Deryn's."

They would have to come up with a plausible reason not to have an escort, or accept the escort and return to Ibai and Akelarre the long and hard way, Jarah thought. The escort could only take them as far as Galon, since to cross the border with a military escort would be considered an act of war.

The escort could not accompany them over or under the mountains either, the route they had taken on their first journey six years ago. No amount of military escort would be able to protect them from the ferocious beasts and monsters that roamed these areas, and in order to survive the trip, they would be forced to use what would be regarded as witchcraft to protect themselves and their so-called protectors. Most importantly, they could not take their children on such a long and dangerous trip. They must convince Deryn and Ambros, without revealing their secrets, to withdraw their offer.

Jarah knew this wasn't going to be easy.

Ambros

After the Six left the room, Ambros noticed Catrin's puzzled look.

"Why do the Six want to leave?" she asked. "They are happy here, and we adore them and their children. They have always felt like family to us." She looked at Deryn to see if he had any insights. He looked at her, but only shrugged.

"If they want to leave, let them go!" Deryn got up and strode out of the room. Catrin knew his show of nonchalance meant just the opposite. Deryn would miss them, he just didn't want anyone to know.

Ambros had nothing to say for a while. He stood, and looked out the window at the city below. He felt Catrin's distress. He turned back to look at Catrin.

"They're not our children," he said at last. "They have lives of their own, and they have a mission to complete. They told us that their life's purpose was to heal the Trueni, and since there are no Trueni here, they must go where they are. It's as simple as that."

"Yes, yes, I know. I think it's difficult for me to accept that they won't be staying here forever, but you're right. At least I still have you and Deryn."

Ambros sat down next to Catrin and put his arm around her. "Look at me," he said. She turned her head and gazed into his blue eyes. "I understand. You have been terribly hurt in your life—abandoned by many you thought you could trust. The worst trust to lose is that of your life's partner. Know that I will never allow that to happen to you again. I am not Brenin. I may be his brother, but we couldn't have been less alike."

Catrin nodded, smiling as a tear ran down her face. She wiped it away with the back of her hand.

"You're right. It's my past that is dictating my reactions now. Ambros, I don't know what I would have done without you in my life. To say I was surprised to find out who you really were is an understatement." She gave a half sob, half laugh. "I will never forget the day I found you at that god-forsaken outpost in Aelfar. You were a rather frightening figure to me and I thought you were the roughest of that gang of bandits. I was so surprised when you protected me and hid my true identity from those men."

Ambros smiled. "I knew who you were right away. You and Brenin had no idea I attended your wedding. How could I forget your beautiful face? You aren't the only one who knows how to wear a disguise!"

They both laughed.

"To think that Brenin would have had you killed if he'd known . . ." She gulped, then took a deep breath. "He told me he'd had a brother, but that he'd died, so I never knew of your existence. And he certainly never mentioned trying to kill you before we married!" She lightly touched the twisting scar on Ambros's cheek. "How I love that scar. It has kept your true identity a secret from those who may have recognized you all these years."

"Yes, it has been my protection, and I'm glad you find it appealing. Maybe you're the only one who does." He winked, but then his face grew serious again. "Brenin still has his loyalists who would want me dead. I'm not surprised you didn't know what happened. He and I were always rivals, for everything—women, sword fights, the throne—except I did not want the throne. He only thought I did. I knew I had to flee the kingdom when he sent assassins after me. They almost succeeded." His hand went instinctively to the scar.

"All Brenin said was that you just disappeared one day, and he suspected you had been killed by enemies. He was rather vague about just who *they* might be. We've talked about this many times, Ambros, and each time we speak of it, I am nearly as surprised by it all as I was the first time you told me."

"I am hopeful for Deryn," Ambros said, changing the subject. He was learning more about Deryn each day. His nephew was not like his father, he knew that, but Deryn hid his feelings well. He was still young, and young men were often hasty and hot-headed. But he knew, deep down, that Deryn had much of Catrin in his make-up. "He will make a fair and just king, thanks to you."

"The next few moons are going to be busy for us with Deryn's upcoming coronation, and I hear that Moran is planning an attack on our territory."

"I've heard that too," said Ambros, his face thoughtful, as he stroked his scar. "In fact, I am almost certain of it."

"We must prepare."

"Yes, we must."

7.

Making Plans

"So what are we going to do?" Kex asked Adain as they made their way through the palace to their quarters. She knew the others would be discussing this amongst themselves as well. They had all agreed to discuss it separately, then meet with their ideas later.

"I really don't know, Kex. It's a problem for sure."

Kex felt annoyed. Adain excelled at stating the obvious. She wanted solutions, and she wanted them now.

Kex had not told Adain what she'd overheard on her trip to find her clan. She was still mulling it over, wondering if she should say something, but her fiercely independent streak prevented her from confiding in her husband. She wanted to be the strong one, and admitting she was homesick and worried was, in her opinion, admitting weakness. It was her experience that weak people did not survive.

She loved her husband, and she would protect both him and their child, Gaiana, with her life. She knew Adain would understand her concern about her family, but Adain was not as skilled in the art of survival as she. He might try and do something separately to help her that would lead to disaster for them all.

She would keep quiet about it. When he asked, she only said she'd located her family, and they were all still alive and well. This was true. The rest was only conjecture on her part. She did not tell him either that her mother and sister had quite possibly seen her. That would have worried him no end.

"We could accept the 'help' and give them the slip while they sleep," she said. She didn't think it was an intelligent idea, but it was a start.

"That doesn't feel right to me, and I don't think the others will like it. Besides, they'll have a guard posted."

They returned to their quarters in silence.

"What should we do?" Djana asked.

Tristan shrugged. "Don't know."

Djana sighed. "We just say *no*. Don't need to explain. We leave, and that will be that."

"We may have to do just that. But we owe Catrin something other than a flat refusal of their help. We're taking the children. Think how worried she will be."

"You're right. We do owe her more. How about we say something like, 'We are grateful for your help, but our friend Irusan will help us again'?"

"Now you'll just be lying, Djana. Is that what you want?"

"No." Djana looked shamefaced. It was so easy to tell a lie of convenience, even to protect someone's feelings.

This was going to be more difficult than she had anticipated.

THE SIX AND ANWYN OF IALANA

The Six met for dinner later that evening in Jarah and Tegan's quarters. The palace was quiet, and the children had been put to bed. Anwyn kept watch over them. No one said anything about their plans until they'd eaten their meal, and then they all walked out of the palace grounds towards the banks of the River Mair.

It was a mild summer evening, and the moonlit water rippled in the gently flowing river. It was their favorite place to meet and talk. The palace was never a safe place to discuss secrets. Brenin had discovered that the hard way. There were always ears pressed against doors, secret listening posts still undiscovered, and servants lurking with the intention of finding useful information about someone. Here, on the banks of the river, they felt completely at ease, and could speak freely.

"Has anyone had any ideas?" asked Tristan. "Because we, sure as the Shadowlands, have not."

"Not for lack of trying," added Djana.

Tegan turned to look at Adain. "How about you and Kex?"

"No."

Kex frowned, but said nothing.

"Well, I think I might have come up with something," said Jarah. He immediately had their attention.

"I had the feeling today that Deryn, in spite of his offer of an escort, may have been relieved to see us go. Without reading too much into that, could we really trust him and his men with our secrets?" He looked around, and even in the moonlight he could see the soft shakes of their heads. They all remembered their betrayal six years ago by their so-called friend, Blaidd.

"Deryn was once betrayed by his own father," said Tegan. Djana nodded.

"He may see us as competitors for his mother's affection," she said. "He is our friend, but he does not share his feelings with us."

"I find him a bit of a mystery sometimes," said Kex.

"He's still young, and I am not sure we should put our trust in him just yet," said Jarah. "I think we can all agree on that. But there is another I am sure of. Someone we could trust with our lives, and our secret."

"Ambros!" yelled an excited Djana.

Jarah laughed. "Yes. I think we do agree on that. He has been one of the most honorable people we've known. I have watched him, and noticed his actions and words always go together. If he makes a promise, he keeps it. He will always tell the truth, and he'll never reveal a confidence. To say he is different from his brother is like saying the sun will rise in the morning. I trust him almost as much as Irusan."

They all nodded again. Irusan, the shape-shifting cat-man who had helped them so many times before, was their paragon of trust and virtue.

"What about Catrin? Do you not trust her, Jarah?" asked Kex.

"Yes, I do, but Catrin has a weak spot. Her son. We may ask her not to say anything to her son, but one day she *will* talk. It is human to do so. Ambros will not. I have never seen Deryn manipulate Ambros, although he does manipulate his mother frequently. I think Ambros understands Deryn better than we do, and that's why I would rather take Ambros into our confidence than either Deryn or Catrin."

"So we'll tell Ambros then. That's settled," said Tristan. "Do you think he will know what to do so our secret will not be discovered by either his soldiers or anyone else?"

"I am sure of it," said Jarah. "Let's talk to him tomorrow."

They sat outside and talked some more. They were all excited now that they'd felt the call to return to their healing contract. They'd spent enough time learning, practicing, and studying the notes that had been given to them by Blaidd.

The notes he'd made on programming crystals, containing all his knowledge from his life in Mu'A, hastily scratched on scraps of papyrus and bundled up and given to Holgar and Adne before he'd completely lost his knowledge. They were grateful to Blaidd. They wondered how he was now. Was he still alive? The pack of wolf-men he'd taken up with and become the leader of was frightening. Even Blaidd's strong and fearful form may not have survived such a brutal lifestyle.

"Do you think we can find him in Mannanon?" asked Tegan. "I would really love to assure myself that he is alive and well."

Jarah looked at her with concern. "What if he's not?" He knew how tender-hearted she was.

"I would be sad, yes, but I hope he is still thriving."

"We can see how things go," said Tristan. "If it looks safe, we will fly over the area we last saw him. Perhaps we'll see him again."

"I'd love to see Finn too," said Kex. "Maybe we can find the portal—the door in the tree—again?"

"I'll ask Anwyn," said Tegan. "She knows more about that than we do."

They discussed their upcoming trip as the stars wheeled in the sky and the moon began to set.

They were too excited to sleep.

8.

The Arrival

Glahivar looked down at her new body. She had awakened on a river bank. The sun was just rising over the trees. She was not pleased. She still missed her old, comely body, and this one looked aged. Not only that, she was completely naked. They hadn't even bothered to supply her with clothing!

She could not see her face, so she crawled on shaking knees, since she could not walk yet, through the undergrowth and down to the water's edge. She felt dizzy and nauseated. Where was she?

The last thing she remembered was undergoing the transformation in the Chambers of Deception. It had been so painful that she'd lost consciousness before its completion. But here she was, and all the pain and suffering had been worth it. To be honest, she told herself, it wasn't her old body, but it was at least better than the spider form.

Her legs were feeling stronger now, and she was no longer dizzy. She stood up. Step by careful step, she walked towards the river. She looked down into a still pool of water near the edge, and the face that looked up at her made her frown. Who would have thought? But it made sense, yes, it did.

"Do I have to tell you everything?" the thin voice sounded in her left ear. She jumped.

"Is that you, Shegami?"

"Of course it is. I can't believe how clueless you are. Are you going to walk into the palace dressed in nothing but your skin?"

"Why didn't you supply me with clothes?"

"Perhaps you've forgotten you can create your own?"

"Oh. Yes, I forgot." Glahivar remembered now. The instructions she'd been given were coming back to her. She closed her eyes and visualized the clothing that would best suit her new role. A rustling sounded, and she felt the soft linens against her skin. Looking down, she was pleased. Yes, she could do this! What about her merkaba? Would it work now?

She closed her eyes again and visualized her orb around her. She opened her eyes again. Yes, there it was. It worked again!

"You will be able to use your vehicle here, Glahivar, even though you won't be as masterful as you were with it before. We can work on that, but you sustained a lot of damage in your previous existence. Remember, I told you the Six all now have working merkabas, and they know how to use them. They will have a tiny advantage over you in that, perhaps in speed, but not in the other things we activated in your new template.

"I will give you something that will take care of their merkabas, but only use it when you absolutely must. They must not suspect anything too soon. There are many weaknesses yet to exploit, and you must not forget about the families of these people. The girl, Anwyn, is our biggest threat, but she is not the only one. Keep your eye on the other children, they have potential.

"When your mission is over, I will come and get you. Until then, you will not see or hear much from me, but here."

Glahivar saw a brief flash, and then heard a soft *clunk*.

She looked down. There was a glint as the rising sun's rays reflected off something lying in the grass.

"We talked about this in Iochodran. This is your weapon against Anwyn and the Six."

The whispery voice faded, and Glahivar picked the crystal up. It was double terminated, one point on each end, about the size of a hen's egg, and inside she could see a faint glimmer of red. She put it in her apron pocket. She would need to keep it with her at all times.

Turning, she slowly walked up to the large stone wall surrounding the palace. Now, where was that gate?

Catrin and Ambros were eating breakfast on the terrace when Lady Corrick approached them.

"Milady, I'm sorry to disturb you, but there is a lady at the palace gate who asks to speak with you, urgently. She says her name is Genove, and she is a farmer's wife—"

"Genove? That is an unusual name. I wonder, is her husband's name Angus?"

"Yes, milady. She says she lost a son—"

"Please, bring her to me at once, Corrick. I would love to speak with her again. I wonder if she would recognize me!"

"Is she the farmer's wife who gave you shelter when you were looking for the healers?" Ambros asked.

"Yes, when I was in my disguise as a boy with Deryn posing as my younger brother. I wonder what she's doing here?"

They didn't have long to wait. Corrick and a kindly faced woman stepped out onto the terrace. Even though it had been six years, Catrin recognized her immediately. Genove sank low in a curtsey.

"Milady," she said. "I need your help. May I speak with you?"

"Of course. What can I do to help you?" Genove had not seemed to recognize her queen as the young boy of so many years ago.

"I seek employment in your city or palace. My husband, Angus, died recently, and I have been unable to work on the farm myself. I have no son, or other children to help, and I am getting older. I have heard of your kindness and generosity towards your subjects, and felt my only option was to come here personally and beg your assistance."

"I am sorry to hear of your husband's demise, Genove." Catrin wondered if she should remind Genove who she was, but she caught Ambros's eye, and he shook his head ever so slightly. "In what capacity should I employ you?"

"I love children so much. Are there any young ones I can take care of within the palace walls?"

"Oh yes! But—" Catrin hesitated. "I don't know how much longer they'll be staying."

Genove's head rose sharply.

"Staying, milady?"

"They are planning to return to their—oh, never mind. Let me just say that we will always have children here. The courtiers have children, so no matter. You will always have a job, Genove."

Genove curtsied again, and Catrin asked Corrick to take her to the housekeeper.

"She will find you quarters and tell you what to do. We always welcome a new nanny in the palace! Our last one left a few moons ago, and we have not yet replaced her. Anwyn has been doing an excellent job with the palace children, but she'll be leaving soon."

Catrin noticed Genove's new interest at the mention of Anwyn. She felt Genove would be an excellent fit in the palace, and she was so happy to have been able to help her.

It was surprising how well this had all worked out.

9.

Anwyn

Anwyn stepped back as the new nanny came towards her. She didn't know why she did that, but her step back was involuntary. Genove looked sweet, and her smile lit up the room. The children loved her already and it had only taken a day, so why did she have this strange feeling in the pit of her stomach?

Anwyn didn't understand herself sometimes. There was no reason not to like Genove. She couldn't tell her parents about the sense of horror she'd felt when she'd first seen Genove. Everyone had loved her on sight, especially once Catrin had told them this was the same Genove who had sheltered her on her trip through Aelfar. She was the only one who felt this way. She must be wrong. Anwyn decided she'd not allow her imagination to run away with her.

She forced a smile and handed Djana's child, Kara, over to Genove.

"There, love! Let me put you to bed with the others!"

Genove kissed the baby on the head and Anwyn shuddered. This was not getting any better. She followed Genove into the baby's room and watched as she placed her in her crib. The baby smiled and gurgled and Genove seemed as comfortable with the baby as the baby was with her. It had to be all in her head, thought Anwyn. Babies were seldom wrong.

She sat next to Genove, and she and Genove sang lullabies to the children, lullabies that she'd learned in Ardvale, and that somehow Genove seemed to know. That was rather odd too, she thought, but maybe the lullabies in Ardvale had been borrowed from Aelfar.

They would be leaving for Ibai soon. Would Genove remain behind? She hoped so. She didn't think anyone would be coming with them since they were using their merkabas to get there, and no one must know about that. Especially not Genove. She hoped they'd stop in at Ardvale, where she grew up. She missed Finn and the other elementals. She knew where the portal was, and she could access it, but her parents could not. Not unless she or Finn was with them.

She had spent what felt like many summers in Ardvale, many more than the thirteen summers she appeared to be here. Time moved on a different track in the land of the Gardeners, but no one ever died there. They just stayed the same and took whatever form they wanted. She knew that unless someone or something deliberately caused her body irreparable harm, she too could live for a very long time. Her template was nearly impeccable in its purity, and in Ardvale she had learned how to shield herself from harmful energies in the material world. She knew how to heal any distortions and imbalances, and how to transmute potentially harmful substances in her body. She spoke to her physical body as if it was aware, which it was, and together they would seek out harmful invasions and transmute them before any damage could be done. She was growing into an adult body here, and it would take yet more years until her family began to treat her as an adult. In the meanwhile, she'd need to—

She looked up. Genove had stopped singing, and the baby was asleep. Genove was staring at her.

She didn't feel comfortable with what she could see in Genove's eyes.

A faint red light shone within. Genove's mouth stretched into a smile, but it looked more like a sneer.

"I think it's time you got to bed too, Anwyn. You are leaving soon, are you not?"

"What do you mean leaving?"

Genove's smile grew even wider.

"The Queen told me you'd be leaving. Where are you going?"

Anwyn shrugged. "I think we're visiting my grandparents. I don't know much about it. The grown-ups don't discuss it with me."

Genove looked disappointed. "Yes, grown-ups can be like that. But you're almost grown-up yourself now, and it isn't fair they don't discuss these things with you. You should know, right?"

Anwyn felt that chill again that sent shivers up her spine. How did she know what she was thinking? She looked at Genove and didn't say anything. She got up and walked out of the room. It felt as if Genove was attempting to separate her from her parents and the other grown-ups. It didn't bode well for them, or her.

She shut the door softly behind her.

Genove

She had to go with them. As soon as the children were asleep, she ran to the queen's private quarters. The uppity lady-in-waiting, Corrick, was on guard, as usual, and would not allow her in to see the queen.

"She's eating her dinner with her husband and son. She's done with court matters for today."

"Tell her I have something important to discuss with her. She knows me well, dear. I am not a mere hireling like you."

Corrick gave her a look that could have withered a snake, but it had no effect on Genove. Without a word, Corrick disappeared into the queen's quarters. A few minutes later, she returned. "She will receive you now," she said, sniffing in disapproval.

Genove entered the room and curtsied.

THE SIX AND ANWYN OF IALANA

The Queen, Deryn, and Ambros sat at a table, eating.

"Milady, I have been told that the children of the healers are leaving with their parents to visit with their families in western Aelfar. I must go with them."

"Why, Genove? It's a long trip, and they'll be going further than western Aelfar. They'll be going through dangerous territory. Even though they'll have a detachment of guards with them, it will still be dangerous. I don't even want them to go, and they're young and healthy. You, on the other hand—"

"Milady, I am healthier than I look. My family farm is on the way. I can always remain there if I am finding the journey too arduous. I feel I need to be there to look after the children. I already love them as my own. I will worry so much about them if I remain behind. Please let me go!"

Catrin thought for a while, then nodded. "Alright. You can go. But the moment you feel it is too much, please find a place you can stay safe in, or return here. Your job will be waiting for you."

Genove smiled. "You are so kind, milady! Thank you!"

She turned and left. Now, she had something else to do. The Queen did not tell her what the destination was, but she felt sure it was not Meadowfield or Potter's Hill. She knew the Queen would keep the secret for fear that she would talk to someone. She wondered if they were returning to Ibai or Akelarre. She could have just let them go and gone there herself in her own merkaba, but perhaps there was something she could do in the meanwhile, before killing Anwyn, to foil their plans. A long trip on the ground would give her plenty of opportunities.

She was sure they'd eventually need to use their merkabas to travel, but she'd be able to follow them in hers. They would not see her. She knew how to stay invisible. She laughed out loud and wished she could see their faces when Catrin gave them the news that she'd be traveling with them.

She returned to the nursery just in time. The nurse-maid was already alarmed at her absence.

"I am sorry I've been gone so long," she explained. "The Queen summoned me about an important matter and I was delayed."

The nurse-maid nodded and left. All was well.

She pulled up her merkaba and sped off, invisible, towards the quarters of the healers. They were not there. It would not take long to find them, she thought. They seldom left the palace grounds so they must still be nearby.

Using her energy sensing skills, she closed her eyes and saw a river bank, the same one she had so recently landed on, stark naked.

10.

Secrets

It was early evening, and the Six sat on the riverbank, waiting for Ambros. They had sent him a message to meet them here, alone, after the evening meal, and not to tell anyone where he was going.

After what felt like a long time, and as the moon rose higher in the sky, Ambros silently appeared. They had not heard him coming.

"Why all the secrecy? I hope all is well?"

"Yes, it is," answered Jarah. "We need to discuss something with you, but first we must have your word you will discuss this with no one but us. Not even Catrin."

Ambros's frown grew deeper. "What is such a secret that I can't speak to Catrin about it? We've never kept secrets from each other."

"I know, and we respect that," said Tristan, "but it is imperative we ask you this. You will understand why when we explain."

"We trust Catrin," said Jarah, "but we do know that Catrin not only does not keep secrets from you, but from her lady-in-waiting, Corrick, as well, and—"

"And Corrick does not keep a secret from her husband, Callum, and Callum . . ." Ambros finished with a look of understanding on his face.

"And so it goes," said Jarah. He had deliberately not mentioned Deryn. "Also, what we have to tell you could potentially put your own life in danger, and we do not wish to expose the Queen or anyone else to our secret."

Ambros frowned again. "In more danger than it already is? I believe my brother's supporters are still out there and would recognize me even with this scar. You'll have to explain before I agree."

They took turns telling him about their adventures, of which he already knew most of, but he had not known the parts that included their stay in Ardvale, and who their daughter really was.

They also told him about their own skills. They told him everything, saying that they'd learned their skills from Irusan, and when they had finished, he sat for a while, thinking. His face did not betray shock or horror, and he did not look at them disbelievingly either. It was as if he heard these stories every day, and this was a normal thing for him.

Finally, he spoke.

"I always felt Anwyn was different, somehow. She is not like other children. Too quiet. She is like a deep ocean. I am not surprised by what you've told me. I did suspect more out of you lot, too. I knew Catrin would not keep you here all these years if you were just ordinary healers.

"Although she does not know all you've just told me, I think she suspects. She told me of some strange things you could do that made no sense to her when you rescued her from the wolf-men and afterwards. She saw you heal that wolf-man, and she also knew the healing of Deryn was far beyond the ordinary. It was not just your crystal, although, that is amazing enough in itself. She does not know of this . . ."

"Merkaba," Jarah finished for him.

"Yes, *mer-ka-ba* . . ."

They nodded.

"She knows nothing of that, and I'll make sure she never will. That is dangerous information, and I see your point. In the wrong hands, it could cause you all kinds of problems. Every warlord and leader in

Ialana will put a price on your head or try to capture you and learn your secrets for their own agenda. Maybe even those loyalists of my brother here in Three Rivers. What wouldn't *they* give for . . ."

He stopped again, and went into more deep thought. The Six patiently waited. They did not want to rush him.

"The question now, is how do you decline the offer to provide you with an escort without raising suspicions or insulting anyone?" He snorted. "It doesn't seem like you need our puny protection now that I know what your capabilities are, but we who would need yours.

"The monsters of Mannanon and the Osgoi are well-known to me. We have little protection against them, and we all know what they did to Brenin's army. We still haven't recovered, and it is only the gods who are keeping us safe from invasion.

"Catrin has told me that Moran Blacktooth, of the Yor Swamps, covets Aelfar and Mernoc. I expect him to invade soon. Catrin and Deryn are building up the defense forces, but not in the same way my brother did. No forced conscriptions. We pay our soldiers well, and they willingly fight for our kingdom. We also train them well, but it takes time.

"I promise not to attempt to use your skills in warfare, but I wish I had them. I won't lie about that." He smiled, and they smiled tentatively back.

It was their biggest fear: that someone would compel them to use their abilities for war, to kill, instead of for peace. They didn't even like using it against their deadliest foes, and they all remembered how they'd used the Crystal to kill the Arrach who attacked them in the tunnels of the Osgoi. It still haunted them, and they would not willingly do it again. They were healers, not soldiers. Even Tristan, who had once been a soldier, now found the idea unappealing. They much preferred to defend themselves by extrication from a sticky situation instead of killing.

"We will protect ourselves, and you or anyone else, if we have to," answered Jarah. "But we will not use our skills as weapons. We want to be clear about that."

"I understand. I really do. It's difficult for me, as a soldier and head of the Army, to comprehend, but now another complication has arisen.

Catrin has ordered your new nanny, Genove, to accompany you on your trip. How would you not frighten her as you take off in your merkabas?"

Tegan's eyes were wide. "She would run screaming to all about the sorcerers!"

"Exactly. And unless you tell Catrin of the pickle you're in, her order will stand, and Genove will accompany you. You may as well need an army escort."

"She'll really slow us down, to put it mildly. What can we do?" asked Tristan.

"I have an idea," said Ambros. He leaned forward and lowered his voice. "Accept my offer of an escort."

He held up his hand as Jarah opened his mouth to protest.

"Wait, let me finish. I told you that the warlord, Moran of Yor Swamps, is planning something. That much is clear. What he is planning remains to be found out. I intend on doing just that, and you will be my cover. Catrin would be horrified if she knew what I was planning, and it is yet another secret I unfortunately must keep from her. I wondered how I was going to do it, but now it is clear to me.

"I will take a handful of men that I trust implicitly with me, plus a few trusted escorts for you. You will leave with us in a week's time. We'll travel together to the road south, towards Galon and the Yor Swamps, and then I and my group will leave you.

"The men I will have with me are all rascals and blackguards, but I know them well, and we will become a band of robbers. We will not rob anyone," he said, as he noticed their looks of alarm. "We'll only scare the skins off anyone who comes near us. The rest of the army escort will go with you as far as Genove's farm, where they will leave her and you will depart in your vehicles."

"You can't leave her there! She will starve!" Tegan said, her eyes betraying her concern.

"You're right." He thought a bit. "Then they can bring her back here and say she was unable to complete the journey due to her advanced years. They will let her know of the consequences if she talks. If she wants to keep her job, she'll say nothing."

"Well then why travel as far as her farm? One of your soldiers could just bring her back after we leave?" Jarah asked.

"And have Catrin wonder why she couldn't travel as far as her farm?

That would make no sense. Her farm, according to Catrin, was about three or four days ride from Three Rivers. We need to do at least that to allay Catrin's suspicions. We could take her someplace and keep her captive, but I can see by your faces you wouldn't like that."

"You're right," said Jarah. "We don't want to cause harm or discomfort to the lady. She doesn't deserve that. I'm sure she'll keep quiet about it if she wants to keep her job here. We'll just have to accept that."

"I only hope that Deryn will not ask to accompany us," Ambros laughed. "But I'll speak to Catrin and make sure she finds enough to keep him busy here. With his coronation coming up in a few moons, there will be plenty for him to do."

"Ambros, I hope your journey to the Yor Swamps will be a safe one," said Tristan.

"It will be anything but safe. That is why I am not telling Catrin. She'll know what I'm up against. This Moran fellow makes my band of blackguards look like children. I hate to keep this a secret from Catrin, or Deryn, but if I told her, she'd either stop me outright or insist on accompanying me. So would Deryn, and he must focus on his upcoming coronation. I have to do this alone."

"How does she know Moran is getting ready to attack?" asked Tristan.

"She has a spy in his camp. A well placed one, apparently. I hope I can make contact with him once I get there, but she refuses to tell me his name. I must admit, that annoyed me a little—doesn't she trust me? That's why I decided to go there and see for myself just what is going on."

"Well, we wish you much luck, and thanks for your help," said Jarah.

They did not notice the glint of red nearby that rose into the air and disappeared back into the palace. They felt relief. With Ambros's plan in place, their trip should be quite uneventful.

Genove

Genove wanted to shout out in glee, but she remained silent as she entered the palace and made her way back to the nursery.

She had been right! The Six were returning to Ibai, and they planned to ditch her along the way. She would show them. She would also show that foolish Ambros a thing or two as well. She had to see the Queen, but she must wait until the morning.

At the first light, she rose and quickly took care of the children's breakfast. Once their parents and Anwyn came into the nursery to play with them, she excused herself.

"I have some urgent business, my dears. I will be back as soon as I can." They didn't seem to notice, and she hied towards the assembly room where the Queen conducted her important business.

It felt as though she waited all day, but at last the Queen had time to see her, even though her lady-in-waiting, Corrick, tried her best to discourage her.

"The Queen is busy with important matters," she'd said, and Genove looked at her with undisguised hatred. She would have to get even with this thimbleskull once her mission was accomplished.

"I really need to see her," Genove responded, working to making her tone humble and sweet. She smiled, even though it took her a lot of effort. "I realize I am only a lowly servant, but I have something important to tell her—for her ears only."

Corrick sighed. She couldn't resist muttering, "And I thought you were no humble hireling . . ." But she made Genove wait. Courtiers came and went, and citizens with long standing appointments were called in one at a time, and still she sat. The sun was going down again, and Genove knew that if she didn't get to see Catrin today, she would be missed in the nursery, and could possibly lose her job. She hoped her unexplained absence hadn't already been noticed.

At last, a footman came to the door and called out, "Genove! The Queen will receive you now."

Almost flying ahead of the footman, who looked at her aghast, she ran into the Queen's audience room and curtsied.

"I am sorry it took so long to see you, Genove," said Catrin, an exhausted look on her face. "But it's been really busy today. So many matters to attend to, and the coronation of my son coming up . . . What is it you wanted to see me about?"

"Ma'am, I overheard a discussion last night that I felt you needed to know about."

"Oh?" Catrin raised an eyebrow. "Please proceed."

Genove gave her a detailed account of what had passed between the Six and Ambros. She did not say how she'd come across this information, only that she'd been close enough to accidentally overhear it. "I don't know what a *mer-ka-ba* is, milady, but it sounds like something they don't want you to know about, and that will enable them to travel without an escort. It sounds like sorcery, to me." She began to sob. "And I dread to think what your husband will encounter in the swamps! Moran is wicked and dangerous."

"Yes, that much is true, Genove. Given all you've said, you should stay here in Three Rivers. I will take care of my husband, and make sure what he has planned is safe."

"No—no, milady. I disagree. I must travel with them. You must act as if you don't know any of this! I wish to ensure that the children are at least safe. If things look as if they are becoming dangerous, then I will take them to my farm until we are able to determine just what is occurring."

Catrin looked long and hard at Genove. "I would feel better if you did accompany them, at least up until your farm. If there is anything going on that makes you uncomfortable, tell the soldiers and they can bring you back here. I am unable to accompany them myself. It seems I have a potential invasion from the south, and I must prepare."

A self-satisfied smirk rose over Genove's lips. She had not, at first, wanted Catrin to know of Ambros's and the Six's plan either, but her own plan was formulating in her head. It was a bonus for her to put a spike in Ambros's plans, if only for the sheer pleasure of it. She didn't care if Ambros went to Yor Swamps or not, but he had become a threat to her now that he knew the secret of the Six.

She turned and left.

Queen Catrin

Catrin was shocked by what Genove had just told her. She didn't know what to make of it. She sat for a long time, just thinking. Was she right to let Genove travel with the six healers? She was an old lady, and what could she do if things became strange? She wondered why the Six had never told her about their—whatever-it-was. And how did Genove know about Moran? She was a simple farmer's wife who would have little knowledge of Moran.

Something did not feel right. She must stay alert. Nothing happened in her land that she did not know about, and she wasn't going to fall down on her responsibilities—the safety of her people and land—now.

Ambros had promised the healers, her friends, that Genove would be returned to Three Rivers, but what really rankled her was that Ambros felt the need to protect her. *Her!* After all she'd been through with his brother. Hadn't she proved she was more than capable of taking care of herself?

The Six had many enemies, many who would wish to know their whereabouts, but in spite of her doubts, she trusted Genove, and wondered if Genove had second thoughts about being in Three Rivers. Perhaps she really did want to return home, even though her husband was dead.

"Corrick!"

Corrick poked her head around the door.

"Please tell my husband I need to see him. Immediately!"

11.

Departure

The day was bright and hot, and the palace was a-bustle with preparation for the long journey ahead. Some servants cried, while others gave explicit instructions for the journey, as if to rather backward children.

They, and Anwyn, only smiled and nodded. They understood just how sad the palace staff and Catrin were at their departure. They were sad too, but they knew they could return at any time, and the palace staff and royal family members, with the exception of Ambros, did not. To them, it must have felt like a permanent arrangement.

Wagons were brought into the courtyard, and each family had a covered wagon that would shelter them from the elements. Other wagons were piled high with food and supplies. Besides the troop of soldiers, and Ambros's rather scruffy group of men, there was Genove and a cook.

The cook was a young man named Alroy. He had red hair and a white-toothed smile. Anwyn liked him immediately. He reminded her of her father, only younger. But Genove . . . she sighed.

It had come as quite a shock to her to hear that Genove was to accompany them. Her parents had finally let her in on the plan with Ambros, and she comforted herself that Genove would not remain long with them.

Finally, the horses and wagons were ready. All the supplies had been loaded, and it was time to say goodbye to Catrin and Deryn. They were surprised Deryn had not insisted on going with them, but Catrin said they had enough to do without leaving home.

Tegan noticed Catrin looking sideways at Ambros, and something seemed to pass between them. Tegan telepathed to Jarah.

We have missed something, Jarah. I have one of my feelings again.

Jarah rolled his eyes in mock annoyance. *Oh no, not one of your 'feelings'!* He pretended to shudder, and they laughed. *Every time you get one, something awful happens. I just want a quiet journey until it's time to leave our escort and fly to Ibai.*

Me too, Jarah. Me too.

Anwyn found her horse, a grey mare named Moon. As she climbed onto Moon, with the help of a guard, Genove walked by and Moon whinnied, a small, sharp sound of fear. Genove stopped, turned, and looked straight into Moon's eyes. Anwyn held her breath. She felt the terror rising in Moon and quickly flung her arms around Moon's neck as the mare reared, neighing loudly and lashing out with her front hooves. Genove was jerked out of the way by a startled guard.

"Move!" he yelled.

The horse's hooves missed both their heads by a fraction, but Moon reared up again, as another guard held onto her reins. Anwyn clung to the saddle now with both hands, trying to stay seated. She looked at Genove. She wasn't imagining it. Genove, now at a safer distance, still stared intently at the horse. She felt the energy that radiated from the nanny, her brown eyes glittering with a red, flickering light. She could sense that Moon was going to bolt with her still on her back, but the guard did not let go of the reins. Ambros ran into the melee and held onto Moon from the other side.

THE SIX AND ANWYN OF IALANA

Tegan shouted for Anwyn to hold tight, "And would someone please calm the horse down!"

Anwyn knew what to do. Closing her eyes, she connected with Moon. It was difficult at first, but she felt the horse's consciousness beneath the thick layer of fear. She sent calming waves of love and reassurance to her.

Moon, you will not be harmed by this diabolic woman. She is out to get me, and she is using you. If you do not allow her to frighten you, she will stop.

Moon gave a final snort, and to everyone's amazement, lowered her hooves and put her head down, trembling and sweating.

"Anwyn, get off that horse and ride in the wagon with us," Tegan commanded.

"Mother, Moon is fine now. She was startled by Genove walking by. I can handle her."

"Genove, are you afraid of horses?" Ambros asked.

"Why yes, milord. I am!"

"That explains it, then," said Ambros. "Horses sense fear and they act up when frightened people are around. Stay away from the horses and ride in the wagons with the others." He mounted Sienna, his favorite horse, and the one that Catrin had gifted him with six years ago.

After much back and forth, Tegan allowed Anwyn to stay on the horse, but kept a sharp eye on her as they once again said their goodbye's. The soldiers, horses, and wagon train left through the front gate as Catrin and Deryn waved their goodbyes.

Anwyn noticed that Genove rode in the wagon with her family, just ahead. She felt that the Genove everyone saw was only a façade. Beneath that, there was so much malice and loathing that she could hardly bear to be around her. Why didn't anyone else notice this? Whoever this *Genove* really was, she was very skilful at energy shielding. If her parent's and the other children could not penetrate that, she was no ordinary human. Of that, Anwyn was convinced. She needed to be on her guard even more now.

But Genove had given her a glimpse of the true entity beneath the veneer. Why?

Genove

Well, that didn't go according to plan, thought Genove, as the wagon trundled down the road. She would have preferred to have her own horse, but now that she was supposedly frightened of horses, that wouldn't work, either. She was confined to the wagons, but it would give her time to think of something else. Anwyn would not be alive for much longer, she was sure of that. She had more tricks up her sleeve.

She now knew too that Anwyn was not fooled by her demeanor of friendliness. She had allowed Anwyn a glimpse of who she really was, the dark energy behind her eyes.

I want her to know what she is up against. I want to see what she is capable of, and therefore I can hone my own skills at the same time. There's no challenge in destroying a mere child, but if she is capable of defending herself, it will pay me in the long run to take my measure of her so that I can develop a plan she will have no defense against.

She was a patient person. She could wait.

She also wondered what had transpired between Catrin and her husband. Apparently, nothing she had said to Catrin had put a crimp in Ambros's plans. She had probed his mind, and he was still going ahead with his plot. Well, she had tried, she thought, and he wasn't her main target anyway. She had just been having a little fun on the side.

The next few days were uneventful. Genove played her part of the devoted nanny to the hilt. She wanted Anwyn to relax, to feel that maybe she was imagining it all, and she didn't want to do anything while Ambros was still with them. He was liable to run her through with his sword if he suspected anything.

As they neared the area where the real Genove's farm was, which she knew because Ambros reminded her as they drew closer, she wondered if she'd be dropped off there. She would try to stay with the group, but if she had to go, she had alternatives.

"We're nearing your old home. Another day's ride, Genove. Would you like to stop in and see anyone there?"

"Oh no, Master! It will make me too sad. I would prefer that we just continue."

Ambros nodded, and Tegan looked at her with sympathy in her eyes. But Ambros, on Sienna's back, continued to trot alongside their wagon.

"My men and I must leave now," he said to Jarah. He looked at Genove. "You can return to Three Rivers, or stay at your old farm. Whatever you choose. You are not continuing on the journey."

Genove, however, was prepared. She had, after all, heard their plans, and this did not come as a shock to her.

"Sire, I must stay! The Queen promised me I could. Do not make me return. I am an old, sick woman, and I really do want to see my old farm. Perhaps if I could travel there, I can die there and won't need to return to Three Rivers. Just let me travel as far as that, then."

Genove felt it safe to give a false promise. Ambros was leaving. She could handle the rest of them.

"Fine then. Go as far as your farm, and I'll tell the soldiers to find a neighbor to look out for you." He looked back to the shocked faces of Jarah and Tegan. "Don't worry, she won't starve. I have a feeling our Genove is more capable than she looks. Also, I'll tell my soldiers to leave all the horses, except for their own, and one or two wagons with her at the farm. She will have more than enough food, and she can sell the horses and make a satisfactory living off the proceeds."

"I was hoping she'd return to Three Rivers," said Jarah, "but if that is what she prefers, then we'll make sure she is taken care of. We'd prefer not to abandon you, Genove, but we do have things to do on our journey that might be dangerous for you. That is why we can't have you along. We'll let the others know." Jarah smiled.

It was condescending smile, Genove thought, and she felt her anger rising. These people did not care for her, for the Genove they all thought she was. She knew it was going to happen, but even so, it was galling. They would pay dearly. All of them.

She forced a smile. Yes, making the choice to return to her farm would suit her better than being put in a cart and sent back to Three Rivers.

They had no idea what she was planning.

12.

Anwyn

It was very perceptive of Ambros to notice that Genove was not the helpless old woman she appeared to be, Anwyn thought as Ambros and his rag-tag band of men took their leave. They cantered down the rough south road that forked away, through the Aelfar forestlands to the Yor Swamps, still several days ride away.

There were now three soldiers left, besides Genove and the cook Alroy, in their support party. Anwyn had talked to Alroy frequently during the trip, and learned that he loved to cook. To him, it was an art he had learned in the army. He didn't care for killing people. He was a gentle soul, and she found him a comfort to talk to.

"Alroy," she'd said just the day before, "I want you to be very careful of Genove. Don't say anything around her about anything. I don't trust her at all."

"I understand," he said. "I get those feelings around certain people too. Now help me fix this stew. I need some more of these herbs that are growing in the field over there. Can you go pick a few for me?" He showed her what they looked like.

THE SIX AND ANWYN OF IALANA

As Anwyn gathered the herbs she felt the hair on her neck rising. She turned around. Genove was watching her. *Odd*, she thought, but she continued to gather herbs.

After Ambros and his men left, they continued on their way, but Anwyn still felt Genove's gaze, and Moon felt it too. As much as she tried to comfort Moon, the horse kept shaking and whinnying in fear. Finally, Anwyn dismounted and handed the horse to Alroy.

"Here, hold her. I don't want her bolting with me. I'll walk." She ran up to Djana's wagon at the head of the wagon train and walked alongside the wagon where Genove couldn't see her. Moon had calmed down, and the day's ride went smoothly as Anwyn alternately walked and rode in the wagons with either Kex or Djana.

That night, they encamped in a field just off the road. A soldier informed them that they were now very close to Genove's farm. He knew where it was because Ambros had given him directions on how to get there before leaving. They would take her there first thing in the morning.

Alroy was preparing another one of his delicious stews. Anwyn enjoyed the early evening fires and the smell of food cooking. She loved to just sit and talk to Alroy, watching him as he worked. The sun had not yet set, and the clear blue sky faded to bright orange on the horizon. They could just see the faint outline of distant hills, hills that her father had told her were close to Meadowfield and the foothills of the Osgoi Range. She'd seen the mountains in her merkaba, but she had not explored them. She'd been cautioned against this by both her parents, and Finn, as "too dangerous." Even so, she would still love to explore them one day.

"I need more of those herbs you got yesterday, Anwyn. I see them over there." Alroy pointed towards a field not too far away, and Anwyn skipped across the field towards the area where Alroy had pointed.

A sudden chill hit her and a raindrop fell onto her head. Startled, she looked up. The sky had been clear just a moment ago. Now a large dark cloud roiled overhead. She could still see the sun shining over the horizon. It was only dark over the field and their encampment. The others had noticed it too, and Tegan shouted for Anwyn to return to the camp, but Anwyn gazed up at the cloud as if hypnotized.

As the cloud above her churned faster and faster, a barely noticeable rotating tendril, black as night, began to form in the middle of the cloud. Anwyn knew what it was. It was the air elementals, but these were not Amun and Ilma, the elementals she knew so well. She sensed a different energy in the cloud, one that had been summoned to do someone's bidding, and she knew who was responsible. She couldn't see Genove, but it had to be her.

The finger stretched towards the frightened people near the wagons, and then twisted up again. Tegan screamed. Like a snake, it slithered through the air towards the field. It was now longer and wider, and Tegan screamed again. Pulling out of Jarah's restraining grasp, she ran out into the field towards her daughter.

No, Mother! Don't come here. I can do this!

Tegan, get back here! Jarah tried to follow, but now Tristan and the others held him back.

Tegan kept running. The wind blew harder as the column got wider and closer. Her hair whipped around her face, and she could barely keep herself upright. The roaring, rotating column was now almost directly overhead. Branches, leaves, grass, and sod flew around them.

Anwyn threw herself on the ground as flat as she could get. Bolts of lightning struck the ground around her as deafening claps of thunder followed each strike.

Panicked horses reared and neighed in the camp, trying to break loose from their tethers, but Anwyn could see as she peered cautiously over the flattened grass that the encampment was not affected by the wind and lightning. It was only here in the field, the field where she lay. Her mother still ran towards her, fighting the wind. Closing her eyes again, she willed her mother to throw herself flat, just like she had.

It worked. Tegan fell to the ground and held onto clumps of grass, anything her desperate hands could grab onto, but her feet were now rising up into the air. Anwyn saw her sandals snatched off her feet by the wind, disappearing into the cloud as the rest of her body slid inexorably towards the dark twister.

Anwyn had to do something, and fast. There was now a dust cloud between her and the camp. Since she couldn't see anyone through the cloud of flying dust and debris, that meant they couldn't see her either.

In an instant, she pulled up her merkaba, and the wind no longer tugged at her. The bolts of lightning flew harmlessly around her. She was witnessing the material dimension from the safety of her vehicle. She could only hope that her mother would do the same. To her immense relief, her mother and her merkaba materialized in front of her. They smiled at each other, and Tegan sent her a thought.

I should have trusted you.

Anwyn smiled, too.

Now I need to go take care of these nasties, Mother. I'll make sure they are neutralized. They won't bother us again.

Tegan felt foolish. She had rushed headlong into a situation without a plan. Jarah was angry, and the soldiers now suspected the worst: their charges were all sorcerers. They had seen both her and Anwyn emerge unscathed from the quickly dissipating tornado.

Only a sorcerer could have survived.

"We can no longer trust the soldiers," said Tristan. "I know how they think. I was one myself not too long ago. Sorcerers and wizards— soldiers are naturally suspicious and hostile towards them. I remember some killings done, just on a suspicion."

"Whoever is responsible for this wanted to expose us," said Jarah.

"Who do you think that could be?" asked Djana. "We are all trust-worthy enough in our party."

Tegan sat silent, with her head down.

Anwyn sighed.

"Not all, Djana." She looked over to where Genove was, in the same field, gathering herbs. Genove had offered to do it after the tornado.

I know Alroy still wants to make supper. Please, you all take a rest while

I look for those herbs. You've all had a nasty shock." She had smiled at Anwyn and Tegan as she played the part of the kindly and motherly servant.

"What do you mean, Anwyn?" asked Jarah, and his face turned red. He'd almost lost his daughter and his wife. He didn't know who to be angry at, and he couldn't hide the fear he felt. They didn't need false accusations flying around now.

Tegan's head came up and she looked at them all, determination in her eyes. "I know who she means."

They all looked at her in surprise, including Anwyn. "I knew it the minute it started. That's why I ran into the field."

"Please explain," said Adain.

Tegan nodded her head towards Genove in the field. "*Her.*"

"*What!?*"

"Yes, Jarah, *her.* I feel a fool for only noticing it now. Now that she almost killed us. Perhaps I didn't *want* to see it before. I had taken Catrin's word that she was entirely trustworthy, and did not use my inner senses at all. None of us did. We're all guilty. Only Anwyn has used them, and we aren't listening to her. I don't blame Catrin, not at all. She didn't know. Whatever is here in Genove's body, or a body that looks like Genove's, is not who we think."

The group now were all agog, focused on Tegan intently, but also shooting furtive looks towards Genove in the field.

"Don't look at her! It must appear as if everything is normal, as if we don't suspect a thing. I can't prove it yet, but let us be watchful. If she is not who she says she is, then she is planning something else, and I feel the target is my daughter, or perhaps even all of us."

"You're right," said Adain. "I think we should be careful now. We have a lot to talk about while she's still in the field. Tell us why you and Anwyn think she's not who she says she is?"

"Right before the tornado hit, while the cloud was still forming overhead, I looked at Genove. She was hunkered down in the wagon where she thought I could not see her, and she was mouthing words up at the sky and waving her hands around. I couldn't hear what she was saying, but I felt the intent of her energy and focus, and a cold terror went through me as I realized she was calling on the air elementals. Not the one's we knew in Ardvale though, but those that are working against all that is loving and benevolent here. When I saw the tornado form, that's when I knew she was responsible, and without thinking, I ran into the field. It was foolish, I know, but my daughter—"

"No need to explain," said Tristan. "We do understand. I'd do the same. I too am compatible with the wind elements, and I felt it was not my friend Amun, the wind element we played with in Ardvale. There was malicious intent directed towards your daughter. We were not taught how to deal with those elementals, but Anwyn obviously was."

"We did cover that briefly while I lived there," said Anwyn, relieved now that the burden she'd been carrying since Genove arrived was out. "I wasn't sure I even had the abilities to neutralize the denizens from Iochodran, but I did my best. They left, but I don't know if it was my doing, or that of . . . *her*." She shifted her eyes sideways to where Genove was still picking herbs in the field.

"Why would she stop, if she wanted to kill you?" asked Djana.

"Because she wants to test me. She wants to see how prepared I am. I think she has something bigger planned, a plan that I have no defense against. She's testing my abilities."

Aghast, they stared at her.

"And she has the added benefit of losing the rest of our guard, now that Ambros has left," said Tristan. "We are going to have to tell them to go back to Three Rivers, to leave us here. They'll be only too glad to do so, unless they decide to kill us in our sleep first."

"Here she comes! Talk about something else."

They quickly changed the subject to discussing their near miss with the tornado, as if they had no idea what had been the cause.

Genove was smiling.

13.

Anwyn

Anwyn watched as Genove walked to the fire where the stew pot bubbled. She watched her place the herbs into the pot, and she noticed that everyone else had noticed it too. She walked over to the fire.

"Thanks, Genove. The herbs will add a lot of flavor to Alroy's delicious stew. Mother said she and Djana need help with the children. We'll call you when the stew is ready."

As Genove walked back to the wagons, Anwyn turned to Alroy. "Do not serve this stew. Don't even taste it. We need to throw it out. Do you have more to make another?"

Alroy looked at her, astonishment in his eyes. "Why?"

"Because these leaves," said Anwyn, as she fished out a partially limp herb from the pot, "are poisonous. She mixed them in with the real herbs."

Alroy gasped. "I should have recognized them. She hid them amongst the others quite cleverly. Should I tell the soldiers?"

"No. We're now aware of her intent. We want to see what else she does. We'll empty this out behind this bush and you can prepare more stew while she's tending to the children. She won't try anything with them. It's me she's after."

"Why, again?" asked Alroy as he surreptitiously dumped the pot out behind the bush. "It's a good thing I had extra stew. I was saving it for breakfast."

"Never mind about breakfast. We'll be gone by then." Anwyn pulled out more herbs from her apron pocket. "I managed to gather some before the tornado hit."

"I wanted to ask you about that. How—"

"We were lucky. It stopped just before it could lift us off the ground." Alroy looked unconvinced.

"The soldiers think—"

"Yes, I know. That we're sorcerers."

"They're ignorant, but I can see why they think that. I ask again, why *you*?"

"Alroy, you're going to have to trust me. I can't tell you. Just know that we're not sorcerers. At least not in the way you understand them. We know some things, and I can only tell you that we will never hurt anyone with what we know. You're safe from us, but you must be careful. Go back to Three Rivers with the soldiers in the morning. Tonight, Tristan and Jarah are going to tell them to return. We will keep watch tonight to make sure nothing else happens, and in the morning we'll be gone too."

Alroy looked sad. "I don't want you to go, Anwyn. You have been a friend to me. I do trust you. I wish you'd allow me to travel with you. I can be of help."

Anwyn smiled at Alroy and touched his cheek with a gentle hand. "I know. I wish you could come too, but it won't be safe for you. You must believe me when I say this." With that, she turned and went back to her wagon.

She would miss Alroy.

Glahivar

They know now who I am, I feel sure. Not just the girl, but her parents and the others too.

They ate the stew tonight and no one got sick. That's just not possible. I told them I had an upset stomach from the traumatic event of the tornado today and I didn't want any, but I watched them, and the soldiers, eat from the pot.

They must have discovered what I did and made a fresh pot when I was at the wagons. I'll put my other plan into action and make sure, they don't discover what I am doing, this time.

Anwyn

Genove is nowhere to be found. During the night, she disappeared without anyone noticing. Not the guards, not me, not those of us who stayed awake to watch both her and the soldiers.

This can only mean one thing.

Whoever—or whatever—she is, she has a merkaba, and knows how to use it.

14.

The Farm

They all felt light-headed from lack of sleep. They had been on alert all night as they watched over the children and the camp. Genove had slept in Djana and Tristan's wagon, but even so, no one had noticed her disappearance. She must be a strong and capable entity, they thought, to disappear from right under their noses. They wondered what, exactly, it was they were dealing with.

They had told the remaining soldiers to return to Three Rivers, and they would "take Genove"—who they said was having digestive problems and was in the woods—to her farm and leave her there, with the extra wagons and horses.

The soldiers obliged, not disguising their haste to leave, but there was a problem. Alroy refused to return with them, and the soldiers did not wait for him to make up his mind. They galloped off as fast as they could down the road, back to Three Rivers.

"So what are we going to do with young Alroy?" asked Djana. "He can't come with us, that much is certain."

"I have an idea," said Tristan. "We'll take him to Genove's farm with the wagons and horses. He'll be alright there, and we'll quickly leave before he knows what we are doing."

"He won't be able to follow us," said Kex. "Not in our merkabas."

"I hope the current residents of the farm won't mind," said Jarah. "I also want to see if the real Genove is there, or if something evil used her body and she's gone."

"How will we know if she's the *real* Genove if she's even there?" asked Kex.

"Use your energy sensing abilities!" said Anwyn, as if this should be obvious to all. "Look in her eyes. If you see a red shimmer anywhere, we will know."

"We should have known to do that right from the beginning," said Djana. She felt as embarrassed as everyone else did.

"I am going to explain a little about Genove to him," said Anwyn, "so he doesn't wonder how she got to the farm, and why—if the real Genove is there—she doesn't seem to know him or us."

"I think you should, Anwyn," said Tegan. "Only don't explain too much!"

Anwyn pulled Alroy aside.

"Alroy, you're probably wondering where Genove has gone."

"I was a bit. I don't believe she's in the woods, as you told the other soldiers, but I see she has caused some trouble for you. I think she is the sorceress the soldiers were so afraid of—"

"Yes, she is. She's a shape-shifter. When we get to the farm she is supposedly from, we may see her there."

Alroy looked alarmed, but Anwyn quickly explained to him that the Genove they may find there would most likely not be the Genove that had traveled with them.

"I will know," she said. "We all will. I'll touch you like this," she touched him on the shoulder, "if it's a different Genove."

They headed off down the road towards the area where they thought Genove's farm might be. No one knew exactly where it was, but they were fortunate to encounter farmers on the road selling their produce to travelers, and they asked them if they knew where they might find a farmer's wife named Genove.

"Surely!" one responded. "Ye might be meanin' Angus and Genove?"

They nodded, and he pointed down the road.

"Go down 'ere a ways and ye be findin' a small cart track towards the forest. Foller this another ways, and ye be comin' up on the farm shortly." They thanked him and continued down the road.

"Well, it appears that both Angus and Genove are alive and well," said Tegan. "Now I really wonder who that person is that has been with us for these past weeks."

"I think we're going to find out soon. Quite soon," said Jarah.

The farm was only a few leagues away, and before the sun had reached its midway point in the sky, they arrived in a farmyard and house that fit the description given by Catrin when she'd told them the story of her stay here. Barking dogs greeted them, and a man tilling with a mule in a nearby field looked up. They waved to him, and he stopped what he was doing and came over, suspicion etched on his weathered face.

"Are you Angus?" asked Jarah, as soon as he was close enough.

"I am. Who are you?"

"We are friends of—" *What was the name she used?*" he telepathed to Tegan.

"*Roland!*" Tegan hissed.

"We're friends of Roland, the boy who came here six years ago. You and your wife gave him and her—er, his brother, shelter."

Tegan glared at him, but Angus did not seem to pick up on Jarah's fumbling. A grin lit up his face.

"*Ah*, yes, we did! I remember him and his younger brother well. Such well-brought up youngsters, with good manners. My wife and I were sorry to see them go. I do hope they fared well?"

"They certainly did. They asked us to stop in and see you. They too hope you are both well."

"Come in, come in!" Angus waved a beefy, sun-reddened arm. "You must meet my wife. She will make you a noon meal. We get so few visitors, but we welcome travelers if they're honest and upright. We get a lot of bandits in these here parts, so we're a little cautious."

"Can't blame you," said Tristan.

"Things are better now that Queen Catrin has been on the throne. We did not fare too well with the King—ah, Genove! Meet some friends of young Roland and Brohan!"

A familiar figure appeared at the farmhouse doorway. It was all the Six and Anwyn could do not to gasp out loud. It was *their* Genove. But, then again, it was not. It became quite clear to them as she approached that the energy from this woman was completely different, even though her appearance was identical.

They relaxed, and introduced themselves and Alroy. Anwyn put a calming hand on Alroy's shoulder.

Genove stared at Alroy. Her mouth fell open, and a tear rolled down her face. At last she spoke.

"Angus! This boy, he looks so much like our son we lost so many years ago."

Angus stopped talking and looked again, harder this time, at Alroy.

"You may be right," he conceded. "He does have that look about him. Same age abouts as when our lad disappeared, too."

The Six knew what had happened. Catrin had once told them. Their son had been conscripted by King Brenin's army, and never been seen again, but they let them tell them the story again. They both felt he was dead, killed in one of the King's endless wars with neighboring territories. Since then, they'd battled to keep their farm together, and now had no one to leave it to.

Genove bustled around the kitchen, and was delighted when Alroy offered to help. Anwyn offered too, and soon a steaming pot bubbled on the old wood stove. Alroy and Genove talked and talked, Alroy telling her all about his own sojourn in the army, how he came to be a cook, and how he had decided, today, that he didn't want to return to the army.

"I would much rather stay with my friends here," he said, looking at Anwyn. "I haven't known them long, but they already feel like family to me. I lost my own family when I was about ten years old, and joined the army to learn a trade. Either that, or starve!" He laughed, but no one else joined him.

Genove looked as if she wanted to cry again, and put her arm around him.

"If you need a family, dear, look no further. These people are nice, but I can see they have something important they must do, or they wouldn't be traveling this *Idris-forsaken* road. Why don't you stay here with me and Angus and help us out on the farm? It's getting to be a little too much for us now. We'll give you a roof over your head, hearty food, and an instant family."

Alroy looked at the Six, doubtful. It was clear he was torn.

"I can see you're not sure, and who can blame you? But if you change your mind, we would welcome you. Are you in agreement, Angus?"

Angus looked befuddled.

"Oh, sure. A fine thing by me."

It was obvious to the now smiling Six, and Anwyn, that Angus was used to being told what to do by his wife, but also that he would be willing to agree to anything just as long as she was happy.

They stayed all afternoon. When they told Angus and Genove they could keep their horses and wagons, along with all the supplies, they were incredulous and alarmed.

"How d'you think you're going to finish your journey without them, and with them babies and young children?" Angus asked. "If your destination is Meadowfield, that's a long ways yet away."

Alroy looked puzzled as well. "I was wondering about that too," he said.

"We have made other plans," said Jarah. "I am sorry, but we can't let you know what they are. Just know that your wife was right. We have something we need to do, and it involves some secrecy. I want to reassure you that we will not be needing wagons or supplies, and the children will be fine with us."

"Well, whatever it may be," Angus replied, "I hope y'know what you're doing. The roads towards the west are dangerous. Not for the faint of heart. We were so worried about Roland and Brohan when they said where they were headed, but we are happy they made it." His eyes went to the children again and they could clearly see doubt in his face.

"They did, and we will too," said Tegan. "Please, don't worry about us. We'll stop in and see you again so you know we'll be alright, and that's a promise."

With that, Angus and Genove relaxed and went out to inspect the wagons and horses. They were very pleased.

"Please take good care of Moon, Alroy, alright?" Anwyn asked. "She's yours now. I know she trusts you, and she's a wonderful horse."

Alroy promised. To their relief, he had needed little to no encouragement to stay at the farm. He was already comfortable with the farmer and his wife, and Anwyn felt a small pang of disappointment. She had really hoped he'd put up a bigger fight, but she knew without a doubt that he had made the right choice. He could not travel with them. She would make sure that she'd visit the farm again, and that this was not going to be a permanent goodbye. That thought gave both of them comfort.

Angus and Genove persuaded them to stay the night, and they agreed, promising to leave early in the morning. They thought they would walk away towards the forest with the children and bring up their merkabas there.

They wouldn't stop until they reached Ibai. All would be well.

With any luck, they'd never see the *other* Genove again.

15.

Ambros

After leaving the healers, Ambros and his men, Bran, Lonan, and Daire, made haste down the south road, towards the Yor Swamps. Ambros had been down this road before. He was familiar with the Yor Swamps.

In his bandit days, he and his men had often traded their stolen goods with the swamp inhabitants, and this time it would be no different. They had even brought some "stolen" goods with them for trade, to authenticate their undercover mission. The three men with him still had a cut-purse look about them, and would frighten anyone on a dark road. Ambros, with his scar and after days of travel, already smelled and looked like the old Ambros.

It would take them a few days yet to reach the swamps, and he hoped that the Six, and Anwyn, would be safe without him and his men. He'd handpicked the soldiers he left to guard them himself, but one could never be absolutely sure of anyone's loyalties. He hoped the strange powers of his friends would protect them.

He had to admit to himself, as they galloped under the hot sun, that he wished he had the Six with them. Their abilities were hard to believe, but if they told the truth, which he was sure they did, he also understood their desire not to use them for power plays. But he had few illusions about himself.

He knew that if he had the same abilities he would not hesitate to use them to conquer his enemies.

Glahivar

Now in her Iochodran body, she felt her huge belly as it rubbed up against the outer shell of her merkaba. There had been no point in staying with the Six. They would be on their guard, and she had other things to do. Something that did not involve the healers. An old score to settle.

Her plans for the Six could wait a bit.

It was still dark, and she sped over the moonlit landscape towards the mountains. She couldn't move as fast as she would have liked. Her merkaba skills were returning to her, but they weren't at the level she once had.

She needed to keep a lookout for something—something on the ground, hidden in the thick forests beneath the Osgoi. She flew low over the forest. She felt more powerful now that she had her spider form back. She could see in all the frequency ranges, and nothing could escape her. Nothing that lived, that is.

Her hearing was also more acute, and she listened for rustles, yelps, or howls. As she approached an area nearer the mountains, she steered her merkaba towards the faint howls in the distant foothills. It didn't take long before she saw them—warm, moving, orange shapes revealed by her thermal vision. They stood out against the cool blues and blacks of the forest. She could still not find the one shape that looked different to the smaller and leaner shapes of the wolf-men. She had to search yet another part of the forest before she finally found what she was looking for. A bellowing roar from below told her that she had, at last, found her target.

She followed the pack, with the largest shape in the forefront as it hunted an unfortunate creature through the forest. She waited as it was mercilessly tracked down and killed, and even then she did not make her move, not until the pack and the large beast eagerly fed at the carcass. When these creatures fed, they were not as alert as usual.

The moonlight gleamed off the long, sharp horns of the largest shape, its white fangs flashing as it ripped at the carcass. Every now and then one of the smaller wolf-men gave a yelp as it approached too close to its leader and the carcass. The big one must eat first. This was the protocol not only of the Vicious Eyes Pack, but all wolf-men.

She descended towards them. Revenge would be sweet.

Yagmak was the first to sense something. He stopped feeding. Blood dripped from his jaws as he sniffed the air. He couldn't see anything, but he felt that eyes watched them. No, not *them*. It was *him* they watched.

Was that a glint of red he saw in the shadows? His yelping pack now tore into the carcass as he stepped back. They still hadn't noticed or felt anything.

Over here, Blaidd—Yagmak—I'm here.

The whispery voice was clear. Yagmak's head jerked towards the sound. He roared, and the forest shook at the power in his voice. The Vicious Eyes Pack growled and howled, but reluctantly, they withdrew from the carcass, crouching behind their leader.

Who are you?

He did not speak out loud. Yagmak was now incapable of human speech, but whoever was watching them was well versed in the mind-to-mind languages of the mutant beast-humans.

You don't need to know who I am, came the reply. *Not just yet. I'll tell you later, dear one. Dismiss your pack. This is just between you and me.*

Yagmak hesitated. The energy behind the speech was vaguely familiar to him, but he couldn't put a name to it. He looked at his pack and motioned for them to retreat. They fell away from Yagmak and the kill, into the shadows, but did not take their eyes off their leader.

Now, tell me, who are you and what do you want with me?

This.

A bolt of blue lightning shot out from the shadows and struck Yagmak fully in the chest.

I trusted you once, Blaidd, but you betrayed me. Now it's my turn.

Another bolt of lightning followed, and Yagmak roared in anguish and fear as he charged, head down, towards where he thought his enemy was. But nothing was there. He stopped, puzzled, and turned just as another bolt struck him again from behind. His fur was now singed, and he smelled burning flesh. The pain drove him to roar again and again, to charge the empty space behind him, but once again he encountered nothing but air.

For the first time in years Yagmak felt acute fear. Another bolt struck him, full in the chest, and he heard despairing howls from his pack. He knew they wanted to run into the forest, to run from this invisible creature with the power of lightning, as did he, but he couldn't. He must stand his ground and defeat this enemy or his days as leader were over. His pack would turn on him, and he would be their next meal.

His breath came in ragged gasps as he turned around and around, trying to find anything he could charge at, but he couldn't even find the red glint that he thought he had seen earlier. Bolt after bolt struck him, coming from every direction now. His roaring grew weaker with each strike as he stumbled around the glade while his pack whimpered and howled from the trees.

Time to finish this off, dear. I don't have all night.

A bolt, larger than the rest, hit him again, and he toppled. The wolf-men took off into the night, howling as they ran. He tried to get up, but his legs wouldn't work anymore. His skin and flesh burned, and he whimpered in agony. He didn't want to be Yagmak anymore. He wanted to be Blaidd. He even wanted his drunkard of a father, and he wanted his warm bed at home. Why couldn't he wake up from this nightmare?

A form materialized in front of his face. An enormous dark figure of something that sent another wave of panic stampeding through him.

THE SIX AND ANWYN OF IALANA

A giant spider. As Blaidd, the young boy, he had always hated them. They'd given him the jitters, and he hadn't wanted anything to do with them. Now, he could see his enemy. His breath came out in rasping sobs and he tried to crawl away, but the spider followed, its red eyes glinting in pure joy.

Oh, how I've waited for this moment, dear one! Now I will tell you who I am, and it's the last thing you will ever hear.

Yagmak looked up at the terrifying shape, his eyes betraying his fear. The spider inhaled greedily, as if his fear was a delicious treat. *Yes, dear! More of that. I love it!* A claw brushed his face and he pulled back in horror. It laughed. *Remember Branwyn?* The tone changed. It was now angry, and he blinked in shock.

Branwyn? This?

Yes, this. Thanks to your betrayal, I lost my kingdom and the war, and I became this. But I always get even, dear.

The spider reared back and a column of fire blasted towards him. It was the last thing he saw before his world went black.

16.

Fire

Glahivar looked down at the smoking, supine form on the ground. It was no longer recognizable as Yagmak. The pack had disappeared, but they would return, and they would feast on what was left of their erstwhile leader. If not them, then something else would. Yagmak, or Blaidd, was finished.

Now she had other business to take care of. She pulled up her merkaba once more and soared into the early dawn sky, towards the northeast. She must get back to the encampment and see what was occurring there. Since she was no longer in the deceptive form of Genove, it would be all-out war. She'd pull out every weapon in her arsenal. She had, after all, just killed Yagmak, and she felt invincible, as if with every moment spent in her spider body gained her strength.

The sun was almost up. She must be quick. She arrived at the spot where the wagons and horses had been. She could still see the wheel tracks in the mud, but they were no longer there.

Growling in annoyance, she remembered that they had talked about going to Genove's farm. The idiots! If they'd known what was in their best interests, they'd have pulled up their merkabas sooner and fled. It would be much more difficult for her to track them, although she did know their final destination. However, she wanted to destroy them all now, as soon as possible.

She sped towards where she thought the farm must be. Yes. There was Alroy, the simpleton cook whom Anwyn had befriended. They must have left him here with the farmer and his wife. He walked, whistling, towards the cow shed, carrying a bucket. She could see the wagons still in the yard, loaded with their supplies. She wondered if the Six and Anwyn were still here.

She slid, silent as a shadow, into the farm house. She'd have to be careful. If The Six were still here, they might sense her.

That whey-faced whelp, Anwyn. She was the one she had to be the most careful of.

Genove was at the stove, cooking breakfast, while Angus sat at the table.

"I know you're worried, Genove, but I have a feeling they'll be just fine."

"Yes, but those children. I don't understand . . . How can they go on foot to Meadowfield with those babies? It's difficult enough with horses and wagons, but *on foot?*"

"I agree with you 'bout that, but Alroy says they're very capable, and he should know. Let's not concern ourselves with things we don't understand. I've a farm to take care of, and that's my main concern right now."

"I thank the gods that Alroy decided to stay. He'll be a big help to us both, Angus. He's already out milking cows!"

Glahivar left the conversation in the kitchen as she inspected the house, but there was no sign of anyone else. The Six and Anwyn had left.

Seething in anger, she flew out of the house, then stopped. Looking back, she chuckled. Her claw rose inside her merkaba and a bolt of lightning streaked towards the thatch roof.

That will teach them!

She must now track down the Six, and it wouldn't be easy. She smirked in satisfaction as she heard screams behind her. The blazing roof lit up the sky with an intensity stronger than the rising sun.

The Six, with the children and Anwyn, had left Genove, Angus, and Alroy before light. They made their way, on foot, through the fields and forest until they felt they were at a safe enough distance to pull up their merkabas. As they rose above the treetops, they could see the rim of the sun just coming up over the eastern horizon. They prepared to set their merkabas to the southwest.

It was then that Kex shouted.

"*Wait*! What is that?" Her sharp eyes had caught a glimpse of another light, one that was not from the sun's rays.

They all turned to look. A wisp of smoke curled up above the treetops.

"It looks like something's on fire," said Tristan.

"Should we take a look?" Tegan wondered. "It's coming from the direction of the farm."

"We really need to keep moving," said Jarah. "The fake Genove might still be out there. We need to move away from here as fast as we can in case she returns."

"Father, please, let us look! We'll be quick. I have a sense that something is terribly wrong."

They now trusted Anwyn's senses, and they needed to at least see what was occurring. Flying towards the blaze, their worst fears were confirmed. The farmhouse roof was on fire. Genove, Angus, and Alroy were pulling up buckets of water from the well, but not fast enough. It wouldn't be long before the whole house burned down.

"We do know what to do, right?" Jarah said, and everyone nodded. Positioning themselves as close to the farmhouse as was safe for them and the children, but staying inside their merkabas, they closed their eyes and focused.

Anwyn felt comfortable with this. Elemental command was her greatest skill, and she knew both her parents were skilled too with the water element. It was *their* element, and they often used it to help in healing.

Tegan remembered how they had enjoyed their training with Arlyn and Nerina, the water sprites in Ardvale. Calling on them now, they asked the air and the water elements to cooperate, and soon they noticed a large, dark cloud boiling above them and the farmhouse. It looked like the same cloud that the fake Genove had conjured up, but this one felt different. It too was black, but dark with water. It rumbled and churned for a few moments, then let its load go, directly over the farmhouse.

Angus, Genove, and Alroy, whose efforts at throwing buckets of water at the roof had become increasingly futile, watched in astonishment as solid sheets of water rained down upon them and the roof. Genove placed the bucket upside down over her head as the water mercilessly pelted down. Angus and Alroy did the same, and they crouched down on the ground, trying to protect themselves from the battering rain.

The Six wished they could offer them some protection, but that would mean giving themselves away, and they could only watch as the roof sputtered and smoked, the water turning to steam and returning to its source. At last, the final ember was extinguished, and as one, they thanked the elements and the cloud slowly dissipated, its last drop spent.

With sighs of relief, the Six turned their merkabas, and sped off towards the mountains.

17.

Pursuit

Glahivar chuckled. Her inadvertent display of temper had reaped results! Overjoyed, she followed the seven merkabas at a distance. Her extra-sensory vision allowed her to see the faint outlines of their vehicles. She knew that since they did not possess the same vision capabilities as she did, they would not see her as she saw them.

She could not get too close though. Anwyn was an adept, skilled with her own senses, and she would feel her energy fields if she got any closer. At the very least, they might see her as a glimmer of light behind them, but with the sun now higher in the sky, that would be difficult.

With the mountains on their right, the Six and Anwyn sped towards the forests of Mannanon. They had one more stop to make before they continued on to Ibai. After the attack on the farmhouse, for that surely was what it was, they realized that Genove, or whatever the entity actually was, had not given up.

"We must make sure the children are safe," said Jarah, and they'd all agreed. There was to be no bickering or disagreement on that, and they realized they could always come back and get the children once they'd neutralized the danger from this unknown entity. If they'd not had the uncomfortable feeling that they were being followed, they would have enjoyed the trip.

Soaring over treetops, hills and forest, they allowed Anwyn to direct them towards their destination.

"It's been a while, but I can find it," Anwyn had said. "I have a homing signal that I activate in my merkaba, and it will always take me to the portal."

She too sensed that they were being followed.

"We must stay closer together," she said. "I am going to speed up my merkaba so that whatever may be following us will not be able to see where we're going. Since you won't be able to see where I am going either, we must all link up hands and not let go."

"How can I link up hands when I'm holding my baby?" asked Kex.

They nodded. Each one was holding a child or baby.

"I realize you don't want to put them down for fear of them falling out, but we must strengthen our merkaba's outer shells. You can do it. It will hold them for the time it will take to find the portal."

Looking at each other, visible fear on their faces, they focused on their merkabas and the outer shells became thicker. The world outside almost disappeared to them, and they placed their children down on the base of their merkabas. Anwyn was right. They held.

"Now, quickly, link up. Let's go!"

In a flash, they disappeared.

Glahivar screamed out all the curses she'd learned while in Iochodran. Where had they gone? They'd disappeared. She'd been surprised to see their merkabas become even more visible for a brief second, taking on a translucent shine. She'd noticed them grouping closer together too. What were they up to?

Then there was a flash, and they were gone.

She rampaged up and down the Osgoi range in her merkaba, at first slow, and then quicker, flashing to Ibai and back, but she realized they had not arrived there either. She hunted over the forest lands and hills all day.

They were nowhere to be found.

But she could wait, she thought. She had patience. She would wait for as long as it took.

18.

The Elemental Kingdom

They were at the portal. The tree, with its door, became visible as soon as Anwyn touched it. Opening the door, they stepped into the little vestibule inside, and then into the outer door that opened into the elemental's world.

Finn was there to greet them.

"How did you know—" began Djana, but Finn interrupted.

"Nerina and Arlyn told me there was some trouble. I was expecting you. I also have something else to discuss with you. There are complications brewing that you will need to protect yourselves from."

"Yes, we know," said Jarah. "We've already encountered them, but we don't know who or what is causing it, or why."

Finn led them to a peaceful bank of a river, and they all sat under the shade of an oak tree as the orb elementals played with the children on the moss-covered ground.

"We need to leave the children here, with you, until we feel it's safe to bring them back into our world."

"We'll be happy to take care of them for you while you're gone," said Finn. "Now, let's discuss what is going on."

They told Finn all that had occurred since they'd decided to return to Ibai. How the fake Genove had fooled them all, except for Anwyn. Finn grinned, but did not interrupt. Finally, when they were finished, he spoke.

"The entity you once knew as Branwyn, or the Raven, is back." They looked at each other, astonishment on their faces. "She spent some time in our counterpart world, the elemental kingdom of Iochodran. I know about the ruler of that lower world. He goes by the name of Astrabal. He's a demon, and he is angry that the six of you, and Anwyn, are healing what he is attempting to destroy. His aim is to lay waste to your world, to reduce it to a pile of ashes."

"Why?" asked Kex as the others nodded their agreement. "Why would anyone want to do that?"

"He and his minions have no purpose other than to destroy. It is what they exist for. You don't need to understand it. Just know that a severe template distortion will cause that kind of behavior throughout the worlds of polarity. Reason and logic are not their strengths. They are driven by hate, envy, and fear. Just knowing that there are people awakening to their divinity in your world infuriates them. Just knowing that Anwyn is now in your world and ready to activate her mission—"

"What is her mission, exactly?" Tegan interrupted, alarm on her face.

"Tell her, Anwyn."

"I am here to help heal the planet. Our world, the dimension of the manifest, has suffered a lot of damage over the eons. It is why I birthed in to you and father, here in Ardvale. I needed the skills to begin the healing process. To undo the damage that has been done. I am originally from Agra-Tan—"

"The same place as Irusan!" Jarah said, amazed.

And we thought our daughter was just a human child.

She is that, but so much more, Tegan thought back.

"*Your* mission," Finn looked at the Six, "was to heal the Trueni. The mutated slaves of Rhiannon and Ibai. But Anwyn's mission is not the same as yours. She will work on the planetary grids, the damaged ley lines of energy that run through the body of the planet. You will remember from your training that we all exist on planetary bodies, even this one we call Ardvale. Ardvale, the land we sit on, is merely another energy body of the planet you inhabit that has a different rotation of particle spin to yours.

"Our fate is inextricably interwoven with yours. If your material planet is destroyed, we too shall suffer the same fate and be absorbed into the vampiristic system of Iochodran. As a result of their own choices made eons ago, Iochodran does not draw energy from the eternal life fields, but rather needs to feed off living systems. We'd all make a nice meal for them. That is why it is essential to us, and to you, that we do not allow this to happen."

"So, the Raven has returned," said Tristan. He grimaced. "How did that happen?"

"Her template was not destroyed. Her energy body still existed after the death of her physical one. It was transferred into a fearsome and monstrous body by Astrabal. Once she allows you to see her, you will see her as a spider."

Tegan made a small sound of disgust.

"The Raven was once from Agra-Tan too, as you may remember."

"Yes, Irusan told us about her. She got angry and jealous and came to the material world to cause trouble."

"And she did, quite a lot of it. Now she has her sights set on revenge. She already has extracted a vengeance on Yagmak—your erstwhile friend, Blaidd."

"Can we help him?" asked Adain. A wave of sadness moved through them all. Although Blaidd had been troubled and twice betrayed them to Amrafalus, he had also suffered much as a consequence of his actions. They remembered how he'd helped them six years ago, and how he had seemed sorry for his actions then.

"Yes, you can, he is still alive, but only barely. When you leave here, we will assist you in finding him. It may be too late already, but there's always still a chance." He reached into his pocket, and pulled out a pink crystal that shone from within with a translucent, white light.

"This is what you will use if you do find Blaidd. It will not destroy him as your other healing crystal will." Jarah's hand went instinctively to the healing crystal, still in a pouch around his neck. He never let it out of his sight, and always wore it. He remembered how Blaidd had tried to obtain the crystal for himself. If he'd succeeded, it may have killed him in his extreme mutation, as it had done with the Arrach.

"Be careful, though. The Raven will be on the lookout for you. I will take you to another portal. One the Raven does not know about. We are short on time. Even though there's no time here in Ardvale, we must get you back out there as quickly as possible, and we'll have to use the portal to get you back out just after you entered. But now I have something else—something even more important than what we've already discussed, to tell you."

His face betrayed a concern that they had never seen before. Finn was always such a jolly fellow, joking and laughing. It was alarming indeed to see that he was worried. The Six looked at each other. What could be more important than the identity of their enemy?

As Finn spoke, their own expressions betrayed their fear. This was much worse than they had imagined.

Irusan, Agra-Tan

A special session of the Council of Twenty-four had convened.

Irusan, as the ambassador to the material plane known as Earth, had been summoned. He always felt honored to be in the presence of the Beings who made up the Council, tall shapes of conscious light and sound. They were not physical as he was, but they were able to communicate with him on their astral plane. Irusan knew that they rarely used this form of communication, but it was evident as they spoke that they felt the situation serious enough to warrant it.

He had not returned to the material plane for some time. He'd spent the last six earth-years healing from his long sojourn on that plane of existence, and he was in no hurry to return. He felt that the six healers no longer needed his mentorship, that they were well able to take care of themselves and that his well-earned rest was deserved.

But the Council had other plans for him.

One of them spoke.

"I am the consciousness known as Artremaya. We called you here, Irusan, to let you know that there are new developments on Ialana's planet that have come to our attention. Dangerous developments. Generally, we would leave this planetary consciousness field alone since free will choices are allowed, but there has been a discovery that could eliminate all life there in a matter of earth-days."

Irusan felt a sense of horror. *Days?*

Artremaya continued. "There was a weapon. This weapon was used eons ago by another race, another civilization, to wipe out most life on this planet. They did not fully understand the power of their creation. They thought it would only destroy that which they hated, and that they could control its immense power. But that was not to be.

"The weapon was activated, and using the energy of the planetary core, they created a plasma conduit by the means of an artificially created crystal. This crystal possessed similar properties to a diamond. They harvested the energy of this plasma and stored it in this crystal. When their enemies entered through portals and attacked, they aimed this crystal at their enemies and it destroyed them, and their portals, utterly.

"However, it was much more powerful than even they had anticipated, and before the scientists could shut it down, it caused the planet's crust to rotate. Can you imagine the havoc and disaster on a planet with that kind of weapon?"

Irusan could. For the first time in maybe hundreds of years, he felt a wave of despair moving through him.

Artremeya allowed a few moments for Irusan to recover his composure before continuing.

"When the planetary crust shifted, it buried the crystal under tons of dirt, debris, and water. Over time, the crystal lost its connection with the planetary core, and it shut itself down, but the damage had been done. Since then, the planet has experienced even more shifts, upheavals, and changes.

"Gradually, Ialana rose up out of the water again. The crystal still lay buried under tons of earth, but all it needed to reactivate itself and reconnect with the core was to be exposed to a chemical sequence that was only found in the DNA coding of the descendants of those surviving scientists who had created it."

"How did it become reactivated?" Irusan asked.

"One of the mine slaves who unwittingly opened up the chamber where it had been buried was a carrier of this code. We understand there are no coincidences. His discovery of the crystal was orchestrated by Astrabal, the demon-lord of the Shadowlands. When the slave touched the crystal, the sweat from his skin was enough to trigger the command for the crystal to release the residual energy still contained within. At this time, the energy contained within the crystal is enough to cause death to anyone nearby. But it is not fully activated yet as a weapon of planetary destruction. It needs to draw upon the planetary core for its energy, and it will not spontaneously release this energy until the command is given to do so."

"But then it may remain inactive as a catastrophic weapon for many years, if there is no one on planet who knows how to give this command," Irusan speculated.

"Not so. It requires chemical DNA from at least three activators from a specific lineage to command it to engage its most destructive state. The three lineages that are required to activate and engage have emerged from the remnants of the scientists who created this weapon. These lineages exist on the planet today."

Irusan sighed. "What about those who can shut it down?"

"There are also some lineages who have the coding necessary to shut it down. Not all of the scientists died in the holocaust that followed. A few, together with their families, found shelter. Not all on the planet today are descended from these particular scientists, but there are many descendants, and not all possess the key codes necessary to control and engage the weapon. The descendants are spread out all over the continent of Ialana. There were even a few that became Trueni after a time, as was the slave who activated the crystal. They were of that lineage, the lineage of the scientist whose coding could activate the weapon.

"One deactivator's coding can temporarily shut it down and place it into an inactive state, but it requires three to shut it down completely once it has engaged.

"The rulers in Rhiannon are aware that something has been discovered, but fortunately, at this time, they have not been able to get near it, and they are not aware of the extent of its destructive power. The energy from it kills almost immediately. It is only a matter of time before the right—or wrong from our perspective—people are able to get close enough for its weapons systems to engage with the planetary core. Therefore, if nothing is done, a repeat of history will ensue."

"Will the weapon not kill those who touch it as it did the slave in the mine?"

"It may, but it wasn't designed to. The slave's DNA was enough to activate it, but not strong enough to put it into its greatest destructive power, or to over-ride the kill factor for him. He was weak due to exhaustion and malnutrition, and his DNA had long ago been mingled with that of an animal so that he could not withstand the residual energies contained within the crystal. It killed him instantly, but it would all depend upon those living today who have the correct sequence of DNA, and their physical condition, whether it would kill them or not."

"Is there any chance of us being able to shut it down before the worst happens?"

"We were, and are, not able to, then or now. We, and you, have different DNA. These scientists anticipated that someone from our dimension may interfere with their choices, and inserted their own coding as the only instructions this weapon would accept. We had to allow it to happen because if we tried to destroy the weapon, they'd create another one almost immediately. They had the knowledge, but not the wisdom.

"Free will choices, even the insane ones, are allowed. The planet, as a whole, was so distorted in thinking that even those who were able to shut it down were blinded by their ambition. Division, subjugation, exploitation, and ambition are only a few symptoms of DNA and energetic convolution in a society. To a society such as ours, these actions would be considered insane."

"So what is different this time?"

"Now we see some opportunity for healing on this planet. After the deluge and destruction, the planet slowly began to heal itself again. There is still distortion and insanity, but also hope. Your healers are instrumental in this, and one of them in particular carries a marker that will allow for a shut-down of this weapon, although it would not be permanent. There must be three people with the coding to shut it down.

"When the weapon was first activated, no one was able to shut it down since the scientists with the necessary DNA were prevented from coming near it."

Irusan looked shocked. "Why? That makes no sense to me."

"The scientist who led the team that created this weapon did not want it to shut down. She feared that they would shut it down too soon once they observed its terrible effects, and that the mission would not be accomplished. So she sabotaged the process, and the three with the coding were not able to reach the weapon in time."

Irusan thought for a while.

"Memories of this period are returning to me."

"Yes, you were there, but not in your current form. Your larger conscious mind remembers this life time. You have been involved with this planet for many eons, Irusan."

"I also remember the scientist who did not want it shut down."

"She is back. She returned to this planet on a redemption contract, and was given the opportunity to heal and learn, but she did not ultimately choose that path. She has returned to the path of sorrow and darkness, and she has been attempting all this time to recreate her one success: the creation of this ultimate weapon. It is only a matter of time before she learns of its reactivation and location.

"She is currently attempting to regain her lost stature on this planet, interfering in the affairs of humanity and claiming back her power. She is no longer the Raven, but is now known as Glahivar, a fearsome creature from the Shadowlands. When she fully regains her memory, and learns of the discovery of the weapon, she will locate those with the codes who can control it so that she can use it again. The demon-lord, Astrabal, will back her, and she will essentially be his pawn.

THE SIX AND ANWYN OF IALANA

"We know that he has become aware of the situation, and will seize the opportunity to reduce this planet to rubble once more."

"How did the progenitors of the genetic lines that are able to shut it down survive the destruction?" asked Irusan.

"There were six scientists who carried this DNA. We assisted by taking them into Ardvale, the elemental kingdom, just before the destruction. They were also barred from entering the escape vehicles operated by the entity now known as Glahivar. Once the planet became safe enough to survive on, they were released.

"They will eventually repopulate the planet, and there will be too many for Astrobal to destroy, although he will always try. But right now there are only a few with this coding left, and Anwyn, the child, is one of them. We are trying to find the others.

"Her parents are the descendants of these fail-safe scientists, but their coding became mixed with others and watered down. The birth of Anwyn recombined it into the correct sequence. That is only one of the reasons she is so skilled at healing and other metaphysical arts. She will be the progenitor of a new generation who can pass this combination down. She will, if she lives, assist in repopulating the earth with humans who possess the full human genetic template that was in the original design, before the mad-scientists of the past meddled in what never should have been changed."

"Yes, I do understand what happened with the experimentation and creation of monstrosities that still exist today. Apparently not all were destroyed during the upheaval and floods."

"They were not. But now you also understand the current situation and how dangerous it is. We wish to see life given the opportunity to thrive and regenerate on the original design, as before, but if Glahivar and others get their way, there will only be a repeat of history, and it will be worse than before."

"You have tasked me with a difficult assignment this time, but I am ready. Where do I start?"

"This is what you need to do," said Artremaya.

19.

The Six

Finn guided them to the portal that would take them into the outer world only moments after they'd arrived at the tree door.

"We're time travelers!" said Djana.

"You are, in a way," said Finn. "We don't have *time* now to explain," he said, and laughed, "but Anwyn will explain it to you one day. We covered this topic with her quite well during her training."

"I remember the time dilation class well," said Anwyn. "I thought it did tax my brain a bit, but I enjoyed it."

"Well, it's a mystery to me," Kex murmured, "but I'm glad it works."

They came out in a part of the forest they had never seen before. Pulling up their merkabas, they felt relief now that they didn't have to fear for the safety of their children.

Except for Anwyn, Tegan thought. She and Jarah tried to remember that Anwyn was a capable being in her own right, but it was difficult. To them, she would always be a child, and their responsibility.

The air elementals, Ilma and Amun, helped guide their vehicles towards a spot near one of the foothills of the Osgoi. The forest there was thick, and they would never have found what remained of Blaidd, or Yagmak, on their own.

They were horrified to see the crumpled figure, almost unrecognizable as the frightening beast he had turned into, lying motionless on the ground. He was hidden by thick undergrowth and bushes, and they had to search a while before the buzzing of insects told them they were close.

Flies had settled on the thick fur, now almost burned completely away from the body. Yagmak's eyes were closed, and Jarah felt for a pulse. He didn't think he had one, but just as he was about to draw his hand away and tell them Yagmak was dead, he felt a faint beat under the charred flesh.

"He's alive!"

They pulled out the crystal, and although they'd been given quick instructions by Finn on how to use it before leaving, they weren't sure if it would work, or even if they were doing it correctly. But they had to try. Blaidd had saved their lives six years ago in this same forest, and they owed him.

As they worked on him, running the crystal over the worst of the burns, they could see a small improvement. Tegan used her healing touch, and she carried a salve with her that she used on scraped knees and small cuts on the children, applying it to some areas. It took them all day, but gradually the monster's heart beat became stronger, and finally, he opened his eyes.

He gave a low growl of alarm and tried to rise. He did not seem to remember them, and Jarah was afraid he would try to kill them.

"Blaidd, it is us! The Six!"

Yagmak, or Blaidd as they remembered him, stopped struggling as Tegan gently rubbed his neck.

"Gh...shheeex?" He couldn't talk. Tegan and Anwyn, taking turns, sent him telepathic messages, since they were the best at that.

Do you remember us, Blaidd? We were your friends once. You helped us escape the Raven and Brenin six years ago.

We have found you to heal you, Yagmak. I am the daughter of Tegan.

A glimmer of recognition began to dawn in Yagmak's red eyes. *Tegan! Jarah!*

Yes. Do you remember us?

I am dead?

No, not dead. We are healing you, Blaidd.

No! Do not heal! I must die. I have been foolish. My pack will kill me—tear me to pieces—if I live . . . Beware . . . she lives! She will find me again. You must kill me, now.

Yes, we do know about the Raven. But you must live, Blaidd. We don't want you to die. Please . . . Tegan begged, her eyes filling with tears.

Yagmak looked stunned. He had forgotten what compassion and love felt like. In his world, only the strong were allowed to live, and he had shown his weakness in front of his pack. It would not be tolerated. If that horrible spider-thing that was once Branwyn wished, she would now rule his pack. He wondered if she had taken over as leader. He was sure she could use them in her vindictive plans.

He carefully got up and felt himself all over, patting his body down. He no longer hurt. His burns had almost healed, but he looked a mess. His fur was almost gone, but he still had his fangs and his horns, and his enormous physical stature. Perhaps . . . perhaps he wasn't so weak, after all. Perhaps he *could* get his pack back.

Hope rose in his heart, and now he didn't feel like dying anymore. He realized that he wanted to live, badly. He wanted revenge. He'd never be Blaidd again, but he was still Yagmak of the Vicious Eyes Pack. He must behave like Yagmak, not like the weak boy, Blaidd.

I owe you a debt of gratitude, he telepathed. *Thank you. I must now try to get my pack back. I am still the strongest beast in the forest. If they want to tear me from limb to limb, I would rather die fighting for my pack than lying here on the ground wishing for death.*

"There's our Blaidd!" said Tristan, and the others nodded.

"Go get your pack back, Blaidd!"

He roared, and the forest shook. They all felt relief and joy that their friend was now willing to live. What happened from here was up to him.

At least they had given him a chance. Bidding the huge beast farewell, they pulled up their merkabas and set their headings towards their next destination. Not Ibai this time, but west, towards the Mines of Amrafalus.

They had another task, and they hoped that Glahivar was not around. They hoped she'd given up trying to locate them.

They had spent a lot of time in healing Yagmak, and they needed to get over the mountains before it was completely dark, but they could not hurry too much. There were markers they had to look for so they would not over-shoot the mines.

As they slowly drifted towards the mountains, intent on looking for their markers, they did not notice when a tiny, red spark flew towards them, or that it now began to follow at a safe distance.

Shegami, Iochodran

"Why am I only hearing about this now?" Astrabal's roar caused his subjects to tremble. They cringed and mewled as they groveled on the floor in front of him. "We've wasted time. Bring Glahivar back immediately!"

"My Liege, we are attempting to locate her before she kills the girl." Shegami knew that this was her last chance. If she and her legions of demons did not find Glahivar, they'd all become food for the hungry imps in the dungeons below. She added, "It wasn't my fault that we weren't told about the existence of the weapon before we sent Glahivar out on her mission—"

The screech that came from Astrabal nearly tore her apart. His courtiers dissolved into dust from the blast from his maw, but she was made of stronger stuff. Now he'd have to find new courtiers. Fortunately, there were plenty of candidates available, she thought. But she had more immediate problems.

She was right. It was Astrabal's fault, not hers. He had known about the weapon for some time now, but he had not known the identity of the activators and those who could stop the weapon. It had come to his ears moments ago that the girl, Anwyn, was the key.

"The imps saw them come out of one of Ardvale's portals and heard them talking," said Shegami. "They came straight to me, and I came directly here. You can't blame me—"

Another screech reduced a few more courtiers to dust, and all the hall-denizens moved back several paces. It wasn't healthy being so close to their demon-lord when he was in one of his moods.

"Without the girl, we cannot get the weapon." Shegami refused to be intimidated. "It is deadly to us, too. We need her to temporarily deactivate it so that we can steal it and put it in a place where it can safely be reactivated."

"Glahivar is the scientist who designed this awesome power." To his subject's relief, Astrabal was simmering down. He didn't have time to be angry. He needed to make new plans. "We need to find her, bring her here, and restore her memory to include this period when she created this weapon. We too can use time portals. Go get her—*now!*"

Shegami scurried out, trailing a legion of imps. Glahivar was most likely still carrying out her mission, to destroy the girl, she thought. They had to find her before that happened. They now needed the girl alive. She rounded up imps, demons, elementals, and every hideous form she could find to look for Glahivar.

She hoped she would find her soon, before Astrabal destroyed them both.

20.

Goodbye

Something was not right. Anwyn felt uncomfortable. They were traveling slowly west, towards the setting sun across the Osgoi Mountain range. They needed to locate the markers Finn had given them that would guide them directly to the mines. She looked behind them again, and thought she saw a glimpse of red, but it could also have been the last rays of the sun that—

It was at that moment it felt as if her merkaba stuttered. It jerked a few times, and then continued to fly smoothly towards the icy peaks ahead. She shrugged.

Must be a gust of wind.

Then, it happened again. This time it felt as if it had dropped a bit. The forest below looked closer. Was there something wrong with her merkaba? It was then that she heard Jarah.

"Down, down, quick!"

They descended as rapidly as they could, but their merkabas were fading in and out, and it was all they could do to descend at a rate that was just slightly less than a deadly fall. The hilly forest below came up to meet them rather too quickly, and it was only by sheer luck that they managed to halt the speed of their plummet just before crashing into the topmost branches of the trees. But they still fell much too heavily through the branches and foliage, and found themselves sprawled on the forest floor.

Shakily, they all got up, feeling for broken bones and bruises.

"Are we all alright?" asked Tristan. "Djana, are you—?"

"Yes, I'm fine Tristan. Just shook up. How about the rest of you?"

After they'd checked to see if everyone was alright, they began to wonder just what had happened. They'd all felt the same thing. The stutter, then the fading in and out, and finally the fall.

"I can understand one of our merkabas not functioning, if the person concerned was not focused well on what they were doing, but *all* of us?" Jarah said.

"And at the same time?" Kex sounded frightened.

They attempted to pull them up, again, but nothing happened. This was alarming, thought Anwyn. She had no explanation. She wished Finn was with them.

They jumped as a breathy whisper came from the trees.

"Say goodbye to your family, Anwyn!"

A red flash, and then they saw her. Even though they'd been prepared for her new form, they couldn't help but freeze, rooted to the ground with shock. A huge claw shot out, and Anwyn felt it close tightly around her. She could barely breathe. In the other claw, Glahivar held a crystal, about the size of a hen's egg. She waved it at them and gave a gleeful chuckle.

"Your merkabas are no longer working thanks to this little crystal. You aren't the only ones who know how to use them!"

"Let our daughter go!" Jarah shouted as Tegan began to wail.

"Oh, I will—*I will*, don't you worry about that, my dears." She laughed again. "But her death might be a lot quicker than yours. Traveling through these forests at night, with no merkaba? Well, I don't need to tell you about that, do I? I have spoken to a nearby pack of wolf-men. They're already on their way." She hee-hawed with laughter as she saw the terror in their faces. "Your friend Blaidd won't be able to save you this time!"

With that, she pulled up her merkaba and shot up into the air, still holding Anwyn. Anwyn saw the ground below her receding fast, and the terrified faces of the Six looking up at her. She looked until she could no longer see them. What was Glahivar going to do with her? Was she taking her somewhere?

As they rose above the clouds, she could now see jagged mountain peaks below them.

"You will not be able to escape your death this time, my dear, but a promise is a promise." She snickered. "I did *promise* your parents I'd let you go. *Goodbye!*"

With that, she let go, and Anwyn plummeted, like a rock, toward the icy peaks below.

The only sound as the forest darkened into the blackness of the night was Tegan's soft sobbing.

Jarah tried to comfort her. She knew that he too felt as if he wanted to scream, cry, and curl up in a ball on the forest floor, but he didn't have the luxury of that now. They had to think of their next step. Things were critical. He must make a decision quickly.

Tristan made some suggestions, as did the others, but no satisfactory solutions arose. Without Anwyn, they could not find the portal again, and without their merkabas, they had no protection. They had no food, no blankets, or warm clothing. They tried to contact the elementals, but in this part of the forest, they felt a strong presence of dark energies that seemed to be seeking something. They felt it was most likely seeking them. It would be unsafe for them to broadcast their plight.

There was already a chill in the night air, and they huddled together as they tried to stay warm and unobtrusive.

They heard the cries, howls, and growls from the surrounding forest, and jumped at every nearby rustle in the undergrowth. Tegan stifled her sobs. They could not allow the sharp-eared beasts to hear them.

"Maybe she's not dead," Tegan finally whispered. The others said nothing. They all felt that Glahivar would destroy Anwyn, and then come back and finish them off if they weren't already dead.

Tegan wished Glahivar had taken her instead of her daughter. She would gladly give her life up to save Anwyn and the others. She had to focus on the possibility—the slimmest of chances—that Glahivar needed her daughter, and would not destroy her.

"I wish Blaidd was here now. I'd feel safe with his protection," Djana said.

"Or Finn. Or Irusan," Kex added. Her small body shook with cold and fear, and her chattering teeth sounded far too loud to her ears.

"Is there some way we can send them a message?" whispered Tristan. "Tegan, you're the best with that. You and Jarah."

Tegan nodded. I am already trying, but I am finding it difficult to focus. I keep seeing Anwyn, but I can't even reach her. She's gone." She moaned softly.

Jarah shook from cold and fear as he tried to reach his daughter, but his thoughts too were fuzzy and unfocused.

"Don't blame yourself. I think that whatever it was that sabotaged our merkabas, has affected our other abilities too," he responded quietly.

They kept trying to pull up their merkabas, hoping that whatever Glahivar's crystal had done to them had now worn off, but to no avail. Their merkabas stubbornly refused to expand around their bodies. It only added to their despair. What if they'd lost their ability for merkaba travel completely? Forever?

"Finn should have protected us," whispered Tristan. "The plan was to retrieve the crystal from the mines and bring it back to Ardvale, where it would be safe. It was far too important a mission to compromise."

"He must have known Glahivar would be looking for us," said Jarah, his voice low. "I can't imagine why he'd allow this to happen."

"I think he knows," said Djana. "Maybe he has another plan."

"And didn't tell us?"

They talked in soft whispers for what felt like hours. The night was long, but Tegan still sat quietly, trying to make contact with her daughter. Jarah was right. It felt as if she was being blocked. She kept seeing Anwyn's face in her inner vision. Perhaps her daughter was dead, and it was her spirit she saw . . . but what if it was her living daughter trying to reach her? What if this was no false image she had conjured up, but—*no*. She could not allow herself to hope. If Anwyn was truly dead, the grief she would feel would be too much for her to bear. Yet a part of her continued to see Anwyn's face. It was insistent. It crowded out everything else in her mind.

It was then that a dark shadow overhead blocked out the moon, then quickly disappeared. What was that? They tried to hunker down under the thick ferns so that whatever it was did not see them. Was it Glahivar, returning?

They looked upwards in fear. There it was again! Whatever it was, it was large, and they could see a glimpse of what looked like red eyes.

The Sentinel

As Glahivar let go of her, Anwyn screamed, but her scream was quickly cut off as icy air hit her lungs. Desperate, she tried to cry out for the air elements to help her, but she could not get a sound out. She tried to telepath to Amun and Ilma, but her attempts only seemed to go as far as her nose, now blue with cold. Panic had set in, and it prevented her from using what skills she still may have that Glahivar's crystal had not touched.

Coughing and crying, she glanced down as a mountain peak rose towards her. She closed her eyes. She did not want to know the moment her body would impact the sharp rocks below. She hoped it would be quick. She hoped her parents would never know how she died, and that they would even think of her as still alive somewhere. Or maybe it was better . . . but she didn't want to think of that now. She must prepare her body to die. Perhaps she could pull out of it just before—she couldn't breathe. The air was too cold. Maybe she should just open her eyes a little, just to see . . .

It was then that she felt an upward jerk that knocked what little breath remained in her lungs completely out of her. *Whoosh!* Her insides felt as if they still plummeted to the ground, but her body was rising, lifting . . . lifting . . . Was this death? Had she already hit the rock face? If so, except for a feeling of tightness around her chest, it had been completely painless.

She opened her eyes, but what she did not see was the tunnel that all the dying entered. There was no light at the end, only a moon up above her and a dark shape. It had her body gripped tightly in enormous claws and its flapping, bat-like wings spread out over her.

Oh no, she thought. *Now I'm food for some mutant bat thing. I think I would have preferred that I was splattered all over a mountain!*

Was it Glahivar? Did she return so she could torture her some more? The humanoid body above her didn't have the spider shape, but it did have red eyes. Those eyes now looked down at her, and it shrieked, its voice chillier than the air around her. She trembled, and its grip tightened. It had arms and legs, with hooks on its wings. At the end of each limb were eagle-like talons. It shrieked again, and she could see gleaming white fangs in its mouth.

She struggled, but the claws only gripped her tighter, and she didn't want to suffocate. A quick fall would have been more merciful, but the thing was not letting go of her. It flew over more mountain peaks, and she could see one of them coming closer, its rock face looming darkly ahead. Would it let her go here? The valley below was so far down she couldn't see where it ended. It would be a long drop.

Just when she thought they would either be splattered against the rock face or the thing would release her, they flew into a dark, almost hidden gash in the mountain. As they glided silently into the cavity, the air felt warmer around them, and she saw that they were in what looked like a tunnel. It was too dark to see much else, but a faint light glimmered up ahead. Was this the tunnel of death? Perhaps she had been grabbed by a demon before she could—but no. She could now see that they had entered a larger space.

It was a cave. A fire that was merely embers glowed in a rock hollow in the center of the cave, and the creature gently dropped her next to the still-warm ashes.

Wary, Anwyn tried to get up, but her feet wouldn't work. They were numb. She rubbed her frozen limbs, and they prickled painfully as the life came back to them. It still hurt to breath, but the air was warmer now, and she knew her body would recover. But to what end? How long would it take before the creature began to rip into her warm flesh?

She sneaked a peak at it again. It had gathered a bundle of firewood from a nearby stockpile and used its bat-like wings to lift itself gently into the air, then down again as it hopped over and placed sticks and limbs on the embers of the previous fire. The fire blazed up quickly, and she welcomed its warmth. The creature stood on the other side of the fire and gazed at her with curious eyes. They were enormous, taking up most of its grey-furred face. She could now see that it was tall, even taller than Yagmak, and bigger. It gracefully folded its wings behind its back.

"*Eat!*" it squeaked. Reaching down, it retrieved a skewer with meat on it from the fire and pushed it towards her.

It spoke! She shook her head. She wasn't hungry, and she didn't know what kind of meat it was, anyway. She looked at the creature again, curious. It did not look threatening. It could have killed her already, but maybe it wanted to fatten her up first?

The creature stared at her as she rubbed her limbs. Finally, she stopped shaking enough to ask, "Who are you?"

The creature observed her a while longer, not answering. Finally, it opened its mouth again and seemed to be forming words. The words came slowly, in a series of squeaks.

"Me . . . Sentinel . . ." It stopped. "See you . . . fall from sky." Another long silence. "Me . . . want know . . . who *you* be!"

It was not comfortable using human speech, she thought. She would try out her mental communication. Maybe that would be more comfortable, and she needed to know what it wanted to do with her.

Can you understand me? she asked. The creature looked at her, surprised.

Of course. I don't come across many of you, it responded telepathically, but with great clarity. *Especially those of you who speak my language. Thank you. I am not much good with human speech. I am sorry if I frightened you, but you just dropped out of the sky in front of me. I thought you were a meal sent from heaven and grabbed you a moment before you hit the peak. How did you fall from the sky?*

Anwyn felt relief. Her telepathic abilities were still intact.

It's a long story. I hope you don't still consider me your next meal.

No, I don't eat human flesh. It made a disgusted squeak with its mouth. *I am, after all, part human myself.*

My name is Anwyn.

And I am 'The Sentinel'. I have no name. That is all I've ever been.

Well, I'm very pleased to make your acquaintance, Sentinel. I was pulled up into the sky by an evil entity who thought she had killed me by dropping me from the clouds. I am grateful to you for saving my life, but I must go. My parents and their friends are in trouble. I need to help them. Can you take me to them?

I am not sure why anyone would want to kill you. You seem harmless to me, but I have eaten for the night, and have plenty of food. He waved his arm around the cave, and Anwyn noticed Arrach exoskeletons scattered across the floor. Chunks of drying flesh hung from the roof of the cave. She felt nauseous. She was glad she had not eaten the meat she'd been offered. *I will take you to find your friends and family after we've rested a bit. Are you sure you won't eat?*

She shook her head, and they rested in front of the warm fire as The Sentinel told her more about himself.

I have been guarding these mountains for longer than I can remember, he said. *I don't remember who put me here, or why. I only know that it is my duty to guard these mountains.*

From what?

He scratched his head. *I wish I could remember. It was after the last destruction of the planet. There were few humans left here after that, and whoever put me here did not tell me why, or I have forgotten. I have stayed here because I know of no other place, and I am happy here.*

THE SIX AND ANWYN OF IALANA

I eat the Arrach, mainly, and there is always a plentiful supply of meat. In summer, I have berries and fish from the mountain streams. I go out at night to hunt, and sleep in the day. My eyes are not able to function well in sunlight. My hearing is better than my eyesight, and I use sound to locate prey. It is how I located you.

Anwyn nodded. *Yes, I know about bats and their amazing ability to bounce sound off objects. You seem more bat than human.*

The Sentinel flapped his wings and rose. *We can go now. Are you warm enough?*

Yes, I think so. I will give you the direction Glahivar came from and we should head slightly northeast—

I don't understand this 'northeast', but just point it out and we'll go there.

The Sentinel gently folded Anwyn into his warm, furry arms—*Better than the claws*, she thought—and they flew out of the cave and into the night.

21.

Flaming Fury

The day had ended admirably, and Glahivar was pleased that she'd been able to pick up the sparks of the seven merkabas just as darkness fell. Her mission had been accomplished, and she'd even managed to exact a satisfying revenge on Yagmak. Congratulating herself, she used her crystal to summon Shegami. Astrabal would be delighted by the news, and she'd be promoted—perhaps even sit at his right hand. Shegami's job was no longer her goal. She wanted Astrabal's!

Shegami's form appeared in front of her, but to Glahivar's surprise, she did not seem pleased.

"Where have you been? We've been searching all over for you. Astrabal will have your head!"

"Relax! What's wrong? I have done what I set out to do—"

"*Oh, Idris!* I had hoped to find you before . . . is she dead?"

"Yes!" Glahivar replied triumphantly. "And so are the Six. Or at least they will be, quite soon. I can go back and make sure."

"You fool. Oh, I don't want to take this news back . . ."

THE SIX AND ANWYN OF IALANA

"What are you talking about? Isn't this what Astrabal wanted?"

"Yes, it was, but things have changed. You must return with me." Shegami's hand shot out and pulled Glahivar into a stifling grip. There was a flash, and they found themselves in Iochodran. Things were not as peachy as they'd first seemed, thought Glahivar. But how could they blame her? She wondered what had happened. Had Anwyn lived? It was just not possible.

Quicker than a blink, the dismal landscape of Iochodran and the black spires of Rhagat Rise appeared. Still pulled by Shegami, they entered the large hall, and now Glahivar felt the familiar fear stirring deep within her. It was not to be the triumphant home-coming she had hoped for. Astrabal's rage enveloped him like a red mist, and even the maggots had been fried by his flaming fury. They popped and sizzled on his flesh like burning bits of bacon.

"Tell me the girl lives!" he commanded.

Glahivar trembled. She could always lie, but Shegami knew the truth, and so would Astrabal. It would have been futile. She hoped her end would be quick, but knowing Astrabal, it would not.

"She is dead, my lord. Dead."

He hissed, and a burned maggot flew into her mouth. *It actually tastes quite delicious*, she thought, as she chewed. *Like butter.*

"And you will be dead soon, as well." As Glahivar crumpled to the ground in shock, her eight limbs trembling, he continued. "But I am sometimes merciful. I see in your mind that there is a possibility—a slim one at that—that the Six still live. You know where you left them. If you'd been smart, you would have finished them off first, but your incredible stupidity saved you this time.

"Go back, and bring all six to me—*alive*. Perhaps they can be useful, especially if they carry the coding for the weapon. I need to see just how much of it they have, if any, or if I have to destroy them. One way or another, I'll find all of those still able to control that weapon."

Glahivar's breath came out in a gasp. She had another chance!

"My lord, you will have them. I don't know what weapon you are referring to, but whatever it is, I will bring the Six to you."

"We already know one of the activators, a Trueni slave. He was killed when he touched the weapon. It is not fully activated though and we need at least three more activators to get it up to its full potential. You, Glahivar, are not an activator.

"Shegami, take her to the records in the Hall of Memory. She must remember something about the weapon and who the activators were. We'll trace the ancestral lines through this memory. She had a hand in its creation too." He snickered. "A big hand. We don't need any more thoughtless actions from this one. Give her the names of the most likely candidates for activating the weapon. She must understand the importance of these descendants, and where to locate them. It is your task, Glahivar, to find them. I want them all!"

"Yes, master! Right away!"

Glahivar and Shegami fled. They had no time to waste.

As the Sentinel, with Anwyn held securely in his warm, fury arms, left the cave and soared over the mountain tops, Anwyn noticed a strange, blue light in the distance.

What is that, Sentinel?

I don't know. It has been there for some time now. I flew over to take a look at it just a few nights ago, and I felt strange emanations coming from it. Fortunately, I noticed birds that dropped dead when they got too close, so I turned around just in time. Whatever it is, it's dangerous. I think it comes from the mines.

So that is the weapon, she thought. *It is where we were headed.*

Anwyn pointed The Sentinel towards the direction they needed to fly, away from the blue light. She tapped him on the arm when she thought they were near the last place she had seen the Six, and pointed downwards.

Flying lower, they set up a search pattern over the forest. Anwyn tried to communicate with her mother. They'd always had strong telepathic links, and she hoped she could now tell her that she was alive and looking for them, but something was blocking her. She didn't know what it was. Every time she thought she'd made a connection, the link went dead. Perhaps Glahivar's crystal had destroyed their telepathic abilities? But no, it couldn't be. She'd had no problem communicating with The Sentinel.

She realized then that her attempts to contact Finn, while in the grip of Glahivar had come to nothing as well. Fear blocked her abilities. So did grief. Her mother would be grieving, and that's why she could not contact her. They would have to do it the hard way and search.

She hoped that they were still alive. The forest was dangerous, and even up here they could hear the frightening howls of the wolf-men. As they flew back and forth over the last place she'd seen them, she wondered if they had set off into the night and were now in a different place. She could hear the high pitched tones of The Sentinel as he bounced his sound waves off objects below. She couldn't decipher them though. Only he could. She would have to rely on his night vision and sound sensors. Her eyes were not designed to penetrate the darkness below.

The Six drew closer together as the large shape glided, soundless, overhead. They could now see its wings. To make things worse, they were not only being hunted from above, but from below, too. The howls and snarls they'd heard in the distance earlier, were much closer now.

"Stay together," said Tristan, pulling his knife out. They were thankful that Tristan still had his knife. It was better than nothing. They stood back to back as their eyes scanned the darkness around them. It wouldn't be long now. They could hear the crackle of twigs and branches as the wolf-men began to close in on their position.

"We still have the crystal," said Jarah. His nervous fingers closed around the bag. "We can keep them at bay for a while."

"Yes, we'll have to use it or we'll be dead in a rather short while," Tristan agreed.

Jarah removed the crystal from its pouch. "When I say the word, begin to tone," he said.

They all cleared their throats. It had worked for them before, when they had been cornered by the wolf-men. The power of the crystal was too much for the mutants to bear, and they had kept their distance until they'd been rescued by the elementals. They hardly dared to hope that this might occur again. Perhaps Finn would—

At that moment, the shadow above dropped down between the tree branches and alit on the ground nearby. Its large, red eyes glinted, and it held a shape in its arms.

The shape ran towards them. "Mother, it's me! Anwyn!"

"Stop!" yelled Tristan, and brandished his knife. "Don't come any closer!"

"It's Anwyn," cried Tegan as she tried to run towards the small figure, but Jarah held her back.

"Tegan, it's not Anwyn. It's Glahivar. Remember, she can shapeshift. She's trying to trick us!"

"Father, I am not Glahivar! Do you remember how we used to joke about the elementals? That day at the river? You told me and El-Azar that we were always overworking the earth elementals—"

"Who is your godfather, Anwyn?" Jarah hardly dared hope this was his daughter. He still held tightly onto Tegan.

"Finn. *Finn!*"

"It *is* Anwyn, Jarah!" He let go of Tegan, and she ran towards her daughter, sobbing. Tristan put his knife away and they all laughed in relief. Anwyn was alive! *But, what was that creature?*

"Quickly, we've got to get out of here," said Anwyn. "This is my friend, The Sentinel." She indicated the large, bat-like creature nearby. "He will take us all to safety. Don't be afraid of him. He's harmless to us."

They had no choice. The red eyes of the wolf-men could now be seen as they fast approached through the trees. They could hear loud howls of anticipation.

"How is he going to take all of us?" asked Tristan.

"He says he can carry us all. It will only be for a short distance, but it will take us out of immediate danger, and then we can think about what to do."

The Sentinel crouched down as Anwyn climbed onto his shoulders. He gently placed Djana under one arm, and Tegan under the other. Tristan and Kex were firmly grasped in a foot claw, while Jarah and Adain felt themselves being lifted off the ground in large, claw-like hands. The Sentinel's wings flapped, and they rose about the height of Tristan into the air.

Not enough! The Sentinel sank down onto the ground again, took a huge breath, and now with fangs that snapped inches below their dangling feet, they rose again into the air. The Sentinel groaned, but with each groan and flap of wings, they rose a little higher. The wolf-men leapt into the air below them, snapping and snarling. If they succeeded in fastening their teeth into only one of them, the combined weight of the pack could pull them all down.

It seemed to take forever, but Tristan and Kex's feet slowly rose, until at last they were out of reach of the creatures below. The frustrated wolf-men, howling in despair, ran in circles below them, jumping and snapping as they made their way slowly and heavily over the tree tops.

They weren't moving fast enough, thought Jarah. These creatures could outrun them, and surely The Sentinel couldn't stay in the air for much longer with their combined weight. They could feel how difficult it was, even for something as large as he, to bear them all aloft. If only their merkabas worked, but then again, they wouldn't be in this pickle if they'd had them.

Where were they going? Was there *any* safe place to go? The wolf-men still followed, and The Sentinel turned and headed towards the mountains. They could not fly over the mountains. They would never make it. But just ahead they noticed a sheer-sided cliff looming in the darkness. Would they make it all the way up there?

The Sentinel gasped for breath, but his wings beat the air even faster, and they rose a little higher with each straining beat. They could see that the precipice, now that they were nearing its sheer sides, was smooth. There were no hand-holds for man or beast, and if he dropped them they'd never be able to climb it themselves. It was also likely they'd crash into the sides of the rocky tor, but The Sentinel, as they got nearer, groaned and made one more effort.

Tristan and Kex felt their feet scrape the summit of the tor, and one by one, they fell or rolled onto the hard rock below.

They were safe, for now.

22.

The Cave of The Sentinel

They sprawled out on top of the rocky summit and, still panting, the exhausted creature rested. At last, his gasps slowed, and they waited until he breathed normally again before anyone spoke.

"Those wolf-men haven't given up," said Djana. "They're still below us." They could hear them baying at the base of the cliff, claws scrabbling at its base.

"They'll find another way up," said Tristan.

"He says he has rested enough. We must go," said Anwyn.

"He can't possibly carry all of us again," said Jarah. "How are we going to escape?"

Anwyn listened, and then spoke. "This is the plan. It's the only one that will work. He will carry three of us to his cave, and then come back for the rest. I am the lightest, so I will wait until the last load to go."

"No!" Tegan and Jarah both spoke at the same time. "You can't stay here. I'll stay," said Tegan. I am light."

"So am I," said Kex. "I will wait."

THE SIX AND ANWYN OF IALANA

Anwyn stood up, her face set into a firm expression that none of them had ever seen before. She looked taller too, thought Tegan.

"You will now listen to me," she said. "I will wait here with three of you, and three of you must go now. The Sentinel says we must distribute the weight evenly so we can all make it. It will take some time for those creatures to find another way up here. The Sentinel says there is an easier back way to get up here, but it's long and difficult, and it will give us a few hours to get away."

After a brief discussion, they decided that Tristan, Adain, and Kex should go on the first trip, and Jarah, Tegan, Djana, and Anwyn would wait for the second trip. No one wanted to go first. It felt unseemly that anyone would leave a loved one behind, but Anwyn tolerated no argument. She firmly stated that this was the only way to do it, and there was no time for discussion. Silently, Tristan, Adain, and Kex allowed The Sentinel to grasp each of them in a claw, and off they flew into the night.

As the four waited on top of the high outcrop, the baying of the wolf-men died down, but they had no doubt they were merely discovering the back way up, and they'd soon be scrambling over its top. They could see a faint glow on the eastern horizon. The sun would be up soon, and Anwyn had told them that The Sentinel had trouble seeing in daylight.

They hoped he would be back soon.

Glahivar had been dropped by Shegami into the area where she'd left the Six. Flying over the night forest, she used every sense she possessed to look for six shapes below, but now there was nothing that looked human in the forest.

She had also used this time to think. Astrabal had been unfair to her. It was not her fault he had not told her about the weapon. After Shegami had taken her into the Memory Records, she understood the reasons Astrabal had not told her before.

He was afraid of her. She had been the scientist behind the weapons project. She had been the one responsible for the destruction it had caused. It was *her* weapon, not his. She would not allow him to get it. She had bowed and genuflected to him, but she'd closed her mind off so that he could not read her thoughts.

He thought she was going to bring the Six, and the weapon, to him. No. She would find them and use them herself, and she would own the weapon once more. She didn't know exactly how she would accomplish this now that Anwyn was dead, but she would find a way. She would also find the genetic offspring of the others. Thanks to the intensive and painful Hall of Memory probings, and her subsequent awakening, she now knew who they were.

But first things first. She must find the Six. Perhaps one of them, or another of their children or family, possessed the right coding.

She was just about to give up searching one area and move on to another when something caught her eye. It was on top of a rocky, nearby outcrop that she saw the moving shapes. There were four, and they appeared warm, human-shaped, and reddish orange in her vision. What would humans be doing up there, and how . . .?

She had no time to waste. She flew to the top of the cliff, hovering just above the human shapes, and looked down.

What she saw made her gurgle with delight. *Well, well, who would have thought?*

She was just about to descend, when she stopped. There were only four of them up here. And—she got closer.

Anwyn?

A jolt went through her like one of her lightning bolts. How did Anwyn survive and reunite with the healers? And where were the others? Perhaps they'd been eaten by the wolf-men. She shrugged. *Oh well.* In a way, she was relieved. She had a sure thing in Anwyn. Her hesitancy and shock in the moment at Anwyn's survival paid off.

A movement, a dark shadow, descended from the sky down to the rocky top.

What is it?

Adjusting her night vision, she could see it clearly now. A human-shaped creature with large bat wings.

She must remain silent and see first what she was up against, and where the others were, before making her move.

Anwyn thought she saw a glint of red, and her heart raced, but it was only The Sentinel returning for them. She climbed up onto his back again while he grasped Jarah, Tegan, and Djana in his claws. They sped through the night with little effort towards the mountain lair just as the sun's rim rose over the eastern plains.

Flying into the cave, they were greeted by a relieved Tristan, Kex, and Adain, warming themselves by the fire.

"We couldn't sleep until you were here," said Tristan, hugging Djana. "And we're glad to see all of you!"

"I never doubted we'd make it," said Anwyn. She thanked The Sentinel, and he told her that they must get some sleep, himself included.

I will go out later tonight and find some food you like to eat. I see you don't like my Arrach meat.

His mouth was unable to form a smile, but they all felt his amusement.

"He'll get mountain trout and berries," Anwyn translated for them, since the telepathic abilities of the Six still seemed to be blocked.

They liked the sound of that. They were all starving by now, and it felt like a long time since they'd last eaten anything at all.

A sound startled them. A flutter of wings from the cave entrance. Alarmed, they jumped up, and Tristan pulled out his knife again. Before anyone could react, an eagle alit inside the cave, changing shape in front of them. A shape that was so familiar they gasped.

Irusan!

23.

Glahivar

B y the gods and all the demons in Iochodran, could her luck get any worse?

An eagle flew towards the cave in the mountain peak. *It may be only an eagle,* she thought, *looking for a nesting spot, but it may also be . . .*

She slowly approached. She didn't want anything to give her presence away. She had to be careful.

As the eagle flew into the tunnel, she followed silently, concealing herself in her merkaba behind a jutting rock. If it was who she thought it was, she didn't want him sensing her. Stifling a hiss of disgust and anger, she watched the seven greet her old enemy with joy on their faces as he changed shape.

"How did you know we were here, Irusan?" they all seemed to ask at once. The Sentinel stood by, keeping a wary eye on Irusan.

"I'm sorry I'm so late," he telepathed as Anwyn spoke it out loud for him. "I have only recently been filled in on the situation here, and I came as quick as I am able to. I was told by the air elementals of your whereabouts, and also that you'd run into some trouble." He looked at Anwyn.

They brought him up to date on all that had happened: the return of the one previously known as the Raven, who now went under the name Glahivar, what she had done, and how The Sentinel had saved all of their lives.

"I am most grateful, Sentinel. I did not know of your existence before now, but I sense you are a compassionate Being."

Anwyn spoke aloud, too, for The Sentinel.

"I am the only one of my kind as far as I know. I have never encountered another of my kind . . ." He looked sad.

"I have not seen any like you in these parts," Irusan continued. "But this is a big planet, and Ialana is not the only continent. There are continents with no humans, only remnants of strange races that somehow escaped the destruction. You seem to have been placed here for a reason. Why? I do not know."

"I do not know either," said The Sentinel, and he sighed.

Irusan turned to the others.

"I understand that Finn has told you about the weapon."

"Yes," said Jarah, "he did."

"You are all still in terrible danger," said Irusan. "I first need to get you to safety at once. I will take you through the same portal I came through. We will work on your merkabas in Ardvale. The problem is a sticky netting that freezes your merkabas and does not allow them to activate. It has also prevented you from using your other abilities, such as thought communication, but I see that Anwyn's is still intact. Thankfully Glahivar did not anticipate that she would survive. We have the antidote for all in Ardvale, but I will have to take you there one at a time."

"I am not sure if I can help with that," The Sentinel said. "I can take three at a time, comfortably, with maybe a lighter fourth, but will have to wait for the sun to go down. I am blind in the daylight."

"We don't have time to wait. I feel Glahivar will find you much sooner." Irusan hesitated, as if something had just ocurred to him, then he turned to them again and said, "I need to speak privately to The Sentinel. I must shield those thoughts from you, Anwyn, but don't feel as if I am excluding you. It is a matter between me and him."

They all nodded. They trusted Irusan enough to know that he had logical reasons for everything he did.

He turned back to The Sentinel. Something passed between them for a while, and The Sentinel also nodded his head occasionally. At one time, he looked startled, flapped his wings briefly in what looked like consternation, but he recovered, and nodded again.

When they had finished their silent communication, Irusan turned back to them and Anwyn heard his thoughts once more as he picked her up. "I'll take her first, since she is in the most danger." He disappeared in a blue flash, and the Six were left in the cave with The Sentinel.

"May as well sleep," said Tristan, and they all settled down again. Tegan and Jarah felt they could sleep now knowing that Anwyn was safe. The Sentinel yawned and flew up into the roof of the cave, where he hung upside down with his bat wings folded over his face.

Glahivar would have laughed if it would not have given her presence away, so instead she allowed a soft hiss to escape her mandibles. Except for the conversation she was not privy to between Irusan and The Sentinel, her patience had paid off. They had been left totally unguarded by Irusan while The Sentinel slept. She came nearer, invisible in her merkaba, and waved her claw over the prone forms. She had to be sure they would not awaken The Sentinel.

It was time to make her move.

Anwyn held on tightly as they flew in Irusan's merkaba towards the portal of the elemental kingdom. She knew she didn't have to, since Irusan would not allow her to fall, but her recent experience still sent chills of fear up her spine, and the ground was a long way down.

As they flew, Irusan spoke to her. He told her of the plan, and that she must not be afraid.

Things are not always what they seem, and when this happens, you might think you have been abandoned. That all is lost. But remember it is part of the plan. I will ensure your parents and the others are safe. I know they're all family to you.

Why don't we just fly to the mines now, and get the weapon ourselves?

Because we'd be intercepted before we could retrieve it. Do you think we are not being watched by Astrabal? It's much too risky. This way we'll have more time to carry out our plan.

As long as my parents are safe, Irusan, I can do it. I know now who I am, and why I am here. I understand the risks, and also that our plan has a good chance of failing, but I am willing to try.

Irusan pulled out a crystal from a small pouch around his neck. *Finn gave this to me. You know what it's for. Carry it with you at all times.*

Anwyn took the pouch with its long, twined loop, and slipped it over her head and shoulders so that it rested snugly around her waist. She took the crystal and placed it into the pouch.

Soon, they arrived at the portal. It was the same one they had exited from not so long ago. It shimmered as Irusan placed his hand into the air in front of them. They were just about to step through when a flash of red appeared next to the portal.

The bulbous shape of Glahivar stood there with two people, one in each claw. Anwyn cried out, her voice betraying her fear and horror.

"Mother! Father!"

Glahivar cackled in derision.

"Thought you were being so clever, did you? Irusan, you're losing your grip. You almost made it through the portal with her. If you'd traveled just a little faster, I might have lost you altogether. But leaving those six unguarded was the worst mistake of your life! Some sentinel that bat-thing turned out to be!" She gurgled again. "Let Anwyn go, give her to me, and perhaps I'll let these two go."

Anwyn shouted out Irusan's thoughts, for the benefit of her parents. "You won't get Anwyn. Give those two up, and we'll forget this happened. You still have a chance to do the right thing, Glahivar. That weapon is not yours to do what you will with it. Astrabal will not go easy on you if he knows what your plan is."

"How do you know what my plan is?" Glahivar said. "But you're wrong. It *is* mine. I created it. I led the team of scientists—"

"Please! Do not give Anwyn up Irusan!" Tegan begged.

"No, do not," Jarah said. "Take her, through the portal, *now*! We don't care what this monster does with us, as long as Anwyn is safe." They looked at him pleadingly.

"Irusan, give me to her right now," said Anwyn. "Take my parents through the portal and get the others to safety."

Glahivar opened her jaws, placing Tegan's head between her dripping fangs.

"I'll bite her head off first, then his, if you don't give the girl to me."

Irusan appeared to be thinking. "If I give her to you, will you let both of them go?"

"No!" screamed Tegan, again. "Please, I beg you!"

"Of course. You'll get both of them. With Anwyn, I have no use for them. Don't worry," she said. "I won't kill her this time. At least, not until I'm done with her. I was a little hasty before. Not my fault though."

"If you promise to release Anwyn once you've used her to get the weapon, then I'll release her," said Irusan. Tegan screamed, and Jarah shouted out in frustration, but Glahivar agreed, and Irusan pushed Anwyn gently towards the fiendish shape. Glahivar was good on her promise. A claw shot out as she let go of Jarah and Tegan, who were still crying and protesting Irusan's decision, and in an instant, she was gone.

Tegan and Jarah looked at Irusan in horror.

"How could you—"

Be quiet. We must go. I'll explain everything when we're through the portal. Shocked that they could now hear Irusan quite clearly, they fell silent as he put one hand on the shimmering area again, grasped both Tegan and Jarah by an arm by the other, and pulled them through.

24

The Mines of Amrafalus

They sped over the mountains, Anwyn once again grasped tightly in Glahivar's claw. Arriving much too soon for Anwyn on the other side of the range, Glahivar steered her merkaba towards thin spirals of smoke on the horizon.

Rocky foothills with scrubby trees flattened out in a dry and empty land that gave way to sandy dunes and higher piles of sludgy yellow tailings, poisonous green ponds, and smoking chimneys.

These were the Mines of Amrafalus.

Irusan had told her what to expect, but she wasn't prepared for the desolation and destruction of the landscape.

There were so many mines she lost count of them. They slowly drifted over the encampments, mine shafts, gaping pits, smelting chimneys, and buildings. Each mine, she had been told, delved for different minerals. This area was rich in metals: copper, iron, silver, and gold. There were thousands of workers—all slaves—but most of them, she knew, remained underground in the dark tunnels. Soldiers and overseers with whips guarded them, and she could hear cries of pain and the crack of whips as they dragged huge carts piled high with ore to the separating areas.

Canals brought water down from the mountains to the dry lands, but it was all used in the mining process. There were no fields of produce or greenery.

She shivered. Djana's parents had once been slaves here. She wondered how they had ever survived.

"Ah, there it is!" Glahivar pointed, jubilant, towards a mine that had been roped off. As they descended they could see the warning signs posted. *No Entry! Danger.*

Soldiers stood on guard at the outside perimeter, but inside the perimeter they could see bodies that still lay on the ground, bloated and grotesque.

"I image there's a safe area still within the perimeter," said Glahivar. She settled her merkaba a few feet from the guards. "I did not lie to Irusan, dear. You will not be harmed, but you must do exactly as I say. Perhaps I'll let you go after that, but we shall see. I only do things that will serve my needs and purposes." She smirked. "If only Astrabal knew what I was up to, he'd reduce both of us to dust! But he won't know, will he? At least, not until it's too late."

Anwyn wondered why Glahivar did not proceed. There were guards, but she could have easily sent them to sleep. As if hearing her thoughts, which was most likely, thought Anwyn—she must be careful—Glahivar answered.

"We'll wait until dark. I can't put soldiers to sleep in broad daylight. They will be spotted, and we need you to get in and out unseen."

She lifted her merkaba up and, still holding tightly on to Anwyn, they retreated to a safer spot.

They could wait.

Tristan opened his eyes. *What time is it?* The fire was almost out, and Djana, Adain, and Kex still slept. *Where are Tegan and Jarah?*

Perhaps they'd gone out into the tunnel. They'd slept heavily, more so than usual, he thought.

He could see the dark shape of The Sentinel still hanging upside down with wings that covered his face. All seemed quiet, but shouldn't Irusan have been back by now for the rest of them? He quietly rose and walked into the tunnel, rounding a curve. The entrance of the tunnel showed the slanting rays of the sun over the mountains. They had slept all day!

Panicked, he ran back into the cave.

"Sentinel, wake up!" he shouted. He shook Adain. "Wake up, all! Irusan has not returned, and I can't find Tegan and Jarah."

The others sat up quickly, rubbing sleep from their eyes. They looked confused. The Sentinel slowly lowered himself from the roof.

"What? What are you talking about? Where are they?" Adain looked confused, as did the others. They turned to The Sentinel, now standing in front of them.

"What happened? Where are our other friends?" asked Djana, her voice tinged with fear. "Why did Irusan not come back for us?"

"He . . . soon come . . . back," squeaked The Sentinel, nodding his head.

"Can't someone try again to telepath?" asked Adain. "I was never any good at it anyway, and his speech is worse than my telepathic abilities. The only person who can communicate with him isn't here."

"I will try," said Djana, and she listened for a while. She shook her head, perplexed. "I'm not sure if I'm succeeding, but something feels as if it's coming through, now, as if it's his thoughts." Incredulous, she put her hand to her head. "If I'm right, I think he's saying that the spider-thing came and took Tegan and Jarah."

They all exclaimed in horror. "What! Why didn't he stop her?"

"He could have at least woken us up."

Djana listened again, he eyes widening in shock, but Kex nodded, as if she was listening, too.

"He says—oh, I hope I'm not right—that he had orders from Irusan to allow it. He saw her take them. His telepathic language is a little different to Irusan's. I can't imagine why he would do that—"

"I told him to allow Glahivar to take them."

They whirled. Irusan stood behind them in the cave. Tristan looked furious.

"You *what*? Have you gone insane, Irusan? Are you now our enemy?" He reached for his knife, but Irusan held up his hand. They were all talking at once.

My, but you're an excitable lot! I understand your concern, but just calm down and I'll tell you what has happened. First though, I must take you to the portal. Jarah and Tegan are safe. The Sentinel will help me.

Once they'd calmed down and didn't look ready to kill Irusan, he told them that although he had just restored their telepathic abilities, they still did not have the ability to use their merkabas.

We'll restore your merkabas in Ardvale.

The Sentinel tucked Tristan and Adain under each arm, while Irusan wrapped his strong arms around Djana and Kex as he brought up his merkaba.

Flying out of the mountain, with The Sentinel not far behind, they flew northeast towards the portal. The sun had now set. It was dark, but Irusan knew where they were. They arrived at the portal, thanked The Sentinel, who merely dipped his head graciously and took off to find his supper.

They tumbled through the portal, and there was Finn, Tegan, and Jarah, waiting for them. Overjoyed, they hugged, and then Djana noticed something.

"Where's Anwyn?"

Tegan sighed. "It's a long story. Glahivar has Anwyn, again. Come with us, and we'll tell you all."

"Irusan has a lot of explaining to do," said Tristan.

Finn looked closely at them. "You are angry too," he observed. "Come along. We have something to do, and I have something to tell you."

They followed him in silence. No one felt like talking, although they were bursting with questions. Finn and Irusan led them up a small path that wound its way through the forest. Elementals followed them, singing, but it did not help their mood. Even Tegan and Jarah looked somber. Each one was deep in their own thoughtful sorrows. Finn and Irusan did not talk either, sensing their need to remain silent.

After a while, the path led to a stone structure in the middle of a glade. It was shaped roughly like a round house, or small tower, with a roof, windows, and a big wooden door. Finn opened the door and motioned for them to go inside. They filed into a circular room with only a low, wooden table in the middle. On the table was a bowl of water. They looked at each other, puzzled. In all their years in Ardvale, they'd never seen this.

"First, I need to tell you what is happening," said Irusan.

"We already know," Adain snapped. "Jarah and Tegan's daughter is in the hands of a foul monster who will kill her!"

"Then you don't know," said Finn. "I understand your anger and sorrow, but just hear him out. Sit."

The Six reluctantly sat, their expressions still hostile and suspicious.

"Anwyn is safe," Finn continued. "Irusan would not have given her over to Glahivar had he not been quite certain of it."

"But we feel so helpless," said Tristan. "Our merkabas were destroyed by Glahivar, and we are unable to bring them back. It is us who should be saving Anwyn and—"

"Irusan was able to restore Djana's and Kex's mental communication abilities when he arrived back in the cave. It was necessary that he do so, but if he had fixed your merkabas there, which he could have done, you would have gone after Glahivar and Anwyn—"

"*What!?*" Tristan leapt up, his face red with rage. "What do you mean you *could* have fixed our merkabas?"

"Settle down," Irusan said. "If I *had* restored your merkabas to their original state, all would be lost now, and Anwyn would be no better off than before. Astrabal would have gotten involved, and quite possibly you'd all be dead."

"Astrabal?"

"Not someone you want to meet. Glahivar's demon overlord in the Shadowlands—Iochodran."

They felt chills go down their spines.

"If you think Glahivar's bad, Astrabal makes her look like an adorable puppy. Astrabal's goal is to destroy all life on this world. You already know about the weapon in the mines from what Finn has told you. But we didn't have time to tell you the details. The *whole* story. It's a weaponized crystal that has the ability to destroy most life on this world. It was created a long time ago, in the dark past of this world. It is before your history begins, but then, you are not the first civilization here, and will not be the last."

Irusan proceeded to tell them about the genetic progenitors and creators of this crystal, and how they were each genetically connected to those lines.

"You do understand what DNA is?" he asked, more as a statement than a question, but they nodded.

"It's the coding in our bodies that tell us how we look. What form we will take," said Djana.

"Yes. All that and more," said Finn. "You each inherited these chemical messengers, or codes from your parents, who in turn inherited it from theirs, and so on, all the way to the beginning of first creation.

"Sometimes there are messengers that have been dormant for centuries, and will pass from generation to generation without turning on, but then in one generation, they will turn on, or activate. This is what has happened here. In years past, many workers could have encountered this crystal and it would have been a mere curiosity to them. Perhaps, it would have been placed on display so people could gaze on its beauty, or even adorned some ruler's palace, with no ill effect to anyone. However, in our present time, the dormant coding was found and activated in seven people, but only six of those are still living."

He looked at the astonished faces that gazed back at him.

"No, it is not the six of you. Not this time, or for this purpose. But it is in someone you know: Anwyn. She does not have the ability to activate this weapon, but she does have the power to deactivate it."

He noticed the looks of relief that passed across the faces in front of him.

"But hasn't it already been activated?" asked Adain. "The Sentinel told us it has killed many life forms already."

"Yes, it was activated by a slave-worker in the mines. It killed him instantly. You may know him. His name was Abban."

"Not—not the Abban who brought Blaidd in his fishing boat, to Galon?" Djana asked.

"Yes, the same, I'm afraid. He possessed the coding, but not the ability to withstand the crystal's energy after he activated it. Unfortunately, there are still three others out there who can activate this weapon and most likely survive the activation."

"That makes four, including Anwyn. Who are the others?" Tristan was doing his best to keep up with Finn.

"We don't know yet. We are still looking for them," said Irusan now, speaking through Jarah. "We don't know exactly who they are. Anwyn is the only one we know of so far who can deactivate the crystal. We hope that Astrabal does not know all of them, either."

A pall of fear came over Tegan. "What will Glahivar do with Anwyn once she's finished with her?"

"Glahivar has plans of her own, as she always has," Irusan continued. "She is no puppet of Astrabal, I'll give her that. If and when Astrabal finds out she is defying him, he will destroy her unless she can escape him. But there's very little chance of that happening. Glahivar's energetic fabric is too mutated to think around corners. She has tunnel vision, and her driving force is greed and the ability to manipulate. Even though she imbued herself with the activation coding when she was the scientist, it has mutated so much over time, and through her different bodies, that she is unable to control the weapon in her current form.

"I have explained the situation to Anwyn, and she agreed to go with Glahivar and deactivate the crystal. Only, Glahivar does not know some things. Some things only Anwyn, Finn, myself, and now you, will know."

"Please, explain!" Kex demanded.

"I will. Now listen." They sat and listened as Irusan and Finn took turns speaking. When they had finished, the Six felt better. They were still alarmed, they still felt fear, and they wondered if the plan would work. So much could go wrong. Their chances of success . . . they didn't want to think about it.

And here they sat, unable to do anything to help.

"That is why we brought you here," said Irusan. "Gather around the table and look into the bowl of water. We will be able to see everything that is going on, and if Anwyn is in danger, well—your merkabas will be working this time. We can get to her quickly."

They all breathed easier, and they moved closer to the table and looked into the bowl of water.

25.

Ambros, Yor Swamps

They knew when they were near the Yor Swamps. Clouds of mosquitoes and biting, black flies swarmed Ambros, his men, and the horses, driving them insane with their buzzing persistence. The sky darkened and it began to rain, a constant, moist drip that only added to their discomfort.

"These things are as big as humming birds," growled Daire. They swatted, futilely, at the hordes, and the horses swished their tails as they bit skittishly at their own flanks.

"We're almost there," said Ambros. "Be on your guard. I don't know how we'll be received."

His hand went to his sword, and so did the hands of the other three, Daire, Lonan, and Bran. They were all nervous, and it wasn't only due to the insects.

After a few hours of riding, the first signs of human habitation appeared. Run-down wattle and daub shacks, roofed with swamp thatch, on the edge of the marshes, and hollow-eyed people that fished from rickety piers, their skins yellow from disease and hopelessness.

THE SIX AND ANWYN OF IALANA

As they rode, Ambros felt his heart sink into his well-made boots. They would be a grand prize for anyone with a mind to relieve them of their horses and belongings. Catrin was right, it was an insane idea, but it was too late now. They couldn't turn back, and he must discover what Moran was up to.

He thought back to their meeting, after she'd found out—she wouldn't say how—about his plan. He trusted the healers. They'd had too much to lose themselves to give away his plan, so he thought it was more likely to be one of the palace rats that had been eavesdropping on them by the river.

He seldom saw Catrin angry, but she had been almost speechless with her fury that day.

"Don't you *trust* me, Ambros?" she'd finally managed to sputter out after confronting him with her knowledge.

"Of course I do. But I knew you'd stop me. I sometimes feel like I'm not doing anything useful here in Three Rivers. I can't expect you to don your male disguise and trot on down to the Yor Swamps and ask Moran what he's up to. I, on the other hand, am a known blackguard in that area. I could be received quite well."

"It's not a choice between me or you, Ambros. I may have even approved had you consulted me first. But instead, you chose to go behind my back. I don't like that."

"I doubt you would have approved. You'd have convinced me to do something else."

"Perhaps, but I also know how stubborn you are." She sighed. "Well, I can see you're set on it, and now I've also been apprised of the rather magical means of journeying by our six healers. Since they won't be needing our help—to my considerable relief—we can make other plans."

"Other plans?"

"To find out what Moran is doing, you lummox. Do you think I'm totally against your idea? I think it was a fair and worth-while plan, but we need to fine-tune it a bit more. We need to be coordinated and know what we're doing."

Ambros shook his head, laughing.

"I really don't know what I'd do without you," he had said.

He laughed out loud as he remembered his conversation with Catrin, then realized his men were looking at him strangely. He had not told them what had transpired between him and Catrin. The less they knew, the less likely they would be to give up any information should their ruse be discovered.

It wasn't long before they were met by outriders, at least a dozen, on horseback.

"Who are you and what is your purpose in coming here?" demanded the leader, a tall man with pockmarks.

Ambros halted his men and approached cautiously, hands visible. He didn't want to look threatening.

"I am Ambros Scarface. These men are—"

The pock faced man held up a hand and spat. "I remember you, Ambros Scarface. We did some business many years ago. We purchased horses from you. They turned out to be older and sicker than you told us. What do you want with us now?"

"I regret the horses were not to your satisfaction, Kromm. I remember you too. My men and I wish to add our numbers to yours."

Kromm's face darkened. "Why?"

"We were set upon by the Queen's soldiers and our gang was almost wiped out. We are the only survivors. As if that was not all, we now have a price on our heads. We wish to join up with Moran. We know his reputation, that of a creative ruler and businessman. We feel our numbers will add to his strength."

Kromm took a moment to size them up, and Ambros could sense the appraisal taking place behind the flat eyes as they carefully scrutinized the horses, the clothing and saddle bags they carried, and, of course, the men themselves. No weaklings would be allowed to join up with Moran's lot.

After what seemed like a long time, Kromm spat again. He nodded to one of his men. "Go quickly. Let Moran know about this." Then to Ambros, "Follow me." Whirling, he and his remaining men took off. Ambros and his men followed at a steadier pace.

THE SIX AND ANWYN OF IALANA

The houses, as they approached the fort, looked less rickety or ramshackle than those further up the road. They were built of wood and swamp thatch, and the village spread out around an enormous stockade of strong poles and wooden boards that had been sharpened into spikes at their tops. They approached heavy doors that were guarded by armed men.

Even though they were now with Kromm, the guards eyed them suspiciously before the doors groaned open and they waved them in. Houses, tents, and lean-to's sprawled throughout the interior of the stockade as far as they could see. They passed a smaller, oval stockade in the interior that surrounded what looked like an arena dug into the ground. The arena was lined by tiered seats, and a raised, covered box, or dais, sat at one end.

Kromm led them to a larger house situated not too far from the arena. It was clear to Ambros that it was Moran's. Kromm dismounted, and so did they. Their horses were led away by Kromm's men. Ambros felt uncomfortable as the horses, Sienna in particular, disappeared to only the gods-knew-where, but there was no turning back now.

Kromm motioned with his head for them to enter. They walked through a narrow hallway, then found themselves in a dingy, wood-paneled room. At a desk in the center, a man leaned back in his chair, and even in the half-dark, they could see a snaggle-toothed moue of derision on his thin face as he laced his hands behind his head.

"Ambros Scarface! I never thought you'd come crawling back to me. This must be my lucky day. The Scarface Gang never did me any favors, so why should I deal with you now? I have a mind to put you to work cleaning out stables, or perhaps. . ."

He ran his tongue over his lips, and Ambros knew that what he left unsaid was probably something horrific.

Ambros regarded Moran for a heartbeat. He had done nothing but think of what he was going to say to Moran once they reached Yor Swamps, and he'd discarded many lies, half-truths, and strategies during mostly sleepless nights, as sounding insincere. He'd finally decided the best way to approach this was to assume Moran knew more than he let on, and to play to his greed.

"My lordship, I know our past business relationship was not always a happy one, but circumstances have changed. I have ridden fast from Three Rivers with my surviving men. I was betrayed by one of my own to the Queen's guards, and we were ambushed in a business deal gone wrong. We were heavily outnumbered, and my men and I were lucky to escape with our lives."

"So why should I care?"

"Because, my lordship, I have valuable information for you."

Moran looked at him, skepticism evident on his rat-like face.

Ambros continued. "Thanks to my spying efforts while in Three Rivers, I know exactly the strength and number of Queen Catrin's army." He didn't know if Moran cared about this information or not. He was going on a hunch, and what they'd heard from Catrin's spy: that Moran was contemplating an invasion.

Moran was silent for what seemed like a long time, and Ambros wondered if he'd miscalculated.

"It apparently didn't do you much good now, did it?"

"No, my lordship. We were still outnumbered. But I did not count on the betrayal of one of my best men. He no longer lives."

Moran laughed, a gleeful guffaw from a rotten mouth. "Can't trust anyone these days. How about these three?" He gestured towards Ambros's men.

"I'd stake my life on the trustworthiness of these men."

"Let's hope you won't have to. If I get wind of any double-dealings from *any* of you, your lives won't be worth a lick." He spat onto the floor for emphasis. "As it is, you'll still need to prove yourself worthy of my regard." He looked at Kromm, who had stood by silently the entire time. "Take Scarface to the arena. Dawla and I need some entertainment."

Zephan

The fishing boat, with an escort of Ibai's Trueni fishermen, pulled up to the dock. It had taken Zephan seven days of fast sailing, alone, to reach Ibai. He had not allowed anyone to accompany him. He had felt it was too risky to arrive in Ibai with back-up.

THE SIX AND ANWYN OF IALANA

He was exhausted, but he had made it. He wore the clothing of a Rhiannon fish merchant: a colorful, but modest linen tunic and robe. The court silks or fine jewel encrusted muslins he usually wore would not endear him to the Trueni of Ibai. Zephan allowed his two Trueni escorts to tie his boat up before stepping onto the dock.

"Who you be?" one of the fishermen asked. His mistrust enveloped him like a thick blanket. Zephan knew the Ibai Trueni were suspicious of strangers, especially human ones. Ortzi was always looking for ways to get information about those who were healed by the Six and their whereabouts.

"I am Zephan. I am looking for my Trueni friend from Rhiannon, Abban. I have not seen him for some time, and thought he may have fled Rhiannon and come back here. I know that he came here six years ago, but he returned. I am concerned for his safety, and want to reassure his family that he is safe."

Zephan didn't really care about Abban. Abban was dead, but he needed to start somewhere.

The two fishermen looked at each other, then shook their heads. "We no know Abban. You go back. Say no Abban here."

"Well, can I stay for a while? I can look for him here, and in Abena. I am also tired, and need rest."

Zephan knew that the Trueni, although riddled with suspicion, were also a hospitable people, and it was against their culture to turn a traveler away without food or rest. He waited as they talked amongst themselves. Another Trueni fisherman, curiosity on his pig-like face, approached the men. Zephan watched as he questioned them, and they continued to talk. Finally, the third man turned to Zephan.

"I Mikel. You come with me."

Zephan followed as Mikel led him through the village of Ibai. It was larger than he had thought, and there was an interesting mix of humans and Trueni. Things were obviously not as segregated here as in Rhiannon, he thought. He wondered if these were the healed Trueni he had heard so much about. Of course, the claims were only rumors. A myth. No one could turn Trueni back into humans. It was just not possible.

These humans must be the outcasts of Abena society. Why else would they live in a Trueni fishing village? He sniffed. The air smelled horrid. What he had to do for Udfa!

They arrived at a small shack on the outskirts of the village, near the Garden River that emptied out into the Bay of Abena. Mikel introduced him to his wife, another animal-like creature that cowered, silent, in a corner. Zephan had never mixed with these degenerates before, and it was harder than he thought it would be. They smelled bad, their speech was barely understandable, and now he had to stay here in this hovel. But it was either this, or return to Udfa with nothing, and that was also unacceptable.

It took him the rest of the day, and most of the night, to build up a foundation of trust with Mikel, but before dawn, he had the information he was after. Zephan was a skilled interrogator. He did not always need to use torture to get what he wanted. Honey and charm worked just as well, and Mikel was no exception. Zephan spun a tale of how badly the Trueni had been treated by their human overlords, and how disgusted he, Zephan, was with Rhiannon.

"I'll be honest with you, Mikel, I don't even feel like going back, except I must. I must tell the family of Abban that he is not here. It will be a very sad home-coming, but I must do what I can for them." At that moment, he knew Mikel would do anything he asked, but Zephan was clever, much brighter than Udfa would give him credit for.

He waited. The time was not yet right.

Mikel, in turn, told him how he had fled Akelarre, the Trueni fishing village across the bay from Rhiannon, many years ago. It was after Mikel, in his broken syntax, told him his life story that Zephan pounced.

"Mikel, I hear there are healers who can change Trueni to human. Do you not wish to become a human? I would help you find them if this is what you wish."

He was startled when Mikel jumped up, his face a rictus of hatred. "Me no heal! Me *like* be Trueni! Me kill healers if come back here. Change too many Trueni to human. Not right. Gods not pleased with change, so bad fish catch as punishment."

Zephan waited, again, as Mikel continued to rant about what was most likely the very people he searched for. He no longer even seemed to remember that it was supposedly Abban's whereabouts that had brought Zephan to Ibai. It was like reeling a fish in, thought Zephan. One had to be careful not to lose the catch before one had it in the net or hand. He waited until Mikel had finished telling him about how there had been six young people here some years ago who healed Trueni with their sorcerer's crystal, and how Ortzi had captured them, but then lost them. Now no one knew if they were dead or alive.

"But Mikel, is there anyone here who would know about them? Where they now are?"

"No one know. We not see since. No one heal since. Gods pleased now. Fish catch better!"

"Did they have friends here? Family?" Zephan knew Holgar and Adne, the parents of one of the Six, had escaped with them. Had they too been lost, or were they—he hardly dared hope—still here? His patience paid off.

"Holgar, Adne. Yes. Father, mother, of Djana. Here in Ibai! Make school for children. No good. Trueni not human. Trueni not need to read, write. Trueni need fish only." Mikel went on in this vein for quite some time, but Zephan wasn't listening anymore. He was making plans in his head.

Finally, he asked the important question.

"Mikel, take me to them. I must speak with them. I must take them back with me."

Mikel nodded, a pleased look on his face. "Yes. Take away. Human not welcome here. Later, I take you."

"No, now, Mikel. *Now.*"

26.

Anwyn

At last, a murky darkness fell over the mines. The work did not stop. There were night shifts as well, and torches lit up the landscape, but it was dark enough that their intrusion would not be easily noticed.

Anwyn felt weak from hunger and thirst. Glahivar had not bothered to feed her, and even if she had, Anwyn would not have accepted it. She wouldn't trust any morsel or drink from this creature.

Using her merkaba, Glahivar once again moved herself and Anwyn, undetected, close to the roped off area. The guards were gathered around a brazier, playing dice games, laughing, and joking amongst themselves. She knew their job was an easy one, as no one would dare approach this mine tunnel, not with the bloated and stinking corpses on the ground near the entrance.

Glahivar stopped, closer to the guards. Raising a claw, she muttered a few words, and the guards dropped, unconscious, to the ground. Since no one dared to come too close to this particular area, the sleeping guards were not noticed. In daylight, it might have been different, thought Anwyn. She too had a vested interest in not being discovered. There were certain things she did not want Glahivar to see either.

Glahivar pushed Anwyn towards the tunnel, but kept a safe distance herself.

"Go!" she commanded. "Bring it back to me. You know what to do, and don't think you can escape out of another exit. I will be monitoring them all from above." She handed Anwyn a candle that materialized in her claw, along with a piece of chalk. She lit the candle with a claw end. "Take this and mark your way. I don't want you getting lost. And look for the newer tunnels. Those that look fresh. They will lead you to the weapon."

Anwyn, now out of the relative safety of Glahivar's merkaba, walked carefully towards the tunnel entrance. So far so good. She continued to move, hoping that Irusan and Glahivar were right, that the weapon would not harm her, but there was always a small doubt in her mind.

Shakily, she approached the tunnel, stepping over bodies, dead birds, dropped whips, pick-axes, and other detritus of a mining operation. The inside of the tunnel looked no better. It smelled worse than anything she had ever smelled in her life before, and she felt faint. Looking back, she could no longer see the faint red spark of Glahivar's merkaba where she'd left her.

She put down her candle and reached into the pouch around her waist. She found the crystal Irusan had given her. She hummed the tones that Irusan had taught her, running the crystal over her body several times. She felt the crystal's energy slice through the sticky cords that surrounded her fields. When she'd cut the last one, she put it back into the pouch, picked up her candle and chalk, and pulled up her own merkaba.

It was a relief to be able to do this again, and she felt safer now. With the guttering candle still lighting her way, she moved quickly down the tunnel. A tunnel that seemed to go on forever. She couldn't move too quickly. She might miss another off-shoot of the tunnel and go down the wrong one.

She looked for signs of fresh workings. Every now and again, she'd find another branch that looked newer than the others, and she'd put a chalk mark onto the wall. She was descending in a spiral, down and down. The further she went, the darker it grew, and she knew that the air must be terribly close and the temperatures unbearable, but her merkaba shielded her well, and she no longer had the stench of death up her nose.

She was amazed by the number of bodies littering the tunnels as she made her way down. Her light cast sooty shadows on the walls that made it look as if the bodies were moving, or coming to life. She wondered where the ghosts of these poor, dead slaves were. She hoped they weren't still in the tunnel.

As knowledgeable as she was about the continuation of consciousness, she still feared ghosts. One never knew what level of consciousness they possessed, and in their confusion, what they might do. But no ghosts reared up to attack or frighten her, and soon she saw a rock wall ahead. A wall that was the end of the tunnel.

Now what? She could see no weapon, not that she knew exactly what that would look like. No one knew.

She saw only a wall.

Ambros

Ambros, at the point of Kromm's men's spears, was prodded into the gate of the central arena.

Moran was already there, sitting in the covered box he'd seen earlier. A woman sat next to him, eyes like grey winter ice on the River Mair. *This must be his wife, Dawla*, thought Ambros. He'd heard rumors of her from his spies. She was not a nice woman, and she had an appetite for men who were not Moran. Kromm placed a small dagger in his hand and gave him a swift kick; a kick that propelled him into the arena.

Kromm will pay for that, thought Ambros. Facing him were three men, all armed with swords. Normally, it wouldn't have been too much of a problem for him. He was skilled with a knife. But it was the man in the middle that worried him most.

He stood like a tree trunk in the middle of the arena, a colossus with a head that looked as if it had once been used as a battering ram, and fleshy hands that could, with a single squeeze, snuff the life out of a man. But the giant stood aside as the two men moved in first, one on each side of Ambros.

The swords they carried were long-swords. Ambros was clearly at a disadvantage with his knife, but by the way they were moving, he could tell they wouldn't have known sword-fighting from a tavern brawl. Ambros had years of experience in both, but even so, he'd need all his knowledge and skills now.

There was no time to think. The first man moved in quickly, while the other circled around. Ambros turned, keeping both of them in his peripheral vision, ready to make a move. He watched as the first man, as soon as he was in range, thrust his sword towards him. He ducked low and whirled under it, coming nose to nose with the startled man, who was now at the disadvantage. Like a striking serpent Ambros's free hand flew up. His palm smashed, with the strength of a hammer, into the man's nose.

It is going to be a tavern brawl, he thought.

The man screamed as a fountain of blood spurted from his smashed nose, but he quickly stepped back, raising his sword up to strike. He was not quick enough. The brief moment the disoriented man took to step back had allowed Ambros to whirl around to his rear and pole-ax him, using his fist, with a blow to the back of the head.

At the same instant, Ambros saw that the second man had already launched himself towards him. As the first man dropped, Ambros, still behind him, held him up, his body acting as a shield as he whirled to face the oncoming threat. Before the approaching man could stop his forward momentum, his long sword had pierced his companion in the chest. Ambros let the body go and with a grunt, the man slumped to the dirt, the sword now protruding from his torso.

A disappointed roar went up from the crowd.

"I'll put down my knife," said Ambros to the second man. "We'll fight fair. With fists."

He was just about to drop his knife, but the second man wasn't having it. He leaned down and quickly pulled his sword out of his now dead partner. He turned to face Ambros, sword at the ready.

"Have it your way," said Ambros. He was relieved to see the giant had not yet made a move. He seemed to be watching the action with a smile on his face. Ambros felt he was just biding his time, and would move in for the kill after—

The second man did not allow him to close in on him as his unfortunate partner had, and warily, they circled each other. Ambros sighed. This could go on all day. He looked at his knife.

Yes, he *could* do it. Perhaps it could work, as it had many times before.

With a smooth movement he lifted his arm and, using all his strength, propelled the knife like a small javelin towards the man who was now closing in, sword raised for a killing blow. Ambros had aimed his knife for the base of the throat, but the man was quick. He saw it coming, and started to duck low, from his knees. Unfortunately for him, it was the wrong thing to do. The point of the dagger pierced an eye and lodged itself, like a spike, into his brain. The man was dead before he hit the sandy arena floor.

The audience once again jeered and booed, but the big man had now moved in.

His weapons were only his size, and his enormous hands. This was going to be much more difficult, thought Ambros. His knife now was embedded in the head of the other man and he didn't have time to retrieve it. Not that it would help him any. Not against *this* man.

He had another plan. One that he hoped would work. In his past career as a bandit, he'd learned many tricks and fighting techniques that did not go by rules. He felt it was safe to assume no one here obeyed these rules either.

The giant smiled. By the look on his vapid face, Ambros knew he thought he was dealing with an easy win. Ambros stooped as if changing his mind about retrieving his knife. He reached down, towards the knife that still protruded from the eye of the prone man on the ground, but allowed his fingers to rake first over the gritty arena.

The giant moved in fast, his size belying a gazelle-like speed. He grasped Ambros around the neck with one hand before he could reach the knife, and lifted him up off the ground as if he were a child's rag doll. Ambros felt as if his neck was in a vice.

In the side of his vision, he could see the giant raise his other fist towards his head. He was sure he was going to pound his head into a pulp first before strangling him. He gasped for air. It felt as if his head was being torn from his shoulders, but he took what little breath he could muster, lifted his fist as far as it would go, and hurled a cloud of dirt and grit into the giant's dull eyes.

The giant roared, his other hand now swiping desperately at his eyes. Ambros felt the giant's grip loosening, but it was still not enough. He lifted his foot, now just below the level of the giant's groin, since he had been dropped slightly, and he kicked upwards as hard as he could. He could feel his boot sinking in to the doughy, unprotected area.

The giant howled again, and the jeering crowd went silent. Ambros still felt as if his head could pop off his shoulders at any moment, and spots danced in front of his eyes. Now for the final move, he thought. He couldn't hold on much longer.

The giant was still howling and clawing at his eyes as Ambros lifted his hand, palm up, smashing it in an upward motion against the man's potato-like nose.

It worked. Ambros fell to the ground and rolled as the giant dropped him, still screaming, his hands trying to grasp his bloodied nose, streaming eyes, and groin, all at the same time. As the giant's body folded onto the stony ground, writhing in agony, Ambros stood up and approached the box where Moran and Dawla sat. The crowd was still silent. No one dared to cheer or applaud. Moran looked stunned, but Dawla had a half smile on her face.

"Do you still want me?"

When Moran found his tongue, he nodded. "No one has beaten Zlatan the Lunatic before."

"Good. Then release my men and my horses to me. We'll be an asset to you."

Moran nodded, again, and Dawla looked at him as if she wanted to lick him all over his sweaty body.

He thought he'd best keep his distance from her.

27.

Zephan

It was not yet sunrise, but the Trueni were already up and out fishing on their boats. Mikel had a sullen look. He obviously did not want to help Zephan, but Zephan was his guest, and he was obligated to offer his assistance.

Zephan understood Mikel's rather simple thought processes quite well after only a few hours with him. He knew Mikel was not pleased he'd get a late start to his day of fishing, but what choice did he have? Zephan could see the conflict in his piggy eyes.

"If you help me, Mikel, I will ensure those six healers never return to Ibai again. I know Holgar and Adne know where they are. I need to capture them and take them to Rhiannon, where they belong."

"Yes, master. I help," he said, reluctance oozing from every word. "But *quick-quick.*"

"Get your knife." Mikel smiled and pulled out the curved blade he used to gut fish. They left the small shack and made their way to the home of Holgar and Adne. Mikel was a familiar sight to the residents, so no-one, even if they were up and about, paid them any attention.

Mikel stopped at a still-dark home. *They must still be asleep*, Zephan thought, as he knocked on the door. He knocked lightly at first, then, after no response, heavier knocks.

"Who is it?" came a voice from inside. Zephan nudged Mikel.

"Mikel!"

"Just a moment."

Zephan was just about to knock again when the door opened. A sleepy man stood in front of him, wearing only a pair of cotton britches.

"Mikel?" He looked confused, then looked at Zephan. Fear rose in his eyes. Zephan did not hesitate. He kicked the door open, and at the same time grasped Holgar in a choke hold with his knife at his throat.

"Make a sound, and we'll kill both you and your wife!"

Holgar looked terrified, but he kept quiet as Mikel strode towards the bedroom. A surprised yelp came from the room and soon he emerged with Adne, knife at throat and a hairy hand over her mouth. Her eyes were as terrified as her husband's as she quickly took in the scene in front of her.

"This is the situation, and I want you to listen well," said Zephan. "You will both go with me and Mikel. Make any sound, any indication that you are in trouble," he looked at Holgar, "and your wife will die." He looked back at Adne. "The same goes for you. No signaling to anyone, and if anyone speaks to you, greet them as usual. Tell them I am an old friend. Do you understand? They both nodded. Zephan took his hand off Holgar's mouth.

"May we please put on some clothes?" Adne asked. "We are in our nightclothes. That will look a little strange."

"Mikel, go with her. Let her get the clothes and bring them in here. No stupid moves now, or he dies."

Adne nodded her head, and Mikel propelled her back towards their bedroom. After a few minutes she emerged with some items of clothing, and Zephan and Mikel watched as they put them on over their nightclothes.

They stepped out of the house as casually as if they were setting out on a picnic with their friends. A few neighbors waved and wished them a good morning, and Holgar and Adne nodded and greeted them back. No one asked them what they were doing or where they were going, and they made their way through the dawn towards the pier and Zephan's boat.

It was just another day in Ibai.

Anwyn

There were only two bodies down here, and both lay close to the end of the tunnel. One had a pick-ax in its hand, while the other still held a whip. They'd died instantly. This must be the right place, but where . . .?

Then she saw it.

She moved her candle slightly. A twinkle of light in the wall, like a star, shined back at her. She moved closer. She could see a hole in the rock, and inside the hole something reflected back her candle flame.

It was not an ordinary rock. Her hand reached out, slowly, towards the shining object. She couldn't see how big or small it was, but she must be certain it wouldn't kill her. As her hand came closer she held her breath. She felt even fainter than before. Was she dying? She continued to allow her hand to move towards the object, and soon she could feel its cool surface.

She could *feel* it! If she could feel it, then she was still alive . . .

Strange that it was not hot, she thought, but rather, she felt a cool energy that came off it in waves.

Putting her candle down on the floor, she reached in with both hands and grasped the object. It was not heavy. She pulled it towards her, through the hole, and looked at it.

A many-faceted, skull-shaped crystal glittered in the light of her candle. It was about the size of a human head. Whoever had shaped it had ensured its faceting would distribute energy in equal parts around it. She felt that it was never meant to be beautiful. It was made to be deadly.

It was at that moment she realized that it was no longer running energy. It felt dead in her hands, as if it were just a common rock crystal.

She didn't have long to wait. Irusan materialized next to her, and she hugged him in relief.

THE SIX AND ANWYN OF IALANA

"I thought you'd never come!"

I can't seem to buy anyone's trust, lately! There was mock severity in his thought, and she could hear the smile behind it.

She handed him the now deactivated crystal.

Ah, so this is what it looks like. Just wait here a bit, Anwyn. It's not over yet. I must take this, but I will return quicker than a blink.

He was right. She didn't even have time to feel nervous when, in a flash, he materialized beside her again.

Quickest trip I've ever made, and I had to use the time portal so I'd get here moments after I'd left.

He held the weapon in his hand and handed it back to her. *You know what to do with this.*

"Yes, I do. Thank you, Irusan, I trust my parents and the others are well?"

Still angry, still untrusting, but quite well!

He disappeared again, and Anwyn deactivated her merkaba, picked up the candle, and, holding the skull-shaped weapon under one arm, she made her way back down the tunnels, her chalk marks guiding her back. Her return now felt quicker than her entry, and soon she saw the faint shape of the tunnel entrance up ahead.

The guards were still asleep, their fire dying from lack of attention, but no one had noticed anything was amiss. She waited for a few moments until she saw the red spark of Glahivar's merkaba descending from where she'd been keeping watch over the tunnel entrance and other possible exits.

"Good. You were smart. Give it to me!" She grabbed at the weapon with two claws. "Yes, I remember it now. What a beauty. It must be deactivated, or I'd be dead before I even touched it."

She looked at it, her eyes glittering. She gave what might have been a shout of laughter, but it came out as a sharp hiss.

"Now all I have to do is find the descendants of the other activators. Perhaps I'll even send them with it through Iochodran's portal! Astrabal will get his weapon, but not in the way he thinks he will." She looked thoughtful. "No, I must stick to my plan, it's—"

"Are you going to let me go?"

"Let you go? What a thought. Hmm…in fact, I've been thinking about that, but you're far too valuable to me to let go of, dear. I'm sorry, but you're going with me. I'll need you later, I am sure."

"But you promised! You told us—"

"I said I *might*, dear. Learn to listen! Words are very important. What did they teach you in Ardvale?

"I feel sorry for you, Glahivar. You continually make the wrong choices. You could have let me go and been no worse off, but you chose to keep me. Know that I will not be kept. Not anymore."

With that, Anwyn disappeared.

28.

Glahivar

Glahivar was stunned. For a moment, she could not react. This girl had somehow gotten her merkaba working again. *Irusan!* Of course. She knew he had to have a hand in that. No doubt all of their merkabas would be working now. She hadn't anticipated that, but she should have.

She kicked the dying brazier over. She didn't care if the coals were setting the guards on fire. They'd wake up themselves, she thought. It didn't matter to her, and she had more work to do. She could do without Anwyn right now. She had accomplished what she'd wanted her for. Astrabal couldn't fault her for not keeping the girl hostage.

Her merkaba arrowed through the sky. She must hide the weapon in a safe place, but where?

Ah! She knew just the place. No one would even think to look there. She flew towards Three Rivers. She also had something, or rather someone, there she needed to see.

She arrived in Three Rivers moments after leaving the Mines. She had no time to waste. Still using her merkaba to conceal herself, she silently entered the palace through the door in the wall by the river bank, the door that opened into the now not-so-secret tunnels and passageways in the palace. But she knew there were other passages that no one knew about yet. They had not been fully explored, and she doubted that even Anwyn would know of them all.

She'd spent the nights exploring these tunnels in her short job as a nanny. She didn't need to sleep. It seemed a useful thing to do at the time, and it had certainly paid off. She was not as short-sighted as Anwyn seemed to think she was. She'd marked the passages, and she knew exactly where she was going.

She manifested a lit candle in her claw, and soon arrived at a dungeon deep within the palace. Within the dungeon was a hole in the floor—an *oubliette*. The wooden trap door had long since rotted away, and the gaping hole presented its own trap to the unwary. Iron spikes rose up from the bottom of the hole. Prisoners had once been thrown down this hole and impaled on the spikes. *Ah, the good old days!* Old bones still littered the floor below.

These dungeons had been in use centuries ago, but one of the King's ancestors, perhaps someone with an unfortunate moral sense, had closed off all inner palace access to them. She wondered if Brenin had known about them when he was still alive. She doubted it, as he would have used them. There was still a passageway that led to the dungeons that had not been closed off, and it had taken her several nights of searching before she'd discovered it.

She carefully descended into the *oubliette,* and, avoiding the spikes, placed the crystal on the stone floor; a floor thickly covered with bones, ancient dirt and dust. Besides herself, rats were the only living thing down here. There was no light, no window to the outer world. It must have been horrific for a prisoner, a slow and agonizing death in the depths.

They probably deserved it, she thought. *How unlucky for them.* But she must get on with her plan.

Covering the crystal with dirt and debris, she left the dungeon and

THE SIX AND ANWYN OF IALANA

emerged out into the night air by the river bank. Astrabal's instructions on how to find her first activator came to mind, and she flew off towards the outskirts of the city.

It took her some time to find the estate of her target, but since it was the largest one in the area, it eliminated many other possibilities. The house was vast and ornate, and surrounded by guards. Not a problem. They wouldn't even see her. She flew like a firefly into an open upstairs window and began her search of the house. While she searched, she completed another phase to her plan, one that she dared not allow her thoughts to broadcast. She shielded her activities well, and found her main target after only a few rooms of sleeping children, multiple wives, and a variety of servants.

He lay in the bed with his mouth open, snoring loud enough to wake the dead. She should have known. She placed him in a suspended state that would ensure he wouldn't wake up until she wanted him to, and lifted him into her merkaba. He was heavier than he looked. Awstin Forkbeard, King Brenin's erstwhile advisor, had obviously been blessed in his retirement.

She headed back towards the palace. He would be safe in the dungeon, if hungry rats didn't get to him first. Now she just needed to hurry before that happened.

She still had others to find.

Finn, Ardvale

"I am not comfortable with this thing remaining in Ardvale," said Finn. "It may have been temporarily deactivated, but not permanently, and it cannot be destroyed. We are not entirely certain what it is still capable of, and while I feel it is safe at this moment, it could reactivate if conditions became just right."

"Perhaps we can throw it into an active volcano?" said Jarah. The Six, and Anwyn, nodded in agreement. The Six had all been relieved and happy when Anwyn had appeared in Ardvale with Irusan.

"No," said Irusan. "That would not work either. It's a diamond. Harder than any substance on earth. Sooner or later the volcano would give it up and someone would find it again. Taking it into another dimension would put that world at risk. We need the original three to deactivate it, more permanently, and then find another way to destroy it. At this moment, it is safe to handle, but if it fell into the hands of the three activators, it would destroy all life on your planet and here."

"Who are the others?" Anwyn asked.

Irusan was silent for a while. He seemed to be listening to something, or someone. Then he spoke.

"The Council has been working on finding the other deactivators. It is quite a task to scan millions of genetic codes but they've just told me they have been successful. We now know who the two others are." Irusan looked at the Six. "You are going to have to find them and bring them to the crystal, and it won't be easy."

"Can we bring them here?"

"No. Unfortunately we can't do that. They may have the coding for the weapon, but they—the two—do not have the correct coding to enter this portal. It would be detrimental to their templates, and may even kill them. You, and your children are currently the only one's who have the right coding to enter. We are going to have to take the crystal to a safe place on Ialana and deactivate it there. When Glahivar finds out she has a dummy copy of the weapon, she'll realize what we did. She'll find out very soon, so we need to have a solution to this before she captures one of us and holds us hostage again. She is clever, and will not make the same mistakes as before. With Astrabal's help, she'll wait for us as we exit any portal from Ardvale. We can't stay here forever, as much as we'd like to, and she will exchange us for the weapon, again."

Tegan sighed. She wondered if they, and their children, would ever be free of this creature. Glahivar would hunt them down for eternity.

"We have a temporary solution right now," said Irusan, "but we cannot leave it like this."

Finn had been silent as they spoke. He did not seem to be listening, but at last he sat up straight and held up his hand for silence.

"I might just have a plan," he said. "But we must be quick. Listen."

29.

Yor Swamps

This morning, Dawla took longer than usual to primp in front of the mirror. She'd had a slave whipped for not having laid out the right outfit for her. She'd wanted her fine, blue linen, not the red. Red always made her look like a swamp-berry.

Her slaves pulled her corset tight around her thick waist, while another slave brushed her thin, dull hair until her scalp tingled. She could not stop thinking about the new man—Ambros. His performance in the arena yesterday was nothing short of spectacular. Even Moran had been impressed. She wondered if he'd noticed her smiling at him. She could be of use to him, and she'd be careful to let him know that without Moran finding out.

Not that Moran would be jealous. She was of as little interest to him as he was to her. Their marriage had been arranged, a business deal between her father and Moran. Neither of them had ever shown any enthusiasm for each other, but he had his pride, and appearances must be adhered to. He had his dalliances, and she kept hers quiet by having the guard or slave sent to the arena to fight Zlatan.

She carefully reddened her lips with berry salve, and her cheeks too. There! If Ambros did not notice her today, then he wasn't the man she thought he was.

She dismissed her slaves, looked one more time into the polished bronze mirror, and was just about to step out of her bedroom to see if Ambros and Moran were together when there was a bright flash of light. Blinking, she let out a squeak of surprise that was quickly stifled as a woman's hand slid firmly over her mouth.

"*Mmm-mmph!*"

"Be quiet," a voice hissed behind her, "or I'll have to put you to sleep. I'd rather talk first."

The hand moved away from her mouth, and Dawla spun around, indignation radiating from her roundness. She would have this woman whipped!

She was just about to open her mouth and say so, when the woman held up a hand and Dawla fell to the floor.

Her eyes were open, she could hear everything the woman was saying, but she couldn't move. She tried to open her mouth, to scream, to cry out, but her muscles were paralyzed. Who *was* this motherly woman who now stood in front of her? She had never seen her in her life before, and it was clear she was not from their settlement. She had not seen her enter either, even though she'd been facing the door.

"You didn't give me much choice, Dawla, but I'd rather talk to you here than at our destination. I've been watching you for a few hours now, and your thoughts are rather interesting. What do you think Moran would say if I told him?"

Dawla began to tremble, and she felt beads of sweat break out on her forehead. Moran would have her whipped, at the very least!

"Yes, he would, wouldn't he?"

Dawla was really frightened now. This woman was reading her mind! *She must be a sorceress.*

"Whatever you say, dear. We don't have time for a debate. I need you in Three Rivers. Don't worry, I won't keep you long. I just need you to do something for me, and then I'll drop you right back here in a wink. Now listen carefully to me. I will only tell you once what you need to do."

Dawla listened, and if she had thought she was frightened before, she was now terrified beyond belief.

Ambros and his men had just finished eating breakfast when a messenger arrived at their small tents. They'd slept two to a tent, as they had not yet merited a wooden home in the fort, but he didn't actually care since they would not be here much longer. He just needed to find out when Moran was going to attack.

That he would attack seemed certain now. Ambros and his men had made a careful reconnoiter of the settlement after he had returned, victorious, from the arena. They'd idly watched as preparations were made for battle. Provisions and supplies were being loaded onto wagons, and weapons were readied. They'd taken count of how many soldiers and fighters Moran had, talked to the guards watching the weapons caches, horses, and supplies, all under the guise of introducing themselves to the inhabitants. No one had suspected their spying activities were anything other than friendliness and a desire to fit in.

But now, the messenger had told them that Moran wanted to see them all, right away.

They hurried over to the large house that was Moran's and were let in immediately. Ambros wondered what was so important that Moran needed to see them now. He sat behind his desk, as usual, but there was someone else in the room with him. His wife, the woman who'd smirked at him after the fight in the arena.

She wasn't smirking now, and could barely meet his eyes. He wondered what she was doing there. He didn't have long to wonder. He had an uncomfortable feeling as Moran's guards stood at the door, blocking his exit.

"So, Ambros Scarface, eh?" Moran's tongue darted out like a snake's, scenting prey.

Ambros looked at him, puzzled. "Yes."

Moran looked at his guards, who came closer, their weapons at the ready. *This is not good*, thought Ambros. He and his men had not even brought their weapons with them; a fatal mistake, no doubt. What had happened to change Moran's trust?

Moran soon enlightened them. He turned to his wife. "Tell them," he said.

She licked her lips, and they paled to almost white. He noticed beads of sweat forming on her forehead that ran down her face in rouge-streaked rivulets. She was not an attractive woman at the best of times, he thought, but now she looked sad and clownish.

Finally, Dawla spoke. "I-I know . . . I know you're not who you say you are." She looked as if she would cry, but she bit her pale lip and continued. "I-I've been told that you are all spies, spies from Three Rivers. Queen Catrin's spies!" She looked bolder now, and her voice became firmer. "You, Ambros, are the husband of Queen Catrin!" she spat. "You are, or were, known as Scarface, but you have not been with the bandits for a very long time. You are here on a spying mission!"

Ambros wondered where she'd gotten her information. She knew too much. Was it one of his men? But they all looked as stunned as he. He turned to Moran.

"Where does your wife get this from? Is there someone who is jealous of my victory yesterday in the arena who wishes to make trouble for me?"

"Speak to me, not my husband! I know. This is my source." She turned, and to Ambros's horror, Genove appeared behind the guards, who parted and let her in.

"Genove! What are you doing here?" The words were out before Ambros could stop himself. Moran looked triumphant, and Genove smirked. Ambros wanted to take back those words but he couldn't. His men looked at him, shook their heads, and put their hands up in surrender. They were now completely at Moran's mercy.

THE SIX AND ANWYN OF IALANA

He wouldn't go easy on them.

This is going well, Glahivar thought. She'd morphed into her old Genove body and told Dawla everything. Ambros would never return to Three Rivers. Now all she needed was to get rid of Catrin and her son, and the Kingdom of Aelfar and Mernoc was hers for the taking, with Moran's help, of course.

She didn't have an army, but she could co-opt one. She'd take care of Moran later, and she needed Dawla for now. The activation of the weapon was within her grasp, but she still had one more person to find.

She waited until Ambros and his men had been taken into custody and locked up in the wooden jailhouse next to the fort's wall before making her next move. Dawla was sitting in her room, where she'd been told to go, silent and still shaking.

"Now you must come with me," she said, and held up her hand. Dawla collapsed, unconscious, onto the floor again, but this time she could hear and see nothing. She did not feel the huge spider's claws as they picked her up, and she did not have a sensation of movement as Glahivar's merkaba sped out, over the fort, northwards.

30.

Cold Bone Clan, Rhagbeneth

Gugun felt that something was wrong. He'd had these feelings all his life, and he knew that if he didn't act on them, he'd regret it. That was why he was the medicine man, and not anyone else.

His eyes narrowed as he thought over what he'd discovered. A potential rival for his position had arisen, and at first it was easy enough to ignore. Firstly, the sister of this rival had left the clan years ago, putting this family into an awkward position, and secondly, the rival was still too young to be much of a threat.

But he must act, and soon. She was showing signs of abilities. Her sister had shown signs too but advising her parents to marry her off to one of the Cold Bone Clan men had been his solution to that. It would have been a brilliant move—if she had not run away. She was probably dead now, but if he was truly honest with himself, he felt she was still alive, and his feeling of disquiet had something to do with Kex.

Saran was now eleven summers, not too young to marry off. He could send her to the Cold Bone Clan as repayment for the broken promises of a runaway bride six years ago. He would do it today, before she could do what her sister had done.

He walked to his tent door and put his hand out to open the flap so he could summon the father, but before his hand could touch the flap, he felt a strange sensation. There was a flash of light behind him, and he couldn't move his hand, or even turn his head to see what it was. He felt himself gripped by a hard coldness, and then his world went black.

"Who are they?" asked Kex.

She'd noticed Irusan giving her a strange look after he'd told them the other two deactivators had been located. She had an uneasy feeling about it. Was it her? But no, he had said it wasn't any of them.

"We are going to need your help on this, Kex," said Irusan. "One of them is your sister, Saran, and the other is Jax, your mother."

Kex felt as if all the air had left her lungs. Her mother and sister? They must get to them before—

"Yes, before Glahivar does. It's only debatable whether or not she now knows their identity. As we were scanning DNA, we sensed Astrabal was just as busy. He may already know. And that's not all. We've also located the three activators. One is Gugun, the—"

"—medicine man of my tribe," finished Kex.

"And the other two have already been taken by Glahivar. They are both in Three Rivers, with the fake weapon. So far, we are still safe, but it could only be a short time before Glahivar discovers the skull is not real once she has all three activators."

"Would she dare to activate it without Anwyn or Saran and . . .?" Jarah asked.

"My mother, Jax."

"No, because it could quite likely kill her too," said Irusan. "She will want either Anwyn, or all of them present before she activates it, and she'll probably withdraw a safe distance herself, killing all—as far as she knows—in the palace. That is where she has placed it and the activators she already has."

"So we have a window of time before we need to take the real one somewhere, along with our three," said Finn. "I have had my elementals out scouring your world for a place that is safe to deactivate it, where Glahivar and Astrabal are unlikely to find it. There aren't many safe places where Astrabal's denizens do not have access, but we have decided on one. It is risky, but we must try it." He stopped and looked at them all closely. "We can bring Kex's family there, all of them, to Mu'A."

"Yes! I would like that!" Kex smiled. "But they are going to be frightened. How do we kidnap them all without scaring the skins off of them? They already think I'm a witch."

"You will have to persuade them first, Kex," said Irusan. "The best thing is to have them remain in Mu'A, but we can't force that on them."

"We don't have time," Jarah interrupted as he quickly grasped the situation. "We can use our crystal to put them to sleep, take them to Mu'A as fast as we can travel, and then explain it to them."

"We don't have time to waste," said Finn. "You must all leave, now, and take the weapon with you.

Gugun had been easy, thought Glahivar. Before he knew what hit him, he was unconscious and in the depths of the palace. She kept all three separate, all in different areas of the secret chambers under the palace. She didn't want them together, conspiring with each other once they woke up. She didn't know how long her sleep spell would work, but it should be just long enough.

She had just placed Gugun in his cell when Shegami materialized in front of her.

"You need to go back to Rhagbeneth. We have located the two other deactivators."

"Where, exactly?"

"Where you just came back from. This time, I'll help. I don't want you messing this up again. I'll find Anwyn, I know where she is, and you take the other two. We'll bring them back here." She directed a poisonous look at Glahivar. "Astrabal is furious. He thinks you're up to something, and I agree with him. Why did you not bring the weapon straight to him when you had it deactivated? Why here?"

Glahivar was ready for that. "Because I needed to get all six of the activators and deactivators in one place, along with the weapon, before I took it all to Iochodran. Can you imagine the weapon activating in Iochodran while we don't have all three deactivators? Who knows what could happen! We don't understand a lot about this weapon—"

"*You*, of all people, should understand it the best!" Shegami hissed. "But you have proven yourself to be so incompetent that we are starting to wonder just exactly what you're up to."

"Well, I suppose I deserved that," said Glahivar. "But I've been doing pretty well, even if I say so myself, since it wasn't my fault in the first place."

"Oh shut your mandibles! Let's go."

31.

Yor Swamps

Ambros, Bran, Lonan, and Daire had been locked up in the fort's jail. Moran had promised them they would not survive the day. There would be a hanging tonight, just as soon as he and his men got back after searching for his missing wife.

"Not that I care about her, but I need to find out how she enlisted the aid of this Genove woman, how this woman knew who you really were when not even I or my spies did, and their current whereabouts. Dawla knows more than she was telling, or she would not have run away. This Genove has disappeared too."

"This 'Genove' you so badly want to find is a *sorceress*," said Ambros. He had come to this conclusion almost immediately. There was no way the elderly and seemingly harmless crone could have traveled the dangerous road all the way to Yor Swamps without the help of sorcery. Perhaps she had one of those . . . flying things, too. He knew she must have something to do with the Six, but what?

He now knew that she had been the source of Catrin's information about his plan, even though Catrin had not told him who had revealed the conversation with the healers on the river bank to her. It was all beginning to make sense.

"I think you're trying to mess with my head," said Moran, a sly look in his eye. "She's an old woman, but she knows more. I will get it out of her."

"Well, good luck with that," said Ambros, and he sat down on the dirt floor of his cell with his head in his hands. There wasn't anything he could do about the sorceress. He just hoped that she had not harmed Anwyn and the Six in any way.

They waited all day. They could see the light beginning to fade from the one barred window high in their cell. Ambros tried to comfort his men. Even though they were all the bravest and toughest men he had, he knew this couldn't be easy on them.

Since they'd left the gang of thieves they'd once belonged to and joined him in Three Rivers, they'd made comfortable lives for themselves in the service of the Queen. They had families, and he was regretful that they would never see their loved ones again.

He hoped Catrin would forgive him for this misadventure, and understand that he'd done it for the kingdom, for her, and for her son. They did not need the treacherous Moran on their doorstep, and he had wanted to wrap it all up before the coronation.

As his thoughts began to drift again towards Catrin, he became aware of a sound outside his cell. It sounded like a *thump*, and then another. He looked at his men and they all looked at each other.

"It's time," said Bran. "They've come for us."

The key turned in the door and it slowly creaked open. Ambros and his men slowly rose. They would not cower or plead for their lives. They would show their bravery right up until the end.

A pale face, surrounded by a hood, appeared at the open gap in the doorway. It looked familiar, but it couldn't be . . . not already?

Catrin?

Catrin put her finger to her mouth and whispered, "*Shhh!*"

Another figure loomed behind her. Ambros and his men gasped. They must be hallucinating. But there was no doubt.

It was Zlatan, the Lunatic.

"We must go, quickly," said Catrin. "I'll explain all later."

Without argument, but with great relief, they silently left the cells, stepping over the unconscious bodies of the guards outside. Catrin and Zlatan had their horses waiting outside the jail, and Zlatan handed them each a robe and silently motioned to them to cover their heads with the hoods. It was now dark enough that they could not be easily identified by the few people who still wandered the streets of the fort.

Ambros thought Catrin had picked the best time—supper. People were indoors. They could smell the aromas from the cooking fires in the houses as the horses silently trotted past. Ambros realized he was hungry. They hadn't eaten all day. As they reached the gate, he wondered how they would bypass the guards. He didn't have long to wonder. There were only two on post and he could see their motionless shapes sitting in the gate. As they came closer, he realized they were unconscious.

That must be Zlatan's doing, he thought.

Once they left the gate, they spurred their horses into a gallop, leaving the road and heading towards the swamps. Ambros was relieved that he had Sienna back. Leaving his horse behind would not have been easy for him.

Zlatan lead them into the swamps, following a road that only he could see: hard, high ground that wove through the fetid water. Ambros knew the swamps were treacherous, filled with quicksand and scaly beasts that could make a meal of a man. He knew too that Moran would avoid venturing into the swamps after them.

Catrin explained to Ambros as they followed Zlatan. "He knows these swamps. He's explored them every day since getting here, and he has found a path. It leads to a forest, surrounded by swamp, where I have hidden our men. Moran will not find us."

The path was dark and difficult to see. Their lives were in Zlatan's hands now, and Ambros hoped that Zlatan could see it better than he could, but soon, stubby tree trunks emerged from the odiferous waters on either side. The single path gave way to firmer ground, and the trees grew thick around them as they continued through the forest.

Ambros started as a figure jumped out at them, brandishing a sword. His hand went to his own sword, returned to him by Zlatan.

"Who goes there?" the figure challenged.

"Queen Catrin!" Catrin removed her hood, and the figure, a soldier in her army, nodded and stood aside as they passed. Entering an encampment, Ambros could not see the end of the camp, or tell how many soldiers were there, but he knew Catrin must have brought at least one Division with her. Four Brigades made up one Division, and those were divided into phalanxes of cavalry, foot soldiers, archers, and swordsmen. Then there would also be support personnel among them. He hoped it would be enough for what they had in mind.

As they dismounted, Catrin looked at him. Her expression in the firelight was exactly as he'd have expected it to be. Now that they had escaped Moran, he could see just how furious she really was with him.

"Let's get something to eat first," she said. "We've ridden hard for many days, and everyone's tired."

Ambros had not expected that Catrin and her men would arrive so quickly. He did not know Catrin had planned to leave immediately after he had left Three Rivers, and he hadn't expected her to arrive here even before he and his men had. He knew it wasn't easy moving an army Division quickly, and it must have been a nightmare as they approached the swamps. There was always the risk they'd be spotted by Moran's outlying spies, so the plan had been to stay off the road as much as possible. Zlatan must have been the coordinator on this end, he thought, guiding the troops and Catrin to the hidden place in the forest.

They had food brought to them, hard bread and stale cheese. No fires were allowed. After eating, Catrin turned to him, sensing his unspoken questions.

"We arrived a day ago, traveling directly south on a shorter, but lesser known road that was nothing more than a slaver's track," she said. "I know you didn't expect us for some time yet, but I had a feeling we must leave right away. And it's a good thing I did. We rode hard and fast. Thanks to Deryn's hard work, the army was well prepared for a sudden departure."

"Did anyone see you?"

"They did, but they no longer live." Her voice was sad. "We couldn't allow them, even though they were slavers and smugglers, to give us away to Moran."

Her eyes glinted with angry tears in the firelight, as she continued. "I went along with your plan because I trust you, but you do know how close I came to losing you over this insane adventure?"

"Yes, I do," said Ambros. "I am sorry. An unexpected twist arose. One that I did not expect." He told them about Genove, ending with, "So she must be a sorceress, and not the lady you thought she was."

Catrin looked appalled. "By the gods!" she exclaimed. "How did I not see that? But she looked exactly like the lady I remembered." She thought again. "Maybe too much like her. How does someone not age . . .?"

Her voice trailed off. She now realized she too had been as much a pawn in the woman's potentially disastrous game as anyone.

Ambros looked at Zlatan. "How did you get mixed up in this?"

"I am Catrin's friend," he said. Ambros' eyebrows rose in surprise, and he looked at Catrin.

"I've known Zlatan for years," she said. "He was once a stable-boy at our estate in Mernoc when I was a child. We grew up together. Zlatan married just after I'd left for Three Rivers to marry Brenin, and . . ."

She stopped talking, looked over at Zlatan, and put her hand over his. He lowered his eyes and Ambros could see the tears form. Zlatan, *crying*? It was inconceivable. He'd wanted to kill this man just yesterday!

"Zlatan's wife and child were captured on a slave raid by Brenin's men and sold into slavery."

"Let me guess—to Moran," said Ambros. Catrin nodded. "Unfortunately, they did not survive."

Zlatan growled. "The whippings. My wife was never an easy person to order around. She did not last long, and then our child—" He stopped, collected himself, and continued. "I vowed to track Moran down and kill him. I allowed myself to be caught on another raid and sold to Moran. I wanted to rip his head off and feed it to the wolves, but then I realized that if I did that, someone else worse than him would take his place, such as his wife, Dawla, or Kromm. There are plenty who are just waiting for the opportunity, and I didn't want that to happen. I wanted to stop this. I got word to Catrin—we have a few spies in Moran's camp—that I was prepared to be her inside man here."

"We wanted to know everything there was to know about Moran and his strengths, his weaknesses," Catrin explained. "Zlatan was essential for this purpose."

"Over the years, I used my strength to convince Moran I was his devoted servant. I pretended to be stupid and crazy. I did everything he asked, even the worst—killing men who did not deserve to be killed. I did not know who you were, Ambros. If I'd known you were Catrin's husband, I would not have been so hard on you in the arena!" He gave a small smile, and rubbed his swollen nose. "It still hurts, and I wonder if I'll ever be able to sire more children."

Ambros smiled. "I'm sorry, Zlatan. At least we didn't kill each other!"

Catrin sighed. "To think the woman I once trusted—Genove—was nothing more than a sorceress. I feel I should have seen through her immediately. I left her in charge of the children!"

"We all make mistakes. She had everyone fooled."

"Well, one fortunate thing is that she was the one who informed on you about your conversation with the Six. If she hadn't, you'd be dead by now. There would be no one to come to the rescue with a queen's army!" She laughed. "I left the kingdom in Deryn's hands—he needs to flex his ruling muscles alone—and told him if we weren't back, victorious, in three weeks, he was to assume he was king with or without a coronation.

"I met up with Zlatan shortly after our arrival. He told me a man named Ambros with a scar on his face had just arrived, and what was going on. Today, we knew you needed rescue. I couldn't have done it without Zlatan."

"You were very convincing," Ambros remarked.

"Being stupid or crazy is one way of hiding in plain sight. No one credits you for anything except banging people's heads together when necessary. I am glad I don't have to do that anymore. I am not really a violent person. It also allowed me to come and go as I pleased. No one dared to challenge me!"

"So tell me your plans of attack, Catrin," Ambros continued. "When do we surprise Moran?"

"As quickly as possible. Tonight. He will be suspicious after your escape, and my men saw him on the north road today, searching for his wife and the sorceress, no doubt. He didn't see us, so probably does not expect an attack just yet, but we must move before he has time to muster his army. He will be hoping to follow you back to Three Rivers and attack before he thinks we've had time to prepare."

Ambros thought for a while and nodded. "As usual, you've got it all covered, Catrin. Let's get ready."

"We *are* ready, my dear. Quite ready."

32.

Shegami

There would be no mistakes this time. Glahivar would pay dearly for her missteps, thought Shegami as she lay in wait outside the portal to Ardvale. Astrabal would not go easy on her or Glahivar should things go wrong again. He had plans for Glahivar anyway, but right now they still needed her, so—

She stiffened, her dark senses alerted her that something was happening. A shimmer appeared near her and she moved to the side. It wouldn't pay to reveal herself too soon. She didn't have long to wait. Irusan stepped through the portal, and behind him were Anwyn and the Six. Invisible in her merkaba, Shegami moved closer.

Irusan looked around. Shegami felt his sensors probing the area, but she had shielded herself well. *No amateurish mistakes from me*, she thought. Glahivar had consistently under-estimated these humans and their tame shape-shifter.

Anwyn, Jarah, and Tegan, you'll come with me.

Shegami heard his thoughts loud and clear. He was not as smart as she thought he was.

Kex, Adain, Djana, and Tristan, we'll meet up where I told you once you have the two others.

Shegami noticed a large package under Irusan's arm. It couldn't be more obvious what it was, and she sucked in her breath in astonishment. She had to act quickly.

Moving at the speed of thought, Shegami pounced, and before Anwyn or anyone could pull up their merkaba, she had Anwyn in her tentacled grasp.

"It's fortunate you're so predictable, Irusan," Shegami hissed as her dark form appeared in front of them. The Six could only look at her in shock and dismay, fear on their faces. She always enjoyed things like this.

Irusan did not betray his emotions, but she noticed him clutch the skull-shaped package tighter to his chest. "You thought you could pull a fast one on Glahivar, but not me. I can kill this one in an instant." She nodded down to Anwyn. "Don't move, any of you. Irusan, hand me the package."

Irusan only grasped the package tighter and shook his head.

"Please, Irusan, give it to this . . . thing!" Tegan's voice sounded desperate. "She has my daughter, and she will kill her if we don't do as she says!"

"She will kill all of us if I do," said Irusan.

"Actually, I won't. Not now. There is plenty of time to kill all of you once Astrabal has all six, and now he does! With Anwyn, that completes the circle. You'll be dead in a few hours anyway, so why waste my energy killing all of you now? Oh, and don't bother flying to Raghbeneth, Kex dear. Your mother and sister won't be there." Shegami cackled and wrapped another tentacle around Anwyn's head. "Come on now, I don't have all day, Irusan. I'll twist her head off—"

"Alright, *alright!*" Irusan looked defeated. His head hung as he handed over the cloth-wrapped parcel under his arm. Shegami reached out with another tentacle, and pulled it towards her, still cackling as she and Anwyn disappeared.

THE SIX AND ANWYN OF IALANA

Irusan and the Six regarded each other silently for a heartbeat, then instantly disappeared back inside the portal again.

As soon as Shegami had left her in Three Rivers, Glahivar flew back to Raghbeneth. She had to move fast now before Kex got there. She hoped Shegami had succeeded in getting Anwyn back. The weapon was almost in her control!

She quickly located the encampment of the Stone Wolf tribe. No one had yet noticed Gugun was missing. People were going about their daily routines as if all was normal and well.

She didn't know exactly where Kex's family tent was located, but it wouldn't take long for her to find it.

33.

Ardvale

"I can't believe we just allowed that to happen," said Kex. They were back in Ardvale, and Finn had rejoined them.

"If this doesn't work . . ." Adain didn't finish his sentence. He knew Kex was as worried as Tegan and Jarah. It was one thing to give up a dear friend or family of your spouse to dark forces, but when it was your own family, it must have been heart-wrenching.

"It *will* work!" Tegan stamped her foot. "It *has* to!" There was a sob of fear in her voice.

Finn placed an arm gently around Tegan, and the other one around Kex. "I have received word from my elementals in Rhagbeneth. Saran and Jax are now in the hands of Glahivar. We would not have made it there in time, since Shegami got involved before you could leave, Kex."

"I regret we had to put them through so much fear and suffering," said Irusan. "We had no choice, and it was the only chance we had. Kex, our plan is still in effect. Tegan and Jarah, we know Anwyn knows what to do. We must now trust, and move quickly. There is still too little time."

THE SIX AND ANWYN OF IALANA

He nodded to Finn, and Finn handed him another cloth-wrapped package. It was the same size and shape as the previous one.

"Now, we must leave for Mu'A."

Yagmak, Vicious Eyes Pack

Yagmak had his pack back, but something was not right. He had a sense of vague disquiet. Getting his pack back had almost cost him his life, but he had prevailed, and the three challengers to his leadership lay dead before him. He allowed Morga, the alpha female to lick his wounds. Her spittle had healing properties, and he would recover well from the gashes in his hide. Compared to what he'd suffered from Glahivar, this was nothing. He had slept well, deep in their cave, but he'd uncharacteristically woken up halfway through the day's sleep.

He felt strange, as if he was no longer a part of his pack. Since he had morphed into Yagmak the monster from Blaidd the boy, he'd felt more in tune with the energies and elements of the forest. He was not feeling that now. Morga, who had lain next to him, woke up too. She licked him, and it was then that he noticed she spat out mouthfuls of hair—his hair. Underneath, he could see pink skin. Yagmak's skin was not normally pink. It was brown and rough, like old leather. It protected him and—

His thoughts were interrupted as Morga whimpered. "Yagmak, something is happening. You are losing hair!" She looked at him, horror on her hideous, wolf-human face. "Your face! It's changing!"

Yagmak put his hands up to his face, and felt himself break out into a cold sweat as he saw pink hands, and fingernails. Long fingernails, but *human* fingernails.

A hand, for that's what it now was, went to his head, and gingerly touched his skull. His horns! He exhaled, a gasp of relief—his horns were still there. As he reached both hands up to grasp them they came off, and disintegrated into puffs of powder in front of his shocked eyes.

Yagmak leapt up and screamed, a high pitched, human scream. "Morga! What is happening to me!" His pack stirred, but they did not awaken.

"Oh Yagmak! You are becoming hideous . . . like one of those humans. You must leave, right away. If you become too human, I will eat you. I am very hungry. I will not tell the pack that you are changing, but you don't have time. You must leave, before the sun sets and the pack awakens. After that, you are on your own. Leave now!"

Yagmak saw the sense in what Morga was saying and without further hesitation, he leapt up and ran out of the cave, past his sleeping pack, and out into the sunlight. He blinked. His eyes did not hurt as much in the sunlight as they used to. Things still looked blurry, but he continued to run, making as little noise as he could, through the forest.

Where should he run to? There was no place to hide, no place that would be safe from his or any other pack, not to mention the plethora of predatory creatures that roamed this forest at night. Fortunately, Morga was right. He was safe until dark. Nothing stirred in the heat of the day, and he must think. Think! A spasm of panic and fear swept through his body as he ran.

He ran, panting, for what felt like hours. He was thirsty. He must find water. He ran on, listening for the sound of a river or stream. He sniffed the air. He had always been able to find water just by its smell, but now he smelled nothing. He was losing his animal senses, it was the only conclusion he could come to. That, inexplicably, he was turning back into his old human form.

Wait! It wasn't inexplicable. Of course! The Six had used a crystal on him, a healing crystal. No doubt it had immediately begun to change him back into his old form, but how much of his old form would he get back? He didn't want to be Blaidd again, the young boy who was always afraid and felt helpless, who was always looking for power outside of himself. He had finally found his real power, and he didn't want to lose it.

As he ran alone with his thoughts, the sun began to sink into the western sky. His body screamed for water, and at last he stumbled upon a small pool in the depths of the forest. He knelt down to drink, and as his head bent towards the pool, he cried out—an agonizing howl that was half human half animal. He could see his face now, a human face. It was Blaidd.

He still had large teeth, and fur clung to his face in patches, but as he raked at his face, it came off in clumps. Crying and slurping, he drank until he was full, then lay curled up in a fetal position by the pool. He would wait for his death here.

34.

The Battle of Yor Swamps

A mbros was proud of Catrin. Nothing had escaped her attention, he thought, as she and Zlatan shared their plan with him and his men. They smiled and nodded their approval, only making a few suggestions and adjustments based on what they'd seen in their own reconnoiter of the fort.

"It should work," said Ambros. Under Zlatan's capable leadership, taking a unit with them, they quietly approached Moran's fort. They needed to attack when people were already settled in for the night, during the guard watch when the men were sleepy and less alert.

"I am sure Moran will be on the alert after our escape, and he has probably noticed by now that Zlatan is gone too, so we need to be extra cautious," said Ambros. Catrin had remained in the encampment, and her duty was to carry out the rest of their plan. Zlatan assured them that the people in the shacks approaching the fort would not alert Moran to their movements.

"They hate him almost as much as I do," he said. "I know many of them, and that they are more than willing to join us once the battle begins."

The night was dark, the moon was on the wane, and clouds scudded across an indigo sky. Ambros hoped they would be able to hit their targets in the dark. A phalanx of fire-archers crouched down within range of the fort walls, their arrows covered in oil and pitch-wrapped rags.

Zlatan, behind another phalanx of skilled crossbow archers, waited in their rear, and behind him was yet another phalanx of cavalry and lancers. They held, silent, until Zlatan gave the signal, and the archers in front lit their arrows.

A cry went up from the guards on the wall. On another signal, the arrows flew, flaming, towards their targets. Before the defenders could fully react, the crossbow archers launched their own bolts. They could now see their targets clearly on the walls, silhouetted against the burning roofs of the buildings behind them. Bodies dropped on and over the wall as many more arrows found their mark. Flames crackled as thick, black smoke rose up against the night sky.

Zlatan yelled, the signal for the siege cart, hidden in a copse of trees, to approach. Behind them, they could hear the heavy trundle of wheels. A cart with a transverse beam affixed to it held, with ropes, an enormous log that had been cut down in the forest that day. A metal ram's head was attached to its business end.

The horses were unhitched, and soldiers pushed the siege cart to the gates. As soon as it was in position, the soldiers began to batter the gates with the ram's head. A cry of triumph went up as the gate splintered, and soon a hole large enough was created so that soldiers began to pour into the fort.

Not all made it. Moran's men were waiting on the other side, and many fell, but they kept pouring in, and by that time the gate had been removed from its hinges completely. The cavalry and lancers now galloped through the gaping hole.

Moran's face was as black as his remaining teeth. Awakened by his men, he heard the screaming, the pounding of feet, and crackling of flames outside.

Moran had suspected something was going to happen after the disappearance of his prisoners, and the defection of Zlatan by helping the prisoners escape, but he had not expected a full-fledged attack tonight. He had thought he still had time to muster his army and meet them halfway, if not in Three Rivers itself.

His spies had reported no troop movements on the north road. They would all be hung, just as soon as he—

His thoughts were interrupted by the arrival of his general who oversaw his men. He looked as if he'd spent too much time before the attack at the home-made brew barrel.

"They must have had their army lying in wait outside the swamps all along! We should have anticipated this!" Moran launched a blow at his general, and then a kick, as he realized the general should have reminded him of that possibility. "Get our men out there, before they get through the gates."

"My lordship, they are already through the gates," the general said, and he ducked, avoiding another blow. "But we are ready, make no mistake. We have the boiling pitch heating up right now in the cauldrons. Our men are gathering their weapons, and the women are putting out fires everywhere."

Moran finished dressing and picked up his sword. If he found Ambros, Zlatan, or any of his men, he'd deal with them personally.

Still muttering to himself, he ran out into the midst of the battle.

35

Blaidd

The man-boy woke. It was dark. Where was he? For a moment he couldn't remember, then it all came back to him, along with a wave of fear. He was no longer Yagmak of the Vicious Eyes pack. He was Blaidd, the human. Was he still a boy? He didn't know, but what did it matter? He would not last the night out in this forest.

He could hear the distant howls of his former subjects. It wouldn't be long before they found him here. His eyes could no longer penetrate the dark, and he would have to wait, helpless and blind, for death. He wished he had died from his wounds. He wished the Six had never found him, and even more, he wished they'd never used their crystal on him. At least he would have died as a powerful beast, and not as a cowering, whimpering boy. He drew his pink legs up towards his naked, smooth chest, and sobbed.

He didn't know how long he stayed curled into a ball. He drifted in and out of sleep, waking with a start at every forest noise. The howls grew louder, and he knew the end was near. They must be following his scent trail. He wondered if he would meet his end by his own pack. Would Morga be among them?

As the howls approached, he became aware of a rustling in the trees nearby. It sounded as if something big was moving through the branches. More rustling, a flapping noise, and a crunch of leaves on the ground. What could be making these noises? It was not the wolf-men. They were moments away, but something else was going to get him before they did. He was sure of that.

He closed his eyes and heard footsteps coming closer, and then he was yanked up by the arm by what felt like a huge claw.

Oh dear gods, what is this? He felt himself rising in the air just as a pack of wolf-men broke out of the trees, baying and howling beneath him.

Opening his eyes now, he looked down. He could see the pack below. It was not his pack, not the Vicious Eyes, but rather the next most feared pack in the area, the Dawnfall Shadows, its leader's jaws snapping just below his feet. He then looked up as they rose above treetops and the pack. He was in the grip of a bat-like creature. He'd be a small meal for this thing.

His pack had once told him about a creature that roamed the skies. He'd never seen it himself, but he'd heard it hunted Arrach, and he wasn't sure if it hunted humans or wolf-men too. Either way, if it ate Arrach, he felt sure it wouldn't object to human meat.

He struggled, trying to escape its tight grip around his chest, but the thing only gripped him even tighter. They soared higher and higher, towards the mountains. He shivered. He might die of the cold before it could eat him. Could he perhaps communicate with this creature? He didn't know if he still had the ability . . .

Yes, you do! came the response. *I can hear you. Do you hear me?*

Oh, thank the gods. You can telepath, and I can hear you too. Who are you?

I am The Sentinel. Your patience please, for a few more moments. I will not harm you. We have much to discuss.

With that, they flew into the cave opening in the mountain, and after The Sentinel had deposited Blaidd onto the floor in front of its warming fire, Blaidd began to relax. He looked at the creature, and it regarded him solemnly too for a while. Then it began to telepath again.

Who, or what, are you? I sensed a human shape in the undergrowth below, and knew you'd be caught by the wolf-pack, so I pulled you out.

I am Yagmak—I mean . . . I don't know who I am anymore. I am morphing into my old shape, that of the boy Blaidd.

Yes, you do look more human to me. I have not encountered humans in many years, and now in the space of a few days, I have encountered seven. Eight, including you, and some other strange creatures as well.

Were those seven others perhaps healers with a crystal?

Yes. Are you in their party too? They didn't mention you.

Not really. I used to be, but then I . . . Oh, it's such a long story.

I have time, said The Sentinel, *and I'll tell you my story too. Let us begin.*

The Sentinel sat silently as Blaidd began to talk. Blaidd told him of all that had happened since he left his boyhood home with the Six, how he'd betrayed them to Amrafalus, then how Amrafalus, in turn, had betrayed him by changing him into a monster with his crystals. He told The Sentinel how he'd ruled over the wolf-man pack for years, and how Glahivar, once known as Branwyn, had found him and wreaked her vengeance on him.

Yes, I saw her in her current form, said The Sentinel. *She came in here and removed two of the Six healers. We did let it happen though.*

As Blaidd's head jerked up in surprise, The Sentinel began to relate, from the beginning, his encounters with the Six and Anwyn, finishing with what Irusan had shared with him during their private conversation.

An incredible tale! Blaidd felt truly overwhelmed. His world with the pack had been so small. Uncomplicated, even.

The Sentinel continued.

I had no memory of who I was, why I was here, or even how long I've been here, but that has changed. When Glahivar appeared, she looked different, and she didn't seem to remember who I was, so I didn't recognize her either at first. But an energy signature always remains the same. It never changes. It jolted my memory. I now remember her as the person who created the weapon. She also created me.

I was to stand guard over this weapon at all times, never to let it out of my sight, but then the planetary changes occurred and the weapon was lost, buried deep underground. I stayed here for eons, watching over something—but never knew exactly what.

I am almost indestructible. She made me that way. Extremely long-lived. With the passage of time I couldn't even remember who or what I was. I only remembered one word: Sentinel. Since my memory sparked, it has all come back to me. I now remember why I was put here in the first place, what it is exactly that I am guarding over.

All that aside, I do believe the Six are in trouble again. Most specifically the girl, Anwyn. I have felt the energies of late, and it has disturbed me greatly.

Blaidd thought-spoke again.

I saw this Anwyn when they used their confounded healing crystal on me. I never thought Jarah and Tegan had it in them to produce such an amazing child. But I am happy for them, and I hope they succeed in getting this—weapon, is it?—neutralized. The old Blaidd would have wanted this weapon for himself, but now. . .

Blaidd stopped, staring into the fire, a far-away look on his face. He thought a bit. Did he *really* desire a weapon of such massive destructive capabilities? He remembered how he'd coveted the healing crystal, thinking it would bring him power, but his actions had only led to misery. He had been at the mercy of evil beings who had used his jealousy and rage for their own ends.

The Sentinel nodded. *I hear you,* it said. *Sorry. I didn't mean to eavesdrop on your private thoughts, but sometimes it's difficult—*

Don't worry. It's past time I acknowledged my mistakes, and you don't look too judgmental to me. I am mostly relieved you aren't going to eat me!

They both laughed, Blaidd in his human way, The Sentinel sending out waves of smiles that tickled Blaidd's body. That made them laugh even more, and then The Sentinel looked serious again.

I also remember the deviousness of this creature, even from that time.

I know she will never rest until she has the weapon in her control again. Irusan told me that she needs to also have the activators and deactivators to operate it. He told me of his plan, to take the weapon to Mu'A, the island that is shielded. But there is something else that Irusan—nobody—knows. No one except me. I will tell you, and then we must make a plan.

Blaidd leaned forward. For the first time since changing into his old form, he felt something that was neither fear, nor powerlessness.

He felt hope.

36

The Weapon

Glahivar and Shegami were back in Three Rivers. The captives were all still unconscious. "We'll keep them that way," said Shegami. "Now show me the weapon."

Glahivar took her to the hole in the ground, the *oubliette*, where she had hidden the crystal skull.

She nodded towards the hole. "It's down there."

"Well, go get it!"

"Afraid of it, are you?" Glahivar snickered. "It's quite safe. I carried it all the way here with no problems." She descended into the hole and soon reappeared with a crystal skull in her grasp. She handed it to Shegami, who only glanced at it, and gave a derisive snort.

"Of course it's safe, you bungler! That is not the real weapon. You were duped, again. *Here* is the real weapon!" With a flourish, she pulled the skull, still wrapped in its package, from where she'd hidden it in her black robe. "I got this off Irusan, who had done a switch on you at the mines. You didn't catch that, did you?"

Glahivar gasped. *It couldn't be! When?*

"When you were looking the other way, no doubt. Now, let's get the six upstairs and take them to Iochodran, along with this—the real weapon." She turned to leave.

"Have you checked that one, yet?" Glahivar asked.

Shegami hesitated in mid-turn.

Glahivar smiled.

"Check it."

Shegami ripped the linens off the skull. Yes, it was a skull, but it was obviously not the weapon. A crudely hewn rock emerged from its wrapping. With a screech, she threw the rock across the dungeon, where it shattered against the wall.

"Who's the fool now? You should be glad I am with you, Shegami. If not, Astrabal would have you turned into one of his maggots. Now, if you're nice to me, I might tell you where they took the real one. And yes, before you ask, I *do* know."

After their arrival in Mu'A, the Six and Irusan were greeted by the Council members and a hasty council session was convened. It felt strange to the Six to be back in Mu'A after so many years. They wished they had more time to spend here, but there was still too much they had to do. They couldn't remain.

Arabed and Mara, two of the twelve council members presided, and Irusan told them all that had occurred from the beginning. The council regarded the skull, sitting on a table, with suspicion and angst.

"Are you *sure* it's safe?" asked Mara.

"No," said Irusan. "We're not. With this thing, one can't be sure. But it's not busy killing anyone right now. We trust that Anwyn was able to deactivate it, but given the right DNA combination, anyone unknown to us with the right combination may be able to activate it again, unknowingly. We also do not know how long a deactivation might last. That is why, too, we must find a safe place to keep it."

"Why here?" asked Arabed. "Why not place it in an active volcano?"

"Astrabal's elementals could easily retrieve it from a live volcano. There are many reasons why that would not do. We thought of Mu'A because the island has shielding. Few know of Mu'A's existence, and even fewer know how to find you. As you all know, if they did come here, they'd only see an uninhabited island and an extinct volcano. One who does not have the access keys will not be able to find this island or get past its shielding."

"Yes, of course, but what if we keep it here, and years—centuries—later, it activates?"

"We have thought of that. In Agra Tan, we have studied the coding of the deactivators. We are steps away from finding the key elements that allows one to deactivate it so we can reproduce it. We will provide every person on this island with the keys, if necessary. You may then keep it on display as a reminder of the folly of man, and touch it as often as you like. That way, it will never activate, and you and all your descendants will remain safe."

It felt, to the Six, that the Council members took much too long to decide as they discussed it amongst themselves.

They were on edge, thinking of Anwyn, Saran, and Jax in the hands of Glahivar and Shegami. If they didn't hurry, they might miss them altogether and lose them to Iochodran, but Irusan had assured them that the discovery of the false skull would delay the departure with the prisoners.

"They would not take them to Iochodran without the weapon. It would be too risky for them," he had said with great confidence. "I feel their priority would be to find the real weapon first." They hoped he was right.

Finally, Mara stood up. "We have decided."

37.

Glahivar and Shegami

The island, a green emerald that rose out of the turquoise Sea of Alania, glowed golden in the first rays of the dawn light. Glahivar and Shegami, along with their burdens, one in each claw or tentacle, alit in their merkabas on the crystalline shoreline and placed the unconscious bodies, none too gently, onto the sand.

"How do you know this is the right island, Glahivar? I don't see any sign of habitation here." Shegami still did not trust Glahivar, but she was going along with her plan, because, she thought, what option did she have?

"Of course you don't, that's the whole point. See that dormant volcano? It's where they live. *Inside* it. I was once one of those from Agra-Tan, remember? We had a lot to do with this island and its people. We helped them move here and helped them develop their shielding. Do you think mere humans could do all this?" She swept her claw towards the peak. "I had forgotten all this in my life as the Raven, otherwise I would have used it to destroy this place earlier. Humans should not be this powerful, and the people on this island must be stopped. That's why we'll start here."

"Alright, then. I agree with that much. But how are you going to alert them to our presence?"

"Just watch. They already know."

The Six had allowed themselves to breath again. The Council had decided that they would accept the weapon, and Irusan said he would ensure they all received the keys that would allow everyone on the island to permanently deactivate the weapon. With their combined power, he had said, it should never be able to reactivate again. In fact, he stressed, it may even shatter the weapon into dust.

"Now all we need to do is to go back to Three Rivers and—" Irusan stopped, mid-sentence. His face changed, and he seemed to be listening. "We must go. *Now.* The elementals have warned me there are Beings on the island, on the beach, who do not belong. Two are from Iochodran!"

A chill swept through the room.

"Anyone want to guess who they are?" asked Tristan. His face was white. "How did they track us here?"

"Glahivar," said Irusan. "She has probably remembered the location of the island. I had hoped she would not, but Astrabal has powerful methods. One good thing is that she will not be able to enter. Let us go see what they want."

The Six followed him down to the beach in their merkabas, arriving almost instantly. Tegan made a small, frightened sound when she saw her daughter lying unconscious on the beach.

Kex cried out, "Mother! Saran!" They, too, were unconscious, guarded by Shegami and Glahivar. There were three other people who also lay in a deep sleep on the sand. One wore a blue dress, the other was clad in strange skins, and one wore what looked like night clothes.

Kex looked closer. "It's Gugun," she cried, pointing at the man in the skins.

"You thought you were being clever, didn't you?" said Shegami. "But you have no idea who you're dealing with here. No more switches, Irusan. Give us the real thing, or we'll truly kill the three deactivators this time."

"If you kill them," said Irusan, "you'll have no way to control the weapon."

"Oh, but we will," said Glahivar. "We have their DNA." She held up Anwyn's limp arm, and they could clearly see a cut on her arm. "See, we took some blood." She held up Saran's arm, then Jax's, and they could see the same cuts on both of them. She then held up two vials. "Here is the blood. One for the activators, and one for the deactivators. So you can see that we don't really need any of them anymore, but we could keep them a while longer, just in case. Soon we will be able to operate the weapon without them. If you want us to return them to you, unharmed, once we're done, we will do so. But there is a price for that. You know what it is."

"How do we know you will keep your promise?" asked Irusan.

"What have we got to lose by not returning them? But if you don't give us the weapon, they will most surely die. In Iochodran."

"*Irusan, we must do it!*" Tegan cried. Irusan bowed his head. Again, he looked defeated, and this time the Six knew it was not an act. Finally, he looked up.

"Arabed will bring it down. I have explained the situation to him."

Tegan began to cry, and Kex sank down on the ground in relief. But, mixed with relief, there was also fear. They all knew the consequences of giving up the weapon to Astrabal. He would use it. There was no doubt in their minds about that. None of them had much longer to live, but at least they'd be with their loved ones, and if Shegami kept her word, they would not die a hideous death in Iochodran.

It took Arabed a little more time, since he had to walk down to the beach from the mountain, but they waited, silently, until he arrived. He held the skull in front of him as if he couldn't wait to be rid of it. Its sinister face grinned at them, and Shegami chortled as she reached out for it with two tentacles.

"Yes! *This* is the real thing. I feel its power!" She caressed it with another tentacle. "We'll keep our promise, of course. We'll leave you here with your family members, and we'll take these three." She nodded towards the sleeping activators. "Glahivar, pick them up my dear."

Just as Glahivar picked them up, Irusan vanished.

"Where did he go?" Tristan asked. There was bewilderment on all of their faces. Arabed frowned.

Glahivar laughed, a wet, smacking, gleeful sound from her mandibles. "Oh, he got out of here fast, didn't he? He knows what we are going to do, and he wanted to save his shape-shifting skin before we did it!"

"We may as well tell you," said Shegami. Her voice betrayed her triumph. She waved a tentacle at the peak of the mountain. "We are going to drop it in there. Astrabal has commanded it."

"How are you going to activate it without killing yourselves?" Arabed asked.

It was the question now on all their minds. The volcanic mountain, although long extinct, still had a crater at its peak. If the weapon was activated and dropped in there, it would destroy all of the island, and eventually the whole planet if it was not stopped.

"We've thought of that too," said Glahivar. "We are going to drop the weapon into the crater, and, seconds later, we'll drop these three activators in exactly the same spot. They will die, of course, but they will also fall right on top of the weapon. The few moments it takes for them to follow the weapon down will give Shegami and I enough time to get out of here."

"We will return for the weapon later," Shegami continued. "Once it has destroyed the planet. By that time, we'll have our activation and deactivation keys ready for use. The Agra-Tanians are not the only ones who are working on this. We have been doing it too, and perhaps we're a couple of steps ahead of them by now."

The Six looked at each other, and they were so numbed with fear that no one knew what to say.

"We must go now," said Shegami. "It's time."

Glahivar held up a claw. "Not so hasty, Shegami, let's not forget—" She took out her crystal and waved it above them. "There, no more merkabas! And for good measure . . ." She reached towards Anwyn's pouch around her waist and removed the crystal Irusan had given her. "Now I'm sure you won't be able to fix your merkabas."

Still clutching the skull, Shegami and Glahivar picked up the three unconscious people and vanished.

38.

Beginning of the End

Irusan was back in Agra-Tan in the blink of an eye after leaving the beach. The Azur'A council met him at the portal.

"We know why you're back so soon. We are not quite finished with the keys yet. We understand the urgency, but we can only work as fast as we can."

Irusan did not often feel frustration, but now he was nearly panicked. He had not felt fear in a long time. Why had he not anticipated that Glahivar would remember the location of Mu'A? His plan had been to render the weapon harmless before Astrabal could succeed, and when the hostages would no longer be valuable to them, he and the Six could rescue them. But that had not been what had happened.

"We understand how you feel and we do know what is going on in Mu-A'Raevia," said Artremaya, one of the Light Beings. "Please be patient. There is something else occurring simultaneously that we are keeping watch over. All is not yet lost."

Irusan let his breath out. He had not even been aware he was holding it.

THE SIX AND ANWYN OF IALANA

They travelled through the night sky, The Sentinel holding Blaidd tightly, still naked, in his claw. Now that he knew he wasn't in danger from the beast, Blaidd allowed himself to relax and, fascinated, he watched the landscape unfolding beneath them as The Sentinel flew effortlessly over it.

The Sentinel was familiar with the mountains, and he carefully found all the routes with the best updrafts to help them cross the Osgoi Range with minimum effort. Blaidd was cold, colder than he'd ever been, but at least this time he wasn't shaking from fear. Finally, they had crossed the mountains and the air felt just a little warmer.

The Sentinel turned, and they headed south, towards the sea.

As they stood, helpless, on the beach, Anwyn began to stir. Tegan and Jarah rushed to her side, cradling her in their arms. Kex and Adain did the same with Jax and Saran. One by one, the three opened their eyes.

Saran began to cry, and Jax looked confused. Her face turned to fear as she saw Kex next to her.

"Mother! It is me, Kex! Please don't be afraid. Saran, you are safe now."

Jax seemed too shocked to speak, her face white and drawn as she looked at her daughter, the daughter she thought was dead.

Anwyn sat up. "Is the weapon safe?" She examined her parent's faces, then looked at the others who were standing over her. Anwyn's face fell. "It did not work? Oh . . ."

"Our merkabas don't work either," said Tegan, "and Glahivar took your crystal." Anwyn looked stricken.

"We are waiting on Irusan," said Jarah in his most comforting voice. "He's in Agra-Tan, and he will be back with the deactivation keys."

What he did not say was that there was no time left. None at all. The sun was higher in the sky, and he wondered what was taking Glahivar and Shegami so long. They should have dropped the weapon by now.

Arabed gasped and pointed. A blue light rose from the top of the volcano. The weapon had activated.

39.

The Sentinel

He had never flown so fast, he thought, as leagues of ocean slipped by under them. He was nearly spent, but somehow he found the strength to continue to fly. He hoped Blaidd was alright. He had not heard anything from him for a while now. Maybe he had fallen asleep, and was not unconscious from the chill air.

There had been no time to stop and find him human clothing. He must wake Blaidd though, as he knew the location of the island. Blaidd had told him before they'd left approximately where to find it, but he needed him to guide him there once they reached the general area.

Blaidd, Blaidd! Wake up. He gently shook his claw with Blaidd in its grasp, and he felt Blaidd stir. *Wake up. I need you to guide me to the island. The sun will be coming up soon and I will be nearly blind in the daylight.*

Blaidd opened his eyes. It was not all just a dream. He really was flying high above the ocean. He could see small whitecaps on the dark water below. They must have been near the island, he thought. He had found the island once before in a fishing boat.

In his last reincarnation, he had been Seryn, from the island. The Seryn that now caused him shame. The Seryn who had betrayed the Six not once, but several times. He had, at that time, regained his memories as Seryn, and try as he might, he could not forget being the deceitful teacher of Mu'A.

But this Seryn, this person he now was, would do the right thing. Closing his eyes, he used his almost-forgotten energy sensing skills. The island could always be energetically sensed by those with a connection to it.

He hoped that he still had a connection.

They continued to fly as the first rays of the sun lightened the sky in the east. Slowly, the orange disk of the sun began to lift above the straight line of the horizon.

Do you feel it yet, Blaidd? I am not seeing much right now.

Blaidd closed his eyes even tighter. There was nothing. This was not going well. The Sentinel was flying nearly blind. Turning his head, Blaidd felt this way, and then that. He was just about to tell The Sentinel to turn around, perhaps they'd flown past it, when he received a *ping* on his inner vision. It showed as a purple dot in his mind that stayed fixed no matter how he moved his head.

"There!" Blaidd pointed towards the south-western horizon. "Fly that way!"

The Sentinel changed course, and they flew on, dropping closer and closer to the water with each league that passed.

I am getting tired, Blaidd. I don't know how much longer I can fly.

The sun continued to rise, and the water was now too close beneath them for comfort.

"Keep flying, Sentinel! We're almost there."

The Sentinel, groaning with each flap, put everything he had into keeping them above the water. Blaidd twisted his head around, and there it was! They were there! The beaches rose whitely ahead, and he could now hear the waves breaking on its shores.

There were people on the beach. He could see them as they drew near, but he couldn't see who they were. They were looking up at the peak.

At that moment, a blue light, like a beam, rose from the peak. They were too late!

Ambros and Catrin

Ambros, along with his three companions, and Zlatan, waited on the outskirts of the battle. Next to them, seated on their steeds, were Catrin's standard bearer and a trumpeter. The battle was chaotic, both within and without the fort. The fort was burning fast, and women, slaves, and children, carrying precious possessions, tumbled out of the front gate past the fighting men.

Ambros had issued orders that no woman or child was to be harmed, and the soldiers allowed them to pass. Moran's men were too preoccupied with their own defense to stop them. The villagers from the shanty-town had joined Zlatan's forces, armed with pitchforks, home-made swords, and weapons of all kinds. They eagerly fought Moran's men, many losing their lives in the attempt. Zlatan knew how much they'd suffered under Moran's rule, and this was their opportunity to either break free, or die with dignity.

But phase two of the battle was soon approaching. Moran and his men still held the interior of the fort. With the relatively few men, less than a quarter of the division that had accompanied them to Yor Swamps, they were unable to make any significant inroads into the fort.

Ambros knew Catrin and Zlatan had this part covered, they just had to wait for the right moment.

It came when Ambros decided he didn't want to sacrifice one more man's life for a strategy. He could see them falling, but the Yor line re-mained steadfast. They were heavily outnumbered, but he must bide his time. Too soon, and his strategy would be revealed. He watched, biting the inside of his cheek, fists clenched, as the battle raged. He so badly wanted to join his men, but he knew that would be folly.

Not yet.

At last, the moment came. Raising his bow and arrow, he fired a flaming arrow into the sky, towards the swamps and the access road. His trumpeter lifted his trumpet to his lips and blew the retreat. One by one, his soldiers began to withdraw from the fort, and Moran's men, shrieking in triumph, gave chase.

As they passed down the road, Ambros, Daire, Bran, Lonan, and Zlatan, from their concealed spot, held their fire. It was not yet time. He hoped his men would survive the retreat, at least until they reached the swamps.

As the last of Moran's men passed them by, they spurred their horses and followed.

Behind him was a third of his army. They had hidden silently in the nearby trees and darkness. They also followed. Catrin had sent a mere fraction of the full division that had accompanied them to the Yor Swamps and into the fort. Catrin, and nearly two thirds of the company, waited in the forest for his signal.

He could now hear the thunder of hoof beats as the remainder of the waiting division approached like a black storm. He could hear the screams of surprise and dismay as Moran's army realized what had happened. They were caught in a pincer formation, their retreat to the fort and the road to the north now blocked. They were the ones now heavily outnumbered. The only option left to them, besides fighting to the death, were the swamps on either side, and the swamps were not a forgiving place for anyone.

As the sun's disc edged over the horizon, the battle ended. Bodies were strewn everywhere, but the swamps had claimed even more lives.

Of Moran, there was no sign.

40.

Mu'A

As the beam rose into the sky, their eyes transfixed on it in horror, they did not see The Sentinel and Blaidd until they fell, sprawling, onto the beach next to them.

"Sentinel!" Anwyn gasped.

"And . . . Blaidd?" Adain couldn't believe his eyes.

They looked on in amazement. They recognized Blaidd. He was rather worse for wear, and totally naked, but it was Blaidd.

"There's no time." Anwyn spoke for The Sentinel. He took a few deep breaths and looked up, with milky eyes, at the beam. "I must get up there."

"What . . .?" Jarah asked. He was as confused as everyone else.

The Sentinel did not wait for the rest of the question, but making a great effort, he flapped his huge wings again He could only see the blue beam. All else was a blur. They watched, mouths open wide in surprise, as he rose into the air.

They continued to watch, silent and fearful, as the ground under them began to tremble. The weapon was building up its store of energy, and the enormous generator crystals under the volcano that powered Mu'A were its conduit to the plasma energies deep in the core. It wouldn't be long before they reached full capacity and everything around them would begin to disintegrate. There was no matter that could withstand the power of the skull, and they were certain The Sentinel would die as soon as he got close enough.

Perhaps this was his way of dying quickly, they thought. He would fly right into it.

He didn't know where he found his strength, but since landing on the beach, The Sentinel had felt a renewed surge of energy through his exhausted body. He rose up, above the beach, and headed directly to the mountain peak. His vision had almost gone, but he could see light and dark shapes, and the beam.

Circling around the beam, he saw its source far below: a small, but fuzzy gleam that could only be the skull. Three darker shapes almost obscured it.

With a high-pitched squeal-shriek, he dropped, like a stone, into the volcano.

He alit near the stone. He could see the shapes now that partially obscured the shining skull. They were three people, and even with his fading vision, he saw that they were rapidly beginning to disintegrate. The ground began to shake, and the skull moved closer to the edge of a dark chasm that fell into the depths of the dormant volcano. *He must get it*! One of the bodies fell, bouncing and breaking apart as it dropped into the crevice.

Without any further ado, he reached out, and picked up the skull, just as it began to drop.

Those gathered on the beach watched, transfixed, as The Sentinel plunged into the volcano. They could barely stand upright now. Saran was screaming, terrified, as the water along the shore-line began to rise, but still they could not move. The sand felt like quicksand under their feet, and they were sinking into it, now up to their knees.

Jarah wondered if they should just wait where they were. The water might rise up and drown them before their bodies began to disintegrate, but he really didn't know what else they could do. He could see the despair and terror in his companions, and he held tightly onto Tegan and Anwyn. Each one of them held tightly onto another, Kex with her mother and sister, and Adain, Djana, and Tristan holding on to each other.

They closed their eyes. None of them wanted to see what else was coming. Blaidd lay supine on the beach, his hands over his head as the sand and water began to cover his body.

It was then that the ground stopped shaking. A large wave washed over their half-buried bodies, then it retreated. They opened their eyes. The water was still shaking, but it was not coming up any higher. No tidal wave! They looked up.

The blue light was no more. It had disappeared. The birds that had flown up, squawking and crying loudly in alarm at the disturbance, had settled down, back into the trees. The jungle slowly returned to it's normal state.

Finally, Arabed spoke. "What *was* that thing?" he asked.

Tegan couldn't help it. She began to giggle. Everyone looked at her in amazement.

"Are you alright, Tegan?" Djana asked.

"I don't know. I can't seem to control my emotions." She giggled and cried, tears spilling down her cheeks. Kex had tears too, and she still hugged her stunned mother and sister as if she would never let them go.

"I hope he made it, but nothing could have survived that activated skull," said Tristan. He looked at the others sadly. "I think—"

Blaidd stood up, shouted, and pointed up towards the peak. "*Look!*"

They looked up, and there was The Sentinel, flying down towards them. He carried something. Could it be?

As he neared them, then alit on the sand next to them, they began to dig themselves out of their almost-sand-tomb. The Sentinel sunk down on the beach, spent, but he held tightly onto the crystal skull in his claws.

"Is it safe?" asked Arabed.

"Yes, it's safe," said Anwyn, stepping forward. "He's deactivated it. I can sense it." She picked up the skull and tucked it under her arm.

The Sentinel looked too exhausted to communicate, even in his telepathic way. He breathed heavily, and they allowed him to rest for a few minutes. Finally, he looked up. His red eyes were completely white, blinded by the sun. He couldn't see at all now! He must have found them again using his bat-sonar senses. They sank down onto the beach next to him, appalled that this amazing creature had sacrificed so much to save them all.

At that moment, Irusan appeared too, in front of them. In his hands, he held a crystal vial.

"I see I arrived too late with this, but thankfully The Sentinel did not."

"What does The Sentinel have to do with the weapon?" asked Jarah.

"I can answer that," said Blaidd. They all turned to Blaidd. They'd almost forgotten he was there.

"Blaidd, we are so glad to see you. You're obviously not Yagmak anymore. How did it happen?" Tristan voiced the question in everyone's mind.

"Your wretched crystal," Blaidd said, an angry scowl on his face. But then his expression changed, and he laughed. "It changed me back to who I was before! But I am now glad, although I wasn't at first. It meant a sure death for me, but The Sentinel saved me. He told me before we left that he used to be the guardian of the skull. He is one of those able to deactivate it."

"I could have done it too," said Anwyn, "But Glahivar used her crystal to sabotage our merkabas again and took away the one I had that would fix it."

Irusan spoke through Jarah. "Glahivar and Shegami made no mistakes this time. We'll get your merkabas working again."

"We must go into the mountain," said Arabed. He looked fearful. "I must see if anyone survived the weapon activation."

THE SIX AND ANWYN OF IALANA

They all gasped. They had forgotten about the Mu'Ans.

"We'll go there straight away," said Irusan. "Arabed, help me carry The Sentinel into the mountain. We must give him to our best healers." He looked at the Six. "You know who I mean."

They nodded, and those of them who could, helped Arabed and Irusan as they each grasped a part of the huge Sentinel and carried him across the beach, through the jungle, and towards to the access door in the mountain.

41.

Aftermath

During the weapon's activation, there had been chaos in the mountain. Like an upturned anthill, many had fled their abodes or places of work, spilling out into the corridors and down the mountainside, while others remained in place. No one had known what to do. Everyone knew though that no matter what they did, they were going to die.

As Anwyn entered, still holding the weapon, people either screamed and ran in fear, or exclaimed out loud in shock and surprise.

"We don't need to fear the weapon anymore," Anwyn shouted out so all could hear. "It's harmless for now, or until we can get the elixir distributed."

Gradually, people began to drift back, and soon a curious crowd had gathered around Anwyn, Jax, and Saran as they made their way to the council chamber. Irusan had taken The Sentinel, along with Arabed, Blaidd, and the Six, to the healing chambers in the mountain.

The healing chambers overflowed with those who had succumbed to fear, or who had been injured by falling objects when the mountain shook. The community's healers were overwhelmed, so Irusan and the Six took Blaidd and The Sentinel to a quieter area to work on both of them while Arabed went off to find Blaidd some clothes. On the beach, Arabed had draped his cloak around Blaidd, but he needed something more permanent since he still shook from cold and fear.

Mara and Almene met with Kex in the council chambers. Those who did not require healing followed them there, and an *ad hoc* council session was convened for one specific purpose: what to do with the weapon now that it was deactivated.

Mara said that crystal programmers were working under the mountain on the huge crystals to ensure they were operating properly. The weapon had overpowered the free will choice of the crystals, and tapped into their energy source without their permission. The crystals now needed healing as much as the people who had been affected by the skull-weapon's activation.

Almene was put in charge of Jax and Saran, who looked as if they had awoken into a never-ending nightmare. She gently led them, silent and unprotestingly, out of the council chambers. She needed to talk with them and reassure them that all was well, and that they'd be returned to their home soon.

Almene was a Mu'An liaison to those from the outside world. Her original mission had been to assist the Six in their healing mission, and the families of the Six were just as much her responsibility as the six healers themselves. She was the one who had, with the help of Arabed, found the Six after their boat had been wrecked by the sea monster, and who had brought them back to the island.

She found a small room that was not currently being used, and she told Jax and Saran to sit. They did not seem familiar with chairs, and they sat on the floor, so she sat next to them on the floor too. She was relieved that the language of Rhagbeneth was similar to their own, and there would be little difficulty in communicating with these tribal people. They still wore their thick clan skins and furs, and Almene asked someone to find them some lighter clothing, since the temperature on the island was much warmer than that of their tundra home. She asked for food to be brought, but when it was, Jax pushed it away.

She looked at Almene as she drew Saran closer to her.

"Are you a witch? Have we died and gone to the Tent of the Moon?"

Almene shook her head. "You are quite alive, Jax. And you and Saran are safe. I understand your confusion, and I want to help explain things to you. What happened."

To everyone's surprise, Saran spoke, for the first time since arriving on the island.

"I know where we are. I know this place. I have been here before."

Almene looked at her strangely. "When were you here, dear?"

Jax put her hand over Saran's mouth, a fearful look on her face. "She doesn't know what she's saying. She thinks she's in one of her dreams. We saw Gugun here. His spirit will be angry if she continues to speak in this way."

"Gugun can't hurt you anymore. I said before, and I'll say it again. You are both *safe*. Saran, you may speak. Jax, remove your hand."

Jax had barely removed a reluctant hand before the words began spilling out of Saran. She'd had dreams of the island ever since she could remember. When she'd tried to tell her tribe about them, she had been threatened by the shaman, Gugun. They all remembered what had happened to Kex.

"I have lived in fear ever since she spoke of dreams," said Jax. "We thought Gugun had killed Kex." Her tears flowed freely now. "One day, just before her marriage, she disappeared. If Gugun had not killed her, then we suspected that she had gone on a last hunt, alone, and the wolves or a cave bear got her. I did see her spirit appear to me not too long ago, and then I knew for sure she was dead. I thought when we saw her again on the big sand by the water that we had been reunited in the Land of the Moon."

"Your Kex is a capable woman," said Almene, a smile on her face. "Don't underestimate her. She is a survivor, and I think she and Saran will find they have a lot to talk about." Almene turned to face Saran.

"You seem to be one of us," she continued. "You must have a purpose connected with that of your sister, or you would not have had those dreams. We will discover what your mission is."

She turned again to Jax.

"You will be returned to your clan. It is probably wiser that you don't tell anyone there what really happened. We—or Irusan—can take you through a portal . . ." She stopped as she saw the confusion on Jax's face. "A portal . . . oh, never mind. It will only mean that you will arrive back at your tent almost at the same time you left it. Irusan knows how to do that, but it's dangerous to attempt except for the most skilled in portal mechanics . . ."

She stopped again and smiled.

"I am confusing you even more. I will just reassure you that when you get back, you will remember nothing, and no one will even know that you left. As for Saran, she will have to go back with you. When she comes of age, Irusan can bring her back here, and we will train her in whatever her true purpose in life really is."

Jax thought for a while. "She would have been married off to another clan anyway," she said at last. "The same as Kex. I see that Kex is doing well, and I think she's married to that ugly, pale man. Not what Keckryn and I would have picked for her. We had already promised her to the Cold Bone Clan. We had broken our previous promise to them, and it started a war between our clans. Now that it will happen again, they won't be pleased." She looked down at her feet and sighed. "We are already outcasts. Maybe they'll kill us all this time."

Almene looked distressed. "I didn't think of your circumstances. Obviously, it's worse than I thought. We can't possibly return you and wash our hands of the outcome. I'll speak to Irusan and Kex. There's a solution in there, somewhere. In the meanwhile, you are welcome to stay here as long as you wish. Kex will be with you soon. She and her friends are taking care of The Sentinel—"

Alarm rose on Jax's face at the mention of The Sentinel. "Do you mean that hideous, flying devil?"

"I can see we have a lot more discussions ahead of us. In the meanwhile, I'll have rooms prepared for you and Saran, and I'll send Kex to you as soon as she's available." It was all Almene could do for them now. She was going to have to take it one step at a time. Saran would be easy to work with, but she had her doubts about Jax.

She sighed.

Holgar and Adne

They sat, miserable and sea-sick, in the hold of the fishing boat. They could hear Zephan on the deck above them, and every once in a while, he'd open the locked hatch and throw food and water down for them. The food was barely edible. Stale bread, mostly, or rancid fish. Adne thought she couldn't possibly vomit up anything more. Her stomach was as empty as her emotional reserves, and Holgar wasn't faring any better.

During the day, they'd felt the sea shake strangely, and the waves rose up higher than ever, washing over the deck. They could hear Zephan up on deck, sliding around as he tried to keep his footing during the turbulence of the waters.

"I hope he doesn't fall off," Holgar said. "With us locked in here, we'd be at the mercy of the sea."

"What do you think they'll do with us?" Adne asked for the millionth time. Holgar answered again, patiently, for the millionth time.

"It must have something to do with Djana and our healers. They—I mean Udfa—is looking for them again."

"I don't know how we can help him," said Adne. "We know that Djana is in Three Rivers, but how will that help him?"

"I don't know," said Holgar. "I don't know. We'll just have to wait and see. This man is telling us nothing."

"I'd like to see Rhiannon again, but not as a prisoner." Adne groaned, and heaved some more liquid from her belly. Their trip had been rough, even without the morning's tumultuous churning of the water, and it was evident their captor was too busy to allow them onto the deck where they could get fresh air. Water spilled into the hold through cracks in the deck, and they were cold. They could tell when it was daylight, since light came through the cracks as well, and they estimated they'd been at sea for nearly two days.

"It's a seven-day journey, if it goes well," said Holgar.

"I don't know if I'll last that long," said Adne.

Holgar just nodded.

42.

Anwyn, the Six

They had finished working on The Sentinel and Blaidd. Both were resting. The Sentinel hanging from a dark and rocky place deep within the mountain, and Blaidd in Jarah's old room, since Jarah would now be sharing Tegan's quarters.

Irusan had quickly returned to Ardvale, coming back with a new crystal to clear the merkaba fields of the Six and Anwyn, and then he, Anwyn, and the healers had gone straight to the council chambers.

"How are they doing?" It was the first thing Mara asked as they walked into the airy cavern. It was a beautiful day outside, and cool sea-breezes flowed through the granite arches and columns of the meeting room.

Anwyn thought it was difficult to imagine that they might never have beheld this sight again if the weapon had worked without interruption.

Irusan answered Mara's question, through Jarah, who spoke for those in the room who could not hear Irusan's thoughts.

"The Sentinel is sleeping, and so is Blaidd. They are both well." He looked at the other healers. "They did an outstanding job of healing them. The Sentinel's sight has been restored, and he is recuperating.

"We also removed the remainder of the coding placed in Blaidd's template by Amrafalus' crystals. He is now the same human—well, maybe with a few differences—that he was before. He is a man now. Now that his template has been allowed to follow his natural growth coding. We saw a boy on the beach, but his normal human growth had been interrupted by the beast code."

"That is welcome news," said Mara. "Let us bring you up to speed on what we've decided about the weapon."

They found places to sit, and she continued.

"Anwyn assures us that the weapon has been deactivated. Irusan, you have the crystal vial with the DNA of the deactivators?"

Irusan began to pat his fur. "I had almost forgotten about that now that the weapon is safe again. I should have given it to you earlier, but I wanted to be sure The Sentinel was taken care of."

Mara frowned, shaking her head. "It was remiss of us not to take it from you. Things were so chaotic here! We'll give it to our scientists, and they will create an elixir that can be given to every citizen of Mu'A. We will use the crystal as a curiosity, a lesson to all, that weapons of great power do not protect, but rather ensure the ultimate destruction of humanity—"

Irusan jumped up, patting frantically now around his body with a panicked look in his large, blue cat-eyes. There was a collective intake of breath, as the people in the large hall looked at him, aghast. Then, smiling, he pulled the vial from his thick fur. It had been in a pouch that hung from a chain around his neck all along.

"Irusan! You scoundrel!" Djana yelled, but she was laughing too. "You almost gave us heart failure!"

"Sorry, I couldn't resist," he at last said, and sat down again. Jarah, in his fear, had almost forgotten to translate Irusan's words.

"Bad joke, Irusan!" said Mara, a stern look still on her face, but as she looked away, everyone could see that she was suppressing her own laughter. Some giggled, and others smiled. Everyone looked relieved.

"We needed to break the seriousness," said Irusan. "Laughter is healing, after all we've been through. I hope I did not scare the skins off everyone."

"You did," said Anwyn, "but it was funny!" She had been one of the gigglers. She laughed some more. "I thought we could use the skull . . ." Her laughter, along with her voice, faded away. She turned and looked outside the archways towards the sea. Her face dropped.

"Something has happened," she said, as she turned back to face them. "Something bad."

Time is Up

Glahivar and Shegami had fled, back to Iochodran, as soon as they'd dropped their packages into the crater. They chuckled, gleefully, as they sped into Rhagat Rise. They felt sure Astrabal would reward them handsomely.

Glahivar, although pleased that their goal—to activate the weapon in Mu'A—had worked, had little hope now of claiming it for herself. She'd been given no choice but to go along with Astrabal's plan once Shegami had shown up, pointed out her failings, and taken charge of the situation.

She had not wanted to destroy the planet. Only Mu'A. She would have liked to keep the planet intact so that she could return and rule it. But she might still have a plan to do just that. She allowed a carefully shielded thought to flit like a shadow through her mind.

Idris's time is up. It's my turn now.

Idris was the God that currently ruled the planet. He was worshipped by all on Ialana, and she would replace him. He was the only Other-Dimensional Being that Astrabal was afraid of. Once she'd taken over, she would replace Astrabal as well.

They were now in front of the towering nightmare that was Astrabal. His eyes looked like coals from a blast furnace. He was . . . angry?

Glahivar was confused, and she sensed that Shegami was puzzled as well. Hadn't they done a wonderful thing? They could retrieve the weapon later. It was not lost. She had just opened her mouth to say this when a blast of hot air hit them with a stench of rotting flesh that was far worse than the flames from his mouth.

Astrabal's wrath prevented him from speaking. Instead, he gestured for a minor demon to bring him a large globe. It was what he used to view events from afar, his skrying crystal. Glahivar knew it was how he often knew what was happening while it was happening.

The demon scurried over and placed the crystal on a table that materialized in front of them.

"Look!" Astrabal hissed, as his voice returned. "Just *look*."

They looked. Then they shrank back, fear rising in their cores.

"I . . . I don't understand," said Shegami, her voice trembling. "It had *activated*! They couldn't have—"

"Oh, but they did," Astrabal hissed again, smoke billowing now from the hole that passed for his mouth. "It doesn't look 'destroyed' to me. How does it look to you?"

"N-not destroyed," said Shegami. "It's still there. And what happened to the blue light beam? We did see it—!"

"I saw it too," Glahivar managed to spit out. "I used my crystal on the girl and the others. Their merkabas weren't working. There's no way they could have deactivated it."

She turned to Shegami, pointing a claw at her.

"It was you!"

"Wh-what? What do you mean it was *me*?"

Glahivar turned back to Astrabal. "I knew she was up to something. She told me when she'd grabbed the weapon from Irusan that she knew it was the right one, when, in fact, it wasn't."

"You nasty piece of—" Shegami spluttered.

"She tried to tell me it was the real weapon, but it was I who had to get the real weapon from the Mu'Ans." She held up the two vials. "And I kept the blood safe. Here it is, labelled nicely."

A minor demon snatched the vials from her, and Astrabal ordered him to take them to the laboratories below. "I want the elixirs produced immediately. Tell them their worthless lives depend on it."

But Glahivar wasn't finished with Shegami. "I think she's playing a game with us. She did something so the weapon did not fully activate. She wants the weapon for herself—"

"What game? Why would I want to gain the weapon for myself, or to save the Mu'Ans? How would it *benefit* me?"

As they argued, Astrabal's head whipped back and forth, looking first at one, and then the other.

He roared.

"Shut up, both of you! Do you think I can't read minds? Shegami, you are innocent, as much as you're able to be innocent of anything. Incompetent perhaps, but certainly not guilty of what Glahivar's accusing you of. And you." He turned to Glahivar. "You are a liar. I like liars, even approve of them, but not when they're lying to *me* and trying to shift blame. You are *both* to blame. Now," he growled, "let's look into the crystal and see what we can do."

"But all we can see is an empty island, still not destroyed," Shegami protested. She still looked befuddled.

"That's not where we're going to look," said Astrabal. "There have been other developments. One of my best men, a human puppet named Udfa, sent his minion, Zephan, to Ibai to take the parents of one of the healers hostage. He has them now, and is bringing them to Rhiannon."

"*Er*, and how is having them going to benefit *us*?" asked Shegami, her voice timid.

"Because, you fool, it will draw out the daughter, at the very least. And if I know these humans, her friends and maybe even the girl, Anwyn, will be there too. We have deliberately allowed this knowledge of their capture to reach them in Mu'A.

"I am counting on the fact that it will take some time yet for the Mu'An scientists to prepare the elixir that will turn every Mu'An into a deactivator, so the crystal, at the moment, has not yet been permanently destroyed."

Glahivar suppressed another thought, that this may be the development she had hoped for.

"So," said Glahivar, "the Six will rush to the rescue. With any luck, the girl will be with them. We'll snatch them all, again, and the Mu'Ans, if they act according to their respect for life, will hand over the crystal—"

"Maybe, maybe," said Astrabal, directing what may have been a fanged smile towards his new star.

Shegami burned with fury. Glahivar was nothing but an upstart, and she would never forgive, nor forget her betrayal.

"But not necessarily," Astrabal finished. "That is not the plan."

It was Shegami's turn to smile now, albeit only inwardly.

Astrabal continued. "We'll have had time too, to prepare our own elixir. The one that will give everyone on the planet the ability to activate the weapon. Irusan and the rest of those do-gooders will be so busy chasing the hostages that they won't ever find out what we're doing until it's too late. That is the second part of our plan.

"For phase one . . ." He gave a self-satisfied smirk. "Well, we won't need a phase one." He savored the stunned looks on the faces of those around him, the minor demons, imps, and Glahivar and Shegami. "We don't *need* the weapon. It can remain in Mu'A."

"Then how—"

"*By Idris,* don't I have any staff who can think for themselves? Just think! How are we going to distribute the elixir?"

Glahivar thought, then snapped a claw. "Through the air and water, of course. We have our own elementals. We just drop the elixir into a major water source and the air, and it will be carried around the globe. People will breathe it in or ingest it in the water they drink. We could potentially turn everyone on the planet into an activator, including those in Mu'A."

"You are promoted to minor demon, Glahivar. Shegami, Glahivar will be *your* superior now."

Shegami hissed. She'd had nothing but bad luck. She too would have come up with the answer had Glahivar not chimed in first.

"So, can we do all this before the weapon is permanently reduced to dust by the Mu'Ans?" Shegami asked, clinging onto a thread of hope that she may yet dazzle Astrabal with her genius. "It takes time for the elements—"

"Not the way I have planned it," said Astrabal. "My air elements can fly, dare I say, *as fast as the wind*?" He snickered at his own joke. "They'll carry the elixir to Mu'A."

He stopped and listened.

"I've just received word that my scientists have almost accomplished what I ordered them to do. They were fast, faster than even I expected." He laughed. "They are also Time Lords. Irusan is not the only one with the ability to use time portals. They are preparing it for distribution now.

"We'll start in Mu'A, obviously." He directed a withering glance towards Shegami. "The Mu'Ans, at some point, are going to have to touch the weapon. That's when it will activate again. And, just in case, we'll drop a massive dose on Irusan, the six healers, and their child as they attempt a rescue of the parents. It will not only change them, but her as well, into an activator. They won't even be aware of it. Their merkabas won't protect them from the elixir, and neither will their island shielding."

"Brilliant!" Glahivar clapped her claws together. "Absolutely brilliant."

43.

Anwyn

They all looked at her in disbelief. *What else could go wrong?*

"The elementals are talking to me," she said. "Give me a moment. I must be certain about this." She pulled up her merkaba and disappeared.

The council and everyone else waited, patiently until she returned. No one had spoken. Even Irusan was speechless. They had looked to him for answers, but he'd only shrugged.

As Anwyn appeared again, the questions began, but she held up her hand and they fell silent.

"I went to Ardvale. I received an urgent communication from Finn through Ilma, the air elemental, that Astrabal has a new elixir. One that has the potential to turn everyone here into an activator of the weapon. He has the DNA of the dead activators, and has found a way to reproduce it in great quantities. One that can be distributed through the air."

They gasped, horror etched on their faces.

"Not only that," Anwyn continued as she looked at Djana, "but your parents have been captured by Udfa. They are on their way to Rhiannon aboard a fishing boat."

Djana cried out and fell, sobbing, into Tristan's arms.

"Finn said that the air elementals intercepted the air elementals of Astrabal, and they are on their way here. It won't be long before they reach Mu'A and drop their elixir over the island. We'll all breathe it in, and it will find its way into our water supply as well, for good measure."

There was chaos in the assembly room as everyone began to talk and shout at once. Irusan stood up, and Jarah, Tegan, and Anwyn shouted out loud for him, so all could hear above the din.

"Quiet! Quiet!" The noise slowly died away, and they all looked at Irusan, hope on their faces. "The first thing we must do, before Astrabal's air elementals reach us, is remove the weapon from Mu'A." He looked at Arabed. "Bring that skull to me. I will take it to Ardvale in my merkaba via the portals. I must take Anwyn with me too, just in case I need a deactivator, and also to remove her from the air here.

"Finn does not wish to hold the weapon for long, but it will give us time. Time to prepare our own elixir. We cannot use the time portals to prepare the elixir. For that to work, as it has for Astrabal, I would need to take the scientists, one by one, through the portals. I am the only one who can do that. That in itself would take more time than we have."

Anwyn screamed as Arabed reached for the skull. It had been placed on a table in the center of the room. "No! Don't touch it!"

But it was too late, his hands were already on the skull, and he withdrew them as if the skull had been a hot coal.

Anwyn looked at Irusan as tears ran down her cheeks.

"They are here. Ilma has told me we've been breathing in the elixir for the last several moments."

The silence in the room was deafening. Every eye was transfixed on the skull.

How long would it take?

THE SIX AND ANWYN OF IALANA

"Stay here," Glahivar said to Shegami. She savored the feeling of ordering Shegami around for a change. It was exquisite. "I have something I need to do." She knew that Astrabal had increased her powers since her promotion, and she would be able to destroy Shegami with a look if she disobeyed. Shegami knew that as well, and she whimpered, but she stayed put.

Slipping unseen out of Iochodran was not easy, but with her new powers, she could do it so not even Astrabal would know. The last thing he would expect was for her to return to a world that was about to be destroyed. This was a weapon that could destroy several dimensions at once, and there were few beings anywhere who were immune to the power of the skull.

She was not immune either. The skull would destroy her just as surely as it destroyed the material world, but she thanked herself for her foresight and skill with sleight-of-hand. She had been too quick for Shegami to notice, and now she must get to the skull before Astrabal realized what was happening. It wouldn't take long for his skrying ball to pick up what was occurring in Mu'A.

Nothing.

Absolutely nothing was occurring in Mu'A, but she had to be quick.

Flying over the ocean, she zipped around in her merkaba, putting out all her energy-sensing skills to find them. At last, she did. A small boat, with a single man on its deck, tossed about on the waves below her. Diving down like a falcon after a mouse, she disappeared into the hold of the boat.

As she reappeared, in her spider form, the woman in the hold began to scream, but Glahivar waved a claw, and Adne and Holgar slumped down, unconscious. She was getting quite adept at this, she thought. Picking them up, she activated her merkaba once more and sped out of the boat and up into the sky. The man on deck was still oblivious, happily humming a tune to himself as he stood at the helm.

In an instant, she was over Mu'A, and she alit onto the beach, still holding onto her hostages.

This hostage thing always works, she thought to herself.

It felt as if everyone held their breath for a long time, and then Irusan spoke.

"It should have activated by now."

"Yes, it should have," said Anwyn. "But it hasn't. According to Ilma, we are still inhaling the elixir of Astrabal."

"Maybe it takes time to work," said Tristan.

"Yes, a little, perhaps," said Irusan, "but not this long. Our people in Agra-Tan calculated that it should hit the blood stream—" He stopped, a strange look on his face. "I have a communication."

Everyone looked up at him expectantly.

"From Glahivar."

Anwyn was as surprised as everyone else. "What!?"

"She's on the beach, and wants us to go down there with the skull."

"Oh no," Tegan gasped. "Here we go again. Who's she got this time?"

"Djana's parents."

Djana looked up, a wild look in her eyes, and before anyone could stop her, she picked up the skull, pulled up her merkaba, and disappeared.

"Oh, by the gods," cried Tristan. "We must go after her!" The Six, Anwyn, and Irusan pulled up their merkabas and flashed out of the council chambers while everyone else took the long way down to the beach.

Triumphant, Glahivar stood over the unconscious forms on the beach. Djana was there, and she held the skull in her hands.

"Let my parents go. I'll give you this, but you must first let them go."

"Oh, I will sweetheart. I will." She looked over towards Anwyn and Irusan. "Glad to see you're all here." She grasped Adne with a claw and brought her up to her mouth, opening her mandibles. "This worked so well with you all last time, I'll do it again. I'll bite the head off your mother, Djana, if you don't give me the skull."

Djana sighed, as tears welled up in her eyes. She looked at the others. "I'm sorry, but I must do it. I can't let my mother die like that."

Tegan nodded. "I understand."

Djana held the skull in front of her and began to walk towards Glahivar. It was then that the unexpected happened.

The skull was snatched out of her hands, not by Glahivar, but by another shape that had materialized next to her.

It was Shegami.

Glahivar hissed. "I thought I told you not to follow me! I'll reduce you to—"

"Oh, just you try, you daughter of a diseased goat! I had a conversation with Astrabal before you left. My powers are restored, and yours have been removed. I had suspected you were up to something, and I was right! We realized what you had done. You had switched the two vials! We are now working on the other one as we speak. The real activation elixir will be in the air in a few moments, but I'll be gone before then. I am not as foolish as you thought I was. I switched them around again and relabeled them. Why you wanted to give us the deactivation vial is beyond me, but we—"

"Oh, you fool! You are so wrong. There were three vials, not two. I switched the activation vial with a vial of dummy blood I'd retrieved from Thane Awstin's household. *I* have the activation vial. She dropped Adne and dug a claw into a pouch that hung around her ghastly head. She held up the vial. "See? This is the real blood. That of the activators."

"Wha-at?" Shegami looked down at the skull. "You mean . . ."

"Yes, I mean—"

Irusan laughed a funny little cat laugh. "We've all been breathing in the deactivation elixir! Astrabal has mass-produced the wrong elixirs!"

Shegami and Glahivar both dived towards the skull, and as they picked it up, each clawing and grabbing desperately for it, the skull shattered. It gave a *crrr-aack*! as thousands of tiny lines appeared, and then the skull disappeared in a large puff of white dust.

"Looks like your and our combined deactivation powers really overwhelmed the poor little skull," said Anwyn, laughing. "Too bad. Well, I guess you all need to go now and explain to Astrabal what happened. I wish you luck."

With a shriek, a screech, and a flash of light, Glahivar and Shegami disappeared.

A wind, colder than a Rhagbeneth winter, gusted overhead, and Irusan breathed in deeply. "That must be the dummy vial elixir coming over us now. Poor Astrabal. He'll never get this one figured out."

"It's like one of those shell-games that the soldiers play in Three Rivers," said Tristan, and he chuckled. "No one ever figures it out and they lose all their wages to scoundrels."

"I wonder what will happen to Shegami and Glahivar," said Tegan. "I feel kind of bad for them." But then she smiled. "Not really."

Djana was cradling her parent's heads, one in each arm, as they began to wake up. She was crying with relief.

"Where . . . where are we?" Holgar asked, looking around him. Adne sat up.

"Djana! What happened . . . where's the boat?"

Djana and Tristan, and several other people, helped Adne and Holgar to their feet, and supported them as they walked to the mountain.

It would be a wonderful reunion for Djana and her parents, thought Anwyn, but they must get them to the healing center. They didn't look healthy at all. They all walked back, talking excitedly amongst themselves.

The fear was over.

44.

Zephan

That evening, he'd opened up the hatch to the hold so he could throw food down, as usual, to his prisoners. To his amazement, the hold was empty. He'd searched it thoroughly, but there was nowhere they could have gone. There was not even a crack they could fit through.

It was sorcery, he was sure of it. Udfa would not be pleased.

He looked at the horizon. And now there was a storm coming. The sky was black in the distance, and it was headed his way. He looked towards the land on his right. It was close enough, but it was mountainous and covered with heavy forest. It was Mannanon, the land of the beasts. Perhaps he could make it there before the storm hit?

He turned his boat and prayed to Idris. He would prefer a death by the beasts of Mannanon than by Udfa.

The Six, and Anwyn, had returned in their merkabas to Ibai, taking Holgar and Adne—with Irusan's help—with them.

Djana's parents had healed well from their ordeal, and they were comfortably settled in their home again. Few had noticed their absence, and those who did were satisfied with the explanation that they'd gone to help a friend in need.

The Six had disappeared into the forest surrounding Ibai on the banks of the Garden River. Here, with the help of Anwyn, Irusan, Finn, and the elementals, they'd created a home that was well shielded from the outside world. While they would not conduct their healing sessions in this spot, they could go in their merkabas into Ibai and heal as many as they could in their homes. If Ortzi heard that they had resumed their healing activities, he'd come looking, but he'd have a tough time finding them.

He did not know, or did not care, about Adne and Holgar, who continued to teach in their school for healed Trueni.

Finn had brought their children back from Ardvale. They all seemed a little older now, and Finn said they'd picked up many skills while in the land of the Gardeners. They all wondered if this was a good, or a bad thing.

"We'll find out, I suppose," said Tegan with a sigh. "I just hope they haven't learned how to use their merkabas yet."

"I hope so too," Djana said. "I don't want to go chasing all over the world after my child."

Finn reassured them that their skills were now age-appropriate.

"You won't find them disappearing unexpectedly like me!" He chuckled as he disappeared.

Before leaving Mu'A, they had visited with Blaidd. He had opted to stay in Mu'A. He wanted to relearn what he'd forgotten and continue to heal, in many more ways than just the physical.

"I have a lot to make up for," he'd said to the Six. "I have damaged my own energetic fabric so much that it may take years, or even lifetimes, to fix it all. But now, I have a goal.

THE SIX AND ANWYN OF IALANA

"I don't miss my pack anymore. I can see how this gave me a sense of power and control, but it was an illusion. As soon as I lost my form, they turned on me. I will no longer seek an external power. I will reclaim my own personal power again, and it is then that I will find true happiness and peace."

They all hugged him, and everyone teared up, even Tristan. Then they had gone to see The Sentinel. He had recovered well from his blindness, and he enjoyed life on Mu'A. He loved his new cave, and he said that the food on the island was better than eating Arrach. He lived mainly off the abundant fruits on the island, and he'd catch fish and insects when he needed protein. He was overjoyed to hear that the skull had been destroyed.

I now have nothing to guard except this island and its people, and that will be my life-long pursuit now. To be the guardian of the Mu'A. Nothing will come near this island that I won't know about.

The Six, and Anwyn, felt it was safe to leave.

Catrin and Ambros

After mopping up what was left of the fort, and making sure the women, slaves and children were removed so they could be taken to Three Rivers to be repatriated to their original homes, Catrin and Ambros began the long trip homeward.

They had not lost as many men as they'd at first feared. They'd burned down the fort and allowed the inhabitants, those who wanted to, to return with them, though. There was still no sign of Moran or his lieutenant, Kromm. Most of Moran's men, when seeing that they were defeated, had given up or deserted their ranks. They'd taken some prisoners, those who still seemed loyal to Moran or Kromm, as Catrin did not want to leave any threats out there to her son's kingdom. She would take care of them now.

Zlatan was now the right hand man of Ambros. He would not abandon him, not even to return to Mernoc.

"There's nothing left there for me now," he had said. "I will come to

Three Rivers with you and the Queen, but I'll still keep looking for Moran and Kromm. I won't rest until I know they're dead."

"I'm with you on that," said Ambros. "I have a bone to pick with Kromm, but I'll leave Moran to you." They shook hands on that, and turned their horses to the north.

END OF BOOK THREE

The Ialana Series

The Six and the Crystals of Ialana
The Six and the Gardeners of Ialana
The Six and Anwyn of Ialana

As an author, I rely on my readers to help me get the word out about the Ialana Series, and you'll be helping me out in a big way if you take a few minutes to write a review.

Every review helps me understand what's important to my readers, which in turn helps me.

By telling others how you enjoyed the Ialana Series, you'll be helping them make a decision about buying the book.

Just go to the Amazon page where you purchased the book and click on "Review this Book". If you are a member of Goodreads, a review here is also appreciated.

www.katlynnbrooke@yahoo.com
https://www.facebook.com/katlynnbrookeauthor/

About the Author

Growing up in Africa during the '50's and '60's, Katlynn Brooke's childhood was an unusual one, even by African standards. While her city peers were learning how to dance to Chubby Checker's *The Twist* or preparing for final exams, she was in a camper travelling through the bushveld penning plays and short stories for her family's entertainment.

As an adult, her many travels took her to India and Indonesia, where she lived in both countries for several years before settling permanently in the United States. She now resides in Virginia with her husband, and a cat.

Katlynn, always an avid and eclectic reader, is still inspired by authors such as Tolkien, Arthur C. Clark, and Terry Brooks. Influenced heavily by her past travels, she draws on her sojourns in foreign lands, and even her dreams, for out-of-the-ordinary settings, intrepid heroes, and the assertive heroines of her epic fantasy adventures.

www.ingramcontent.com/pod-product-compliance
Lightning Source LLC
Chambersburg PA
CBHW050029180626

46810CB00002B/643